SISTER
WHERE
ARE YOU

ALSO BY A.M. STRONG & SONYA SARGENT

THE PATTERSON BLAKE THRILLER SERIES

Sister Where Are You

Is She Really Gone

Coming Soon

All the Dead Girls

PATTERSON BLAKE PREQUEL

Don't Lie to Me

SISTER
WHERE
ARE YOU

A PATTERSON BLAKE THRILLER

A.M. STRONG
SONYA SARGENT

**WEST
STREET**

West Street Publishing

Cover art and interior design by Bad Dog Media, LLC.

ISBN: 978-1-942207-21-4

For Tiki and Gidget, who will always be here in spirit. Also for Izzy and Hayden, who make sure we don't write for too many hours by demanding their walks!

PROLOGUE

SIXTEEN YEARS AGO

S he surfaced to a sensation of motion and a world of darkness. At first her thoughts were disjointed, as if she were coming around from a night of heavy drinking. Her throat was dry too, and it hurt when she swallowed. But she hadn't touched any alcohol. This was different. She had been drugged. It was probably the glass of iced tea she'd drank to stave off the terrible thirst that had become her constant companion.

She was dressed now, but not in her own clothes. Those were long gone. The garments she currently wore felt baggy on her size six frame—at least three sizes too big. She couldn't remember getting dressed, which meant he put them on her after she passed out. That she wore no underwear was further proof she had not dressed herself.

"Where are we?" she asked in a croaky voice, as the realization dawned that she was being carried over her captor's shoulder like a sack with her arms pulled behind her back, wrists tightly bound. "What's going on?"

Silence was her only answer. He rarely responded to her

questions, no matter how many times she asked. He had spoken little during her months of captivity, and when he did, it was to issue terse commands like *take your clothes off*, *stop crying*, or *look into my eyes*. He said that last one the most, forcing her to gaze at him while he abused her. Now, though, something had changed. Instead of leading her from the block building to his cabin, nestled among densely packed elm and cedar trees, he had knocked her out.

This frightened her more than anything. She knew there had been others before because she'd found a name scratched into a floorboard under the metal frame bed with the stained mattress.

Helen.

She'd tried to add her own name but hadn't succeeded. There was nothing inside the room with which to make a mark except her fingernails, and all she'd managed to do was break two of them. Afterward, she'd cried for a long time, not because of the pain, but because writing her name alongside that of a previous captive made her feel less alone, even though she suspected Helen was long since dead. Now she wondered if her predecessor had awoken one night, groggy and afraid, being carried half-naked through the woods, just as she currently was.

"I'm uncomfortable," she said, trying again. "Can you please let me walk?"

"We're almost there," her captor responded, hitching her further over his shoulder and gripping the back of her leg with a powerful hand.

"Almost where?" She tried not to let the fear show in her voice. From somewhere behind them, she could hear the distant sound of lapping water. Was there a stream nearby? A lake?

"You'll see."

She lapsed into silence, realizing the futility of her questions. Besides, the answer might be worse than not knowing. She suppressed a sob, swallowing hard to contain her terror. The filthy outbuilding he'd kept her in for so long didn't seem so bad now she was faced with the unknown. She almost begged to go back there but knew it wouldn't work, just like all the begging that preceded it hadn't.

Not that it mattered. He was slowing up now, coming to a halt. He pitched her forward off his shoulder and let her slide to the ground. Leaves crunched underfoot as she struggled to maintain balance. Then he shoved her forward toward a black shape looming up out of the earth.

She realized it was an old automobile with sweeping lines and chrome hubcaps surrounded by whitewall tires, the air inside them long since escaped. Leaves and other decaying matter covered the hood and roof in a thick vegetative carpet. The car was reminiscent of the one her grandfather kept in a garage at the back of his house and only drove when he was going to auto shows, except his vehicle didn't have vines growing up over the wheel arches and dirt caking the windshield.

He steered her toward the derelict vehicle and tugged at the rear door, pulling it open on protesting hinges.

An odor wafted out, pungent and ripe.

Ignoring the smell, her captor lifted a foot and put it behind her knee, applying enough pressure that she buckled, even as he placed a steering hand atop her head and pushed her forward with the other. She felt herself pitching into the car, and found the will to fight back, digging her heels into the soft earth next to the vehicle. She twisted and bucked, overcome with a sudden sense of her own mortality. But her captor was too strong, and she was soon bundled inside, hands still restrained behind her back. The stench was worse now. Like rotting cabbage tinged with garlic. She gagged and tried to hold her breath.

A flashlight clicked on, bathing the car's interior with a dull yellow glow. Then she saw the chain, one end draped over the front seat. The other disappeared underneath.

The man reached in and took the chain. He looped the free

end around her neck a couple of times, tight enough that she gasped for air. A padlock appeared from his pocket, which he inserted between the loops and clicked shut. He tugged on the chain to make sure it was secure, then stepped back, dangling an item between two fingers for her to see. A pair of small silver padlock keys. He dropped them into the leafy detritus on the hood too far for her to reach. Then he leaned in close, his mouth inches from her ear, and spoke in a soft voice. "I'll never stop thinking about you."

With those parting words, he slammed the car door and stepped back. He watched for a moment as if admiring his handiwork. Then he turned and retreated through the forest, the beam from his flashlight getting fainter until she was left alone.

Except she wasn't totally alone.

As the moon emerged from behind scudding clouds, a ray of silvery light spilled through the back window, illuminating the chained corpse sitting next to her in the back seat. In the front was a second body reduced to little more than skeletal remains with patches of dark, mottled skin attached. She knew it was female only by its clothes. A rotten sweatshirt and a stained yellow skirt. The corpse sat bent slightly forward, giving the grimy windshield a dead stare, one bony hand shackled to the steering wheel with a set of rusty handcuffs.

She screamed and flinched away from her long-dead companions, tugging at her restraints in a desperate attempt to escape. But it was no use. The chain was too tight, and there was no one around to hear. Except for the man who had brought her here, assuming he was still within earshot. Which was why she cried out for his help, even though she knew it was useless.

———

Her captor did hear the girl's terrified pleas. He turned off the flashlight and stood in the darkness, soaking up her terror as she shrieked and begged for him to return. Then, after the screams had given way to exhausted whimpers, he continued down the overgrown woodland trail with a satisfied smile on his face. And as he went, he wondered how long it would take her to die.

FAMILY STATEMENT

IN THE DISAPPEARANCE OF JULIE BLAKE
— SEPTEMBER 20, 2005

On September 20 of this year, our 19-year-old daughter, Julie Blake, was reported missing to the Los Angeles Police Department after she did not return home from a summer cross-country trip. All attempts to contact her have failed.

Julie is a wonderful and vivacious person. Her love for adventure and passion for life have inspired her family and friends in so many ways. We do not believe she would voluntarily break off contact.

If anyone knows where Julie is, or they have information regarding what happened to her, we urge them to contact the LAPD or their local police. Callers may remain anonymous if they so desire.

Julie, if you are out there and see this, please call. We are worried and want to know that you are safe, regardless of whether you wish to return home. We love you, always.

— Mom, Dad, and Sis.

POLICE STATEMENT

IN THE DISAPPEARANCE OF JULIE BLAKE
— NOVEMBER 14, 2005

The Los Angeles Police Department has concluded its missing persons search for Julie Blake, a 19YO student attending college in Chicago, Illinois. Julie was reported missing by her family after she failed to return from a summer road trip, however we have uncovered no evidence that she disappeared under suspicious circumstances. We are no longer actively looking for Julie. We would like to thank all those involved in the investigation. Out of respect for the family, we will make no further statements at this time.

ONE

FBI Special Agent Patterson Blake weaved her way through the mess of rusting farm machinery clogging the barn she had entered moments before. She moved forward on high alert, gripping her Glock 19M service weapon with both hands, trigger finger pressed to the frame. Although it was pointed downward, Patterson was ready to bring the gun up at a moment's notice, but she hoped it wouldn't be necessary.

From somewhere outside the barn, in the direction of the dilapidated farmhouse, she heard shouts—other agents identifying themselves prior to entering the structure. More agents would be fanning out across the property, fifteen of them in total, all with the same objective. To locate the man who lived here and any victims that might still be alive.

Patterson slowed her step, searching the gloom between the pieces of equipment. To her left was a tractor, the back wheels almost as tall as she was. Next to this was a plow attachment with three large blades. Further away she could make out what looked like a tiller. The other side of the barn was crammed with oil drums, an old truck with the hood missing, and a riding mower. It was clear that none of it had moved in years.

She reached the middle of the aging structure. Ahead of her another set of double doors just like the ones she'd entered stood open, spilling an oblong patch of sunlight across the barn floor. She took one more look around before moving faster again, deciding she was alone. But as she neared the exit, a faint noise somewhere behind the tractor drew her attention.

Patterson swiveled, raising the gun.

The sound came again. A faint scrabbling that sent the hairs on the back of her neck standing on end.

She aimed toward the movement and spoke with all the authority she could muster. "Armed federal agent. Keep your hands where I can see them and show yourself."

Her command went unheeded.

Patterson stood listening to the stirring air within the barn, waiting for something to happen. When it didn't, she repeated her warning and edged forward, stepping between the tractor and a multi-bladed attachment that looked as much like an ancient torture device as it did a piece of farm equipment. But when she reached the other side of the tractor, nothing was there.

She felt her thumping heart ease up, just a little. She turned to make her way back toward the barn doors, lowering the gun once more, just as the sound came again. This time though, she caught movement from the corner of her eye. Bringing the service weapon back up, Patterson curled a finger around the trigger ready to fire. But she didn't need to. Instead of the suspect, she saw a furry gray body hightail it in the opposite direction, ringed tail scraping the ground.

A big fat raccoon.

Patterson felt a rush of relief, but at the same time, she'd had enough of the barn. She circled back around the tractor and hurried to the doors, stepping out into the bright June sunshine. To her right was the farmhouse, a two-story shingle-clad structure with a wraparound porch. It had once been painted white but was now weathered to a silvery gray with only the barest hint of paint remaining. One of the porch's corner posts had rotted causing the roof above to sag. She saw a figure standing near the front door, wearing a baseball cap above a blue nylon raid jacket with the letters FBI written across the back in blocky gold lettering.

Behind the house, across what had once been an open farm-yard ringed by a decaying picket fence, stood a second barn, smaller than the one she just searched. It was to this that she now set off, determined to complete her sweep of the outbuild-ings. She was three quarters of the way across the open area when something caught her eye near the fence line. An oblong spot of disturbed earth that looked darker than the soil surrounding it. It was barely noticeable. In fact, she would have walked right past had the sun not been slanting down at the right angle to cast a shadow across the unusual depression.

Patterson changed course and approached the anomaly. Now that she was closer, it looked less like a depression in the ground and more like something buried. She holstered her gun and kneeled down, then brushed the loose soil away to reveal a sheet of pockmarked and eroded metal. It extended way beyond the area she'd first noticed. A pair of hinges were attached at the far end. Closer, near her knees, a piece of rope was tied through a roughly hewn hole.

This was no sheet of metal. It was a trap door.

Patterson stood and brushed herself off, then gripped the rope and pulled. The makeshift trapdoor swung upward to reveal a dark space beneath. Fetid air belched out. She heaved the door all the way up, then let it fall open with a thud. Pulling a flashlight from her pocket, she dropped to her knees again and leaned over the gaping chasm, turning the light on at the same time.

She aimed the beam down through the hole and was shocked to find an oblong room with corrugated metal walls. With a jolt, she realized it was a shipping container, buried deep in the earth and covered over again to conceal it. Several inches of stagnant water sat on the container's floor. A noxious odor of decay wafted up.

Patterson leaned in further, sweeping her flashlight beam around the concealed space until it picked out a small figure huddled in one corner. A thin young woman wearing a stained and torn blouse, and not much else. She sat with her knees drawn up to her chest, arms folded around her breasts, and head bent low. She wasn't moving, but the barely perceptible whimpering sounds escaping her lips proved the woman was alive. Then, as if sensing the FBI agent's eyes upon her, the girl lifted her head and looked up.

Patterson felt a stab of icy shock. She almost dropped her flashlight. She squinted into the darkness, studying the features of the young woman that gazed back at her, stunned and confused. It was impossible, she knew, yet she could not deny her own eyes. She recognized this girl. A wave of dizziness overcame her, and she reached out, gripping the edges of the trapdoor to stop herself tumbling forward. The world compressed down until there was nothing left but herself and the woman in the shipping container. She gasped for breath, too stunned to move. Until she heard pounding footsteps approaching from her rear. She glanced up to see a middle-aged man, shirtless and obese, lumbering toward her with a pitchfork gripped in his meaty hands. A sheen of sweat covered his doughy skin. His eyes glinted with anger.

Patterson fell backwards and raised her arms in defense, even as the pitchfork arched down toward her chest. The man behind it snarled in anger. She flinched away from the sharp tines, expecting to be impaled at any moment.

Instead, two sharp cracks rang out. The burly man tottered a moment, looking surprised, then fell forward. The pitchfork clattered harmlessly to the ground next to her.

Patterson lay still for a moment, recovering her senses. The girl's face swam in front of her eyes. The face of a person she hadn't seen in sixteen years. She blinked to clear the illusion then glanced up to see Lance Driscoll, one of the senior agents at the New York Field Office, standing several feet away with his gun extended. He approached the man he'd shot, kicking the pitchfork away before kneeling and checking for a pulse. He shook his head. "Dead."

But Patterson wasn't listening. She rolled over and scrambled back to the dark opening in the ground, completely oblivious to the agents descending upon the scene from all directions. She reached into the shipping container, extending a hand toward the figure that still sat huddled in the corner. And as the tears started flowing, she uttered a name over and over again. A name she hadn't said aloud in a very long time. Julie.

TWO

The Federal Bureau of Investigation's New York Field Office occupied the twenty-third floor of Federal Plaza on 26th Street in Lower Manhattan, a stone's throw from the Brooklyn Bridge. Patterson Blake sat outside the office of the Criminal Investigative Division's SAC, or Special Agent-in-Charge, and stared straight ahead, ignoring the curious secretary, who was surely wondering what the lowly agent had done to find herself in such a predicament. You didn't receive a summons to see the SAC unless you were being congratulated or about to receive a dressing down. The look on Patterson's face was enough to tell the secretary she wasn't here to collect a heaping of praise.

The phone on the secretary's desk buzzed. She picked up the receiver, listened, nodded, and then set it down again, before turning her attention back to Patterson. "The SAC will see you now."

"Thank you." Patterson stood and tugged at the hem of her jacket, then turned toward the door. She stepped inside to find Madeline Khan, the Special Agent-in-Charge, perched behind an imposing antique oak desk. Jonathan Grant—late thirties with short cropped dark hair and a muscular build barely hidden by his white shirt—occupied one of two chairs on the other side of the desk. He was the assistant SAC and presented a more youthful contrast to Khan's austere features and authoritative demeanor. He was also Patterson's immediate boss.

"Special Agent Blake," Khan said. "Please, take a seat."

Patterson nodded and slipped into the chair next to her boss. She forced her hands into her lap and took a deep breath.

"I'm sure you know why you're here," Khan said.

Patterson nodded again. "Yesterday's farm raid."

"That's right," Khan said, nodding. "Jeffrey Dutton, fifty-three years of age, single, and the only occupant of his family's ninety-acre farm near the town of Ticonderoga in upstate New York. A quiet man, by all accounts. Kept to himself and rarely left his property, except when he was abducting and murdering young women, that is. At least eight of them. You would've been number nine were it not for Special Agent Driscoll's quick actions."

"Yes, ma'am." Patterson dropped her eyes. "I made a mistake."

"You lost focus, Special Agent Blake," Khan replied. "More than that, you appeared to be under the illusion that the young woman being held captive in the shipping container was your older sister, Julie."

"Yes," Patterson said stiffly.

"Julie went missing sixteen years ago while on a cross-country road trip. Is that correct?"

"It is."

Khan nodded. She picked up a folder and opened it, reading for a moment before continuing. "At this time, she remains unaccounted for, it appears."

"She does." An image of the captive girl flashed into Patterson's head. The young woman wasn't her sister. She knew that now. The age was wrong. She was nowhere near Julie's last known location. Yet in the moment…Patterson shrugged off the image, focused her attention on the SAC. "The police couldn't find evidence of foul play, so they stopped looking."

"Which is most unfortunate, but not uncommon," Khan said. "Over half a million people go missing each year in the United States. At least fifteen percent are never found."

"I'm aware of the statistics."

"Then you surely know that many individuals don't want to be located."

"My sister wasn't a runaway."

"I never said she was." Khan closed the folder. "We're not here today to dissect your sister's case, Special Agent Blake, sad as it might be. We're here to discuss your actions in the field. There are clearly unresolved issues."

"I realize that," Patterson responded. "Now."

Grant cleared his throat, spoke for the first time. "The girl in the container did bear a passing resemblance to Julie. Given Special Agent Blake's past, it must have come as a shock to see her." He glanced quickly toward Patterson, then back to Khan. "I would also like to point out that if it weren't for Special Agent Blake, we might not have found Dutton's final victim in time to save her life, if at all."

"True. And I commend Special Agent Blake for being alert and finding the concealed victim." Khan leaned on the table and made a tent with her hands, fingers pressed together. "But the fact remains that she lost her objectivity when confronted with a deadly situation. In this instance it was her own life on the line, but it could very well have put other agents in danger under different circumstances."

Grant rubbed his chin. "I realize that, however—"

"If you're about to defend your agent's actions, you might want to stop and think," Khan said. "You will, after all, be sitting in this chair one day if all goes well. I don't intend to remain SAC forever. There are bigger opportunities. Your own success in following me up the ladder will depend upon the decisions you make now."

"I was merely going to say that Special Agent Blake's work has been exemplary, outside of this one incident. I see no need for a formal reprimand to be placed on her service record. I'm sure Special Agent Blake has learned from this mistake and will not allow her personal life to impact her work in the future." He shot Patterson a quick glance, green eyes flashing, then turned frontward again.

"That may very well be the case." Khan sat back in her chair and observed her underlings with a thoughtful expression. "But I'm responsible for more than just this one agent. I need to be sure she won't choke the next time a dangerous situation develops. We work as a team, and each of us depends on the others to have their back. I would be remiss if I did not take action."

Patterson felt her chest tighten. She steeled herself for what was about to come. Beside her, Grant remained quiet, no doubt thinking of his own career.

Special Agent-in-Charge Khan milked the silence for a few moments, then cleared her throat. "There will be no formal reprimand. However, I'm removing Special Agent Blake from duty for the time being."

"What?" Patterson could hardly believe her ears. "You're suspending me?"

"No. I'm not suspending you. I do want you to take the rest of the week off though, to clear your head. Upon your return, you will be placed in an administrative position until I trust you to perform your duties without endangering others."

"You can't do that," Patterson protested.

"I already have," Khan replied. "Furthermore, you will be required to complete a psychological evaluation and be declared fit before going back into the field."

"But that's not—"

Khan held up a hand, silencing Patterson. "I would advise you to think hard about what you're going to say next. So far, your conduct during the raid has not resulted in any significant damage to your career, but the wrong words right now might change all that. Do you understand?"

"Yes." Patterson nodded, swallowing her unvoiced protest.

"Good." Khan looked at Grant. "I trust the current course of action meets with your approval?"

"It does," Grant said, keeping his eyes fixed forward.

"Is there anything else you would like to add before we bring the meeting to a close?"

"Not at this time." Grant folded his arms, a look of stoic resignation on his face.

"Excellent," Khan said. "In that case, this meeting is adjourned. Grant, I shall expect you to keep me appraised of Special Agent Blake's progress, and we shall revisit this matter in due course."

"Very good," Grant said, standing.

Realizing this was her cue, Patterson vacated her own chair, cheeks flushed with pent up anger. She wanted to ask how long *due course* might be, but she didn't. Instead, she moved silently toward the door. As she stepped through with Grant following behind, she could feel Kahn's gaze heavy upon her back. It was only when Grant turned and closed the door that she could breathe again.

THREE

Out in the corridor, Patterson turned on Grant with anger flashing in her eyes. "You threw me under the bus in there."

"That is absolutely not true," Grant retorted, defending himself. "I tried my best to minimize the damage, and it worked."

"Unbelievable." Patterson folded her arms and waited while a pair of agents she didn't recognize passed by with file folders clutched in their hands. They ignored the pair and continued on their way, deep in conversation. When she was sure they were out of earshot, she continued. "You didn't do a damn thing. You let her send me home like some kid being punished. And when I *am* allowed back, I'll be stuck doing admin for months, maybe years."

"Don't be so dramatic. You've been given a few days off, that's all. A free vacation. When you come back, you'll do some time behind a desk. Big deal. It'll be a matter of weeks before you're back in the field. You mark my words," Grant said. "And regardless of what you think, I did have your back. There's no formal reprimand on your record, is there?"

"No," Patterson admitted, grudgingly. "This still sucks,

though. I worked hard to become a special agent, and now I'm sidelined. Worse, I have to go through another psych eval."

"And who's fault is that?" Grant kept his voice low so he wouldn't be overheard. "You're the one who went to pieces in the middle of a raid. You could've gotten yourself killed."

"Not that you'd care," Patterson replied.

"That's not true, and you know it."

Patterson shrugged.

"Whatever. I don't have time for this. I have work to do, even if you don't." Grant turned and started down the corridor toward his office. He entered and closed the door. Before he was halfway to his desk, the door flew back open and Patterson stomped in, slamming it hard enough to make the frame shake.

"We haven't finished talking yet."

"I have," Grant replied, walking around his desk to sit down. "Do what the SAC told you. Go home and simmer down. Take this time to evaluate what happened. I'll apprise you of your new assignment next week."

"You mean you'll show me the pile of paperwork I'll be shackled to."

"Something like that." Grant leaned on the desk and looked up at Patterson. "I really don't know what you want me to do here. It wasn't my call, and you know that."

"I want you to support me," Patterson replied.

"And I did." There was a sliver of pent-up anger in Grant's voice.

"Not enough." Patterson moved closer to the desk. "If it were anyone else, this wouldn't hurt so much. But it's not anyone else. It's you."

"I was wondering how long it would be before you brought that up." Grant sighed and rubbed his temples. "Just because we've been seeing each other doesn't mean you get special treatment."

"That isn't what I'm asking for."

"Sounds that way from where I'm sitting."

"Well, it's not."

"Then quit being so belligerent. I'm not the enemy." Grant stood up. He approached Patterson and reached out, but she flinched from his touch and took a step back. He lingered, perhaps hoping she would change her mind. When she didn't, he retreated to his own side of the desk and stood looking at her, arms folded, jaw clenched. "Go home, Patterson."

"Is that an order?"

"No. It's advice. Madeline Kahn was the one who gave you the order."

"What if I don't want to go home?"

"Then it *will be* an order."

"Fine." Patterson spun on her heel and made her way toward the door.

"I'll call you later. See how you're doing," Grant said as the younger agent tugged on the door handle, fumbling to escape in her anger. "After I've finished work."

"Don't bother." Patterson finally got the door open and stepped through. She turned back toward Grant. "I don't need you checking up on me."

"That isn't what this is."

"Yeah, right. Just like I'm not suspended."

"For heaven's sake, Patterson. I'm worried about you."

"Don't be. I'm a big girl."

"I never said you weren't. I'm still allowed to worry. That's what people in relationships do."

"Then maybe we shouldn't be in a relationship." Patterson regretted the words as soon as she said them. "I mean…"

"I know what you mean." Grant turned his back on her and moved to the window, staring out over the New York skyline beyond. "Just go. I'll see you next week."

Patterson stood in the doorway, hesitant. She wanted to retract her words, was unsure how to do it without looking weak. Besides, the anger was still bubbling beneath the surface. She felt hurt. Betrayed. She didn't know what she had expected of Grant. She realized on an intellectual level there was nothing he could do, but on an emotional level it was different. He wasn't just her boss. He was so much more. But none of that mattered, because right here and now, he had to be her boss. And nothing else. With a lump in her throat, she turned and left, pulling the door closed behind her. She navigated the narrow corridors, ignoring the curious glances of those who noticed the dour look upon her face, and took the elevator down to the ground floor. Her FBI badge weighed heavy on her belt. As she exited the building, she reached down and touched it. At least Grant hadn't asked for that back. Yet. On the sidewalk, she stopped and took a deep breath. The anger was ebbing away now, to be replaced by a resigned acknowledgment of her situation. She turned and headed toward the subway, then followed the stream of people down into the bowels of the earth where trains rumbled and heaved their way to the distant corners of the city and beyond. And as she went, her thoughts turned to that girl in the shipping container. A girl who looked, briefly, like her lost sister, Julie, gone for so many years, yet never too far away. And she couldn't help but wonder if her sister really was out there still. Alone and afraid. Just waiting for someone to find her.

FOUR

Patterson stood in the shower and let the steaming water cascade over her hair and shoulders. Normally she would find the massaging spray relaxing, but not today. Her meeting with the SAC, and subsequent argument with Grant earlier that afternoon, was still fresh in her mind. It would take more than a few minutes under the shower to wash away the sting of being pulled from the field, slapped on the wrist, and sent home like a naughty schoolgirl. She turned the water off and reached up to her hair, wringing the excess wetness from it before stepping out and grabbing a towel. She rubbed herself dry, then wrapped the towel around her body before moving into the bedroom.

A slant of light shed by the evening sun spilled through a west-facing window onto the wood plank floor where it created a pattern of squares that matched the windowpanes. The sparse furnishings in the room—double bed and a single night stand—highlighted the fact that she was rarely home. The other two rooms in the tiny apartment were equally bare, with the living room containing a loveseat and side table upon which sat the room's only lamp, and a kitchen-diner combination that housed a high-top with two seats. The kitchen counter contained a coffeemaker, toaster oven, and not much else. Patterson didn't cook, preferring to dine in the myriad restaurants surrounding her cramped apartment on the second floor of a brownstone in the Queens neighborhood of Astoria. The accommodation was expensive, eating up a good portion of her paycheck, but offered the convenience of an eclectic lifestyle and an easy commute into Lower Manhattan on the N train.

Patterson got dressed and walked to the living room, dropping the towel into a laundry bin on the way. It was past six in the evening, and she was getting hungry. She hadn't eaten since breakfast, skipping lunch because she was nervous about the afternoon meeting with Madeline Kahn, the Special Agent in Charge. The summons had come minutes after she arrived at work that morning, and it had occupied her thoughts during the hours that followed, mostly because she suspected what it would be about. She had been right. Now, though, despite her lingering frustration, she needed to eat.

She picked up her phone, intending to place a takeout order from the Chinese restaurant at the end of the block, but it rang before she had the chance.

It was her father.

She answered with a terse hello that came out sharper than she intended.

"Peanut?" Her father's baritone voice filled the earpiece. "Is everything okay? You sound flustered."

"I'm fine," Patterson replied, attempting to sound upbeat and failing.

"You sure?"

"U-huh." Patterson shifted the phone from her ear and put it on speaker. "Bad day at work, that's all."

"Been there, done that," the elder Blake said. "Sounds like this is a job for pie. How about we meet at Park Pizza in an hour, and you can tell me all about it."

"Thanks for the offer, but I was thinking I'd just get takeout and veg on the couch," Patterson replied. "If it's all the same with you."

"You're bailing on third Tuesday?" her father said. "That's not like you."

"Oh, shoot. That's right. It's the third Tuesday of the month," Patterson groaned. Every first and third Tuesday, they met up at a different restaurant for dinner. It was a tradition that had been going on ever since she'd returned from Quantico and started at the New York Field Office as a new agent trainee. Her father still lived in the same Ozone Park house she'd grown up in. The tree-lined suburban neighborhood was nestled in the southwestern section of Queens, nine miles from her current digs. She rarely missed their bimonthly dinner dates, begging off only when she was working late, or if a blizzard shut the city down. "It completely slipped my mind."

"No worries." Her father sounded disappointed. "If you really don't feel like it..."

"No. It's fine."

"You're sure?"

"Yes. I'm sure," Patterson replied. "But I can't guarantee I'll make good company."

"Not asking you to. I can be jolly enough for the pair of us."

Patterson smiled despite herself. "In that case, how can I refuse."

"That's my girl. Seven-thirty sound good?"

"Sounds great."

"Perfect. If you get there first, find us a table by the window. I like to people watch."

"They only have eight tables, so that shouldn't be too hard," Patterson said. "See you in an hour."

"It's a date," her father responded, offering a quick goodbye before the line went dead.

Patterson looked down at her clothes. A faded tee and blue jeans with ripped knees. She wondered if she should change, but then decided it wasn't worth the bother. Besides, Park Pizza was hardly haute cuisine. The place had been in the same Ozone Park building for over fifty years and looked like it hadn't received a fresh lick of paint in just as long. It was a popular local hangout that served slightly burned brick oven pizza over a worn melamine counter that had once been bright yellow but was now faded almost white. The beer was cold, and the pies were thin and crispy, just as New Yorkers liked them. Just thinking about the place made her stomach rumble. She returned to the bathroom and ran a brush through her shoulder-length blonde hair, which was now mostly dry. The person staring back at her looked tired. Her eyes, normally a dusty pale blue, appeared a flat gray. Her face was haggard above her slight frame. Even so, she couldn't be bothered to put on makeup—not that she owned much. An occasional application of lipstick was about as far as she usually went, and even then, it had to be a special occasion. Deciding she'd done enough, Patterson turned away from the haunted image in the mirror and hurried back through the apartment, scooping up her keys and phone. Seconds later she was out the door.

FIVE

I t took the better part of thirty minutes to arrive at the pizza
joint. When she entered, Patterson saw her father immediately. He was sitting at a corner table near the window with a
mug of beer in his hand. When he saw her, he raised the other in
greeting.

"How long have you been here?" Patterson asked, eyeing the
half-drunk beer and second empty mug that adorned the table.

"Not long," her father replied. "Fifteen minutes. Place is only
a ten-minute walk from the house, so I thought I'd arrive early
and get us a table."

"Right. Because it's so busy." Patterson glanced around the
dining room. Only two other tables were occupied. A couple
more customers lingered at the counter, waiting to collect
takeout pizzas.

"Tuesday's a funny night. You never know if it will be
packed or not."

"Sure. We'll go with that, and I'll ignore the fact that you've
drunk a beer and a half already."

"I work hard. I'm allowed a couple cold ones." Her father
shook his head. "You sound more like your mother every day."

"I'm just looking out for you," Patterson replied, sitting

down opposite her father. When the server came over, she ordered herself a beer and asked for a side of garlic knots while they decided on their pizza.

"I take it we don't intend to practice what we preach?" Her father asked with a raised eyebrow.

"We do not. It's been a rough day. I was intending to order Chinese food and open a bottle of wine, but pizza and beer will hit the spot."

"Perp give you a hard time?"

"Not so much. More like my boss."

"Ah. That boyfriend of yours losing his luster, already? I told you, workplace romances never work out."

"How would you know? You've never had one."

"I've never had a fistfight with a black bear either, but I know it's not a good idea."

"Touché." Patterson smiled despite herself. "And no, it isn't Jonathan. It's the boss above him. Madeline Kahn. She's Special Agent in Charge of the Criminal Division."

"Fancy title. Sounds high up."

"High enough." Patterson fell silent while the server brought the beer and knots. She took a long swig before continuing. "It's my fault, though. I brought it upon myself."

"Want to talk about it? Problems sometimes don't seem so bad when you voice them out loud. Kinda puts things in perspective."

"I'm not so sure that's true." Patterson took another long sip of her beer.

"If nothing else, it will make you feel better."

"I don't want to discuss it." Patterson plucked a garlic knot from the plate and bit into it, savoring the crispy exterior and the buttery flavor that filled her mouth. She chewed heartily and swallowed, then condemned the remaining dough to a similar fate. Afterward, Patterson licked her fingers and looked across the table at her father. "Can we talk about something else?"

"Whatever you want, Peanut." Her father smiled and met her gaze.

"All these years and you never stopped calling me that. It's like I'm still your little girl."

"You are my little girl—always will be—even if you carry a badge and a gun." Her father nodded toward the paper menu sitting on the table in front of her, which also served as a placemat. "You know what you want on your pizza yet? We can do half and half if you're getting fancy toppings."

"They do fancy toppings here now?" Patterson asked, glancing down at the menu.

"Yeah. Anything but pepperoni."

"Gotcha." Patterson shrugged. "I'm down with pepperoni. Keep it simple."

"Sounds like a plan." Her father raised a hand to attract the server's attention and placed their order. While they waited for the pizza to come, he settled back in his chair and sipped beer. Eventually, he spoke again. "It was your mother's birthday last week. I hope you sent her a card."

"I sent a card," Patterson replied. "Although I'm not sure why you'd care either way."

"Because she's your mother."

"Right. And she also walked out on us. Turned her back and left like we were nothing."

"She walked out on me. Not you."

"That's not how it looked when I was trying to finish my last year of high school and she wasn't around anymore."

"And I'm sorry for that." Her father sat up straight and reached across the table, taking Patterson's hand. "I really am, even all these years later. I know how much you struggled back then."

"Ancient history." Patterson pulled her hand away and downed the last of her beer just as the pizza came.

A silence fell between them, which they filled with eating. Their biweekly dinner dates didn't usually devolve into such prickly affairs. They were filled with laughter and gripes about work and life in general. Patterson wondered if her own foul mood had set the tone of tonight's meal. Any other evening, she would have responded to her father's questions with less vitriol. She felt bad about that and determined to ease up on him.

When they'd had their fill of the pizza, her father rose and grabbed a box from a table near the door and slid the remaining slices into it. He closed the box and looked at her. "You want to take this home for later?"

"No. It's bad enough on the subway without carrying a pizza box." Patterson shook her head. "You take it. There's probably no food in the house anyway so you'll need it tomorrow."

"I have food. Even without your mother around I still cook once in a while."

"I know that." Patterson reached out and took her father's hand again. "I'm sorry I snapped at you. Like I said, it's been a rough day. I guess I'm just taking it out on the easiest target."

"Don't worry yourself." Her father paused. A distant look passed across his eyes. Then he smiled at her. He drew in a sharp breath. "Your mother leaving really wasn't anything to do with you. To tell the truth, it wasn't even anything to do with me. We were arguing, for sure, but there was a deeper cause. A rot that set in the summer your sister went missing. She never got over it. The grief consumed her, ate her up inside. By the time she left, all that remained was a shell. I think that if she hadn't gotten out, walked away from us and the house, and everything that reminded her of what happened, even that shell would have eventually crumbled."

"And what about you?" Patterson asked. "Do you still think about her? My sister I mean."

"God, yes. All the time. I talk to her every night before bed and hope she's out there somewhere listening." Her father's brow furrowed. "Why would you ask me that?"

"It's the reason I'm in trouble at work," Patterson admitted. She let the statement hang in the air, expecting her father to comment. Instead, he stared at her with wide, searching eyes. When she realized he wasn't going to say anything, she continued with a trembling voice. "I saw her, dad. My sister. I was on a derelict farm in upstate New York. We were in the middle of a raid. Went there to arrest a man who'd killed a bunch of young women. And I saw Julie, right there, as clear as I'm looking at you now."

SIX

Patterson waited for her father to respond. When he did, there was soft concern in his voice. "You can't have seen Julie, Peanut. It's impossible."

"I realize that, dad. I know it wasn't Julie. It was some other scared, abused girl. But for a brief second, I could have sworn it was my sister being held in a shipping container buried under the earth at the home of a psychopathic killer. I was so lost in the shock of seeing Julie, I didn't hear the man we were looking for coming up from behind. He had a pitchfork. He almost killed me. Almost certainly would have if it weren't for the quick action of another agent. I messed up bad. I lost it in the field, which is the worst thing an agent can do."

"Surely not," her father said. "Mistakes happen."

"This wasn't a mistake, dad. It was a serious error of judgment. Sure, the girl looked a bit like Julie, but there was no way it could have been her. She was too young given how much time has passed and she was thousands of miles from where Julie went missing." Patterson wiped a tear from her eye. "The crazy thing is, I wasn't even thinking of Julie before that. I mean, she's always at the back of my mind, but it wasn't like I was expecting to find her there. I could've gotten myself and other people killed."

"I don't know what to say. I never realized it still affected you this much."

"How could it not?" Patterson leaned on the table. "She was my big sister. When we were growing up, we used to call ourselves PB&J."

"I remember." Her father smiled. "Your mother and I never did that on purpose. It wasn't until afterwards that we realized what your initials spelled out. I think it was your sister who started the whole thing. Patterson Blake and Julie. Peanut Butter and Jelly. Even now I smile when I think about that."

"She was almost six years older than me, but she was my best friend. At least until she went to college."

"And after that, you kept in touch all the time. She was always emailing, sending you a letter, or mailing some trinket she'd seen and thought you'd like. I always felt lucky to have two such wonderful and close daughters."

"So why would you think her disappearance didn't affect me?"

"I don't know. It's just been so long. Sometimes I feel like I've led two different lives. The one before Julie, and the one after."

"Me too," Patterson admitted. "I went into law enforcement because of her. After I arrived at the New York Field Office, I had Jonathan pull the LAPD file on her disappearance. I wanted to see if there was anything they'd missed."

"And was there?"

"There was barely anything at all. They looked into it, but had no firm leads, or even evidence of a crime. She just vanished. In the end they assumed she just didn't want to be found. It happens. One thing I've never understood, is why everyone was so convinced she disappeared in Los Angeles. The file even claimed there was correspondence that placed her there, but I know that's not true. She was traveling all the way from Chicago to LA with her friend,

Stacy. That's a lot of miles. I know she was safe until Oklahoma City, because that's where she and Stacy had an argument and parted ways, but there's a whole heap of empty road between there and California and we don't know who she might have met, and what their intentions were." Patterson took a breath. "For the life of me I don't understand why Julie kept going on her own."

"You know what your sister was like. Always so headstrong. Never wanted to admit defeat or leave a task half done. That was her special power and also her downfall."

"I get that. I always admired her strength of character. But it still doesn't explain why you filed the missing persons report in LA. She was sending me postcards along the way, but she never mailed one from Los Angeles. The last postcard was sent from Oklahoma City, fifteen hundred miles to the east. I know because I still have them. She could have disappeared anywhere before California."

"That's not strictly true." Her father looked uncomfortable. She caught the twitch, barely perceptible to an untrained observer, that tightened the muscle under his right eye. She'd seen the same involuntary reaction when interrogating a suspect who was afraid of her, trying to cover their nerves, or both. It was a stress indicator the instructors at Quantico had taught her to look for. She hadn't expected to see it from her father.

"What aren't you telling me?" Patterson asked with a sudden sense of dread.

"It's nothing, really." Her father's gaze drifted to the left, toward the counter and the server who stood there engaged in idle conversation with the overweight middle-aged man who spent every evening sliding pizzas and garlic bread into the brick oven. A sure sign that whatever he was about to say was anything but nothing. "You have to understand, you were so young. Still in junior high. Your mother and I didn't want to burden you."

"I'm not in school now," Patterson snapped. "I'm twenty-nine years old and I chase bad people for a living. Whatever you're holding back, I'm sure I can handle it."

"You're right, of course." Patterson's father dropped his head. He studied his empty beer mug, still unwilling to meet her gaze. "There were more postcards we never showed you."

"What?" Patterson felt like someone had slapped her in the face. "You knew there were more postcards all this time, and you didn't share that information with me?"

"We didn't say anything because you were just a teenager. After Oklahoma City, there were no new postcards until the end of August. We didn't worry right away. She called twice in between. Left a voicemail the first time and spoke with your mother the second. Said everything was great and they were having a good time, except her the phone had gotten damaged, that she'd dropped it and would get it fixed when she could. That was a lie, of course."

"I know about the cell phone. It was in the police report. You bought it for her before the trip, to use if there was an emergency. It got stolen. That was what caused the argument in Oklahoma City, after which she and Stacy parted ways."

"Yes. They were staying at a budget hotel. After they arrived in the city, they dropped their bags in the room and went out for food. When they came back, someone had broken into the room and went through their stuff. Most of their money was gone, whatever they didn't have on them, and the phone too."

"Which is why Stacy wanted to go back to Chicago. She called her father, had him buy her a bus ticket home. Wanted Julie to leave too and come here, to New York, for the rest of the summer."

"Except Julie wasn't having any of it. She wanted to continue the trip even though they were broke. She swore Stacy to secrecy about the phone. She didn't want us to know it had been stolen because then she would have been forced to admit what happened in Oklahoma City, and that she was now traveling alone."

"She knew you wouldn't approve."

"And she was right. We would have been beside ourselves. As it was, Stacy went home to Chicago while Julie continued their trip all by herself and vanished. I often think about that decision. About how one seemingly innocuous choice can change the trajectory of so many lives. If only she'd come home, Julie would still be with us."

"You still haven't told me about the postcards. How many more were there?"

"There were two. They came about ten days apart. When the first one arrived, we felt uneasy, but tried to shrug it off. We didn't want to admit anything was wrong. Then we got the second postcard. That's when we realized something was very wrong. The tone of those last postcards was different, and we couldn't ignore it anymore."

"Different how?"

"They didn't sound like Julie. At least not to us. And our calls to her cell phone went unanswered even though she'd promised to fix it."

"Except she couldn't fix the phone because it had been stolen."

"Right. That's when we reported her missing. We couldn't get the authorities to take the matter seriously, though."

"The two postcards—the ones you kept secret all these years —where were they mailed from?" Patterson studied her father's face, just as she would a suspect in an interrogation. "Tell me."

"I can do better than that." Her father motioned the server and asked for the bill. He paid in cash and left a generous tip. Then he stood and turned toward Patterson. "I can show you."

SEVEN

Patterson paced the living room of the home where she grew up, a boxy detached two floor single-family with four steps leading up to the front door. It was painted a pale yellow, as it had been for as long as Patterson could remember. The backyard was still covered with the same pavers she had scraped her knees on while learning to ride her first bicycle when she was five. In fact, the entire house was a time capsule to her childhood, inside and out. Photos adorned the living room wall closest to the kitchen-family portraits, images of Julie and Patterson, and some older black and white pictures of her grandparents. There was even a photo of her father receiving a service award from the MTA, New York's Metropolitan Transportation Authority, where he'd worked for the past thirty years sitting in a booth dispensing tickets.

She perused these surroundings with a detachment born of familiarity and waited for her father to return from the upstairs bedroom. When he did, he was carrying a shoebox, which he placed on the coffee table before settling into his favorite wingback chair. He took the lid off the box and rummaged inside before finding what he was looking for. Two postcards, one with a creased corner.

He waited for Patterson to approach and handed them to her. "I never intended to show you these. Couldn't see the point after all this time."

"Then why are you showing them to me now?" Patterson asked. "Why did you mention them at all?"

"You didn't give me much choice." Her father chuckled, the sound mirthless and hollow. "I can see why you make a good FBI agent. You certainly tripped me up with your cross-examination back in the pizza parlor."

"I wasn't cross-examining you. I was just saying that I've always carried the memories of Julie with me. After I read the LAPD report and realized there was nothing of significance there, I thought I'd worked past my issues with her disappearance. Came to terms with it. After what happened on the raid, I guess I was wrong."

"That's the real reason I told you about these postcards tonight. Ever since Julie disappeared, I've tried to shelter you from the worst of it. I hoped you'd move on and live your life without this demon on your back. Heaven knows, I carry enough guilt about her disappearance for all of us. I should have banned her from going on that road trip. I should've told her it wasn't safe to travel all that way like that. I should've done so many things."

"She was an adult. You couldn't stop her." Patterson turned the postcards over in her hand. "And trying to protect me from the hurt and the worry was an admirable thing. I was a child. But now I'm grown up. I see bad things every day and I could've handled this."

"I was just doing what I thought was right for our family."

"I know." Patterson looked down at the postcards, noting with surprise that one of them was from Las Vegas. This was nowhere near Julie's intended route which should have taken her to Flagstaff and then south, through Sedona, and down to Phoenix, where her traveling companion, Stacy, had arranged for them to stay with an old friend from school who'd moved there. Then they would have turned west once more to LA. Except that she never made it that far, or so Patterson had always thought. She turned the postcard over and read the message on the back.

Hey,

Los Angeles can wait. I took a brief detour to Sin City. Who wouldn't? Going to hang here a week or two before I head back to Chicago. I might be too busy to write, but don't worry about me. Having a blast.

Forever,

Julie

XXX

Patterson read the card again, her eyes flicking to the postage stamp in the top right corner, and the date on the postmark. The end of August. Weeks after the last card Patterson had received from her sister as a teenager. The one from Oklahoma City. What had happened to Julie in that time, and why had it taken her so long to reach Vegas? The postcard offered no details. She flipped it over and studied the image on the front. An aerial photo that showed the Stratosphere, and the now long-gone Stardust hotel. She turned her attention to the second postcard. This one was from Los Angeles and appeared to confirm that her sister had indeed arrived there, albeit later than expected. According to the postmark, almost two more weeks had passed. It was now close to the middle of September. Julie should have been back in school already. Not that it mattered, given the message on the back of the postcard.

Hey All,

Finally made it to Tinseltown. Wow. Look at me out in Hollywood

like some sort of movie star. Vegas was fun. LA is better. Think I'll stay
a while and see where life takes me. School can wait for now.
    Later,
    Julie
    XXX

Patterson read this second postcard with a growing sense of unease. She could see what had bothered her parents about these communications back when they first arrived, and why they had kept them from the teenaged Patterson. The messages didn't sound like her sister. Especially the last one. Julie was an extravert, could be strong-willed, but she was a bookworm who loved college and was looking forward to her sophomore year. Her friend Stacy was the wilder of the pair. She would have been the more likely one to abandon her studies to hang around Los Angeles. Then there was the sign off. Julie had used her first name.

"This isn't right," Patterson said, a cold tingle worming its way across her skin. "She called me PB and signed all the other postcards with her nickname. Jelly."

"I know that." There was a somber look on her father's face. "Believe me, we tried to tell the police. They wouldn't listen, said it proved nothing. That's when we hired the private investigator."

"You hired a private investigator?" Patterson's head was spinning. There was so much she didn't know about her sister's disappearance. So much her parents had kept from her. "I never knew that."

"Why would you?" Her father shook his head. "You were a kid."

"So, what came of it?"

"Nothing. The guy asked around, looked into it, but came up blank. He even contacted Stacy's friend in Phoenix to see if Julie had gone there, but she hadn't. He didn't think that meant much, since Julie didn't actually know the friend and her showing up there alone would have been awkward."

"How long did he look for Julie?"

"Not long enough. Cash was tight. We could only afford to hire him for a few weeks. We used the last of the money from a home equity loan we'd taken out to help support Julie in Chicago. She was the first in our family to attend college. We were so proud."

"I know that." Patterson felt the postcards weighing heavily in her hands. Just holding them brought back pain of that awful time in her life.

"After the private investigator turned nothing up, and the money ran out, the arguments started. I'm not sure if your mother was blaming herself or if she blamed me. Perhaps she thought we were both to blame."

"It was none of that," Patterson said. "Julie was the one who went on that trip. She was the one who refused to call it quits after they got robbed. She should never have continued on her own."

"Didn't stop it from driving a wedge between me and your mother. I'm surprised she stayed as long as she did."

"What's done is done," Patterson replied. She looked down at the postcards. The Hollywood sign, set against the bright blue sky, stared back at her from the front of the last postcard that Julie, or maybe someone pretending to be Julie, ever sent. "Do you mind if I hold on to these?"

Her father shrugged. "Be my guest. Just promise me something…"

"What?"

"You won't let what happened to Julie wreck your career. I came to terms with her loss a long time ago, and you need to do the same. Some things just can't be fixed, no matter how badly we want them to be."

Patterson nodded. She glanced toward the door. "I should go. It's getting late."

Now it was her father's turn to nod. He observed her with narrowed eyes, perhaps wondering if he'd stirred a hornet's nest by showing her the postcards kept hidden for so long. But he said nothing more. Instead, he just walked her to the door and said his goodbyes, then closed it softly as she descended the front steps and started back toward the subway station and home, with the postcards still held in one hand.

EIGHT

Patterson sat cross-legged on the bed with the postcards in front of her. Near her left knee was a small pile with the five postcards that her sister, Julie, had sent during that last fateful trip so many years ago. Next to her right knee were the two new postcards her father had given her just this evening. She had placed them picture side down, so that the writing on the back was visible. Her eyes flitted between the two clusters of postcards, noting the similarities and discrepancies between them.

The handwriting matched, or at least, that's how it appeared to Patterson. The way her sister completed descenders, especially G's and Y's, with their fat, rounded tails that looped back upon themselves. The crossbars through her T's and F's, which ran slightly upward in a left-to-right stroke. The letters all slanted forward in a neat feminine hand. There was no visible hesitancy or excessive pen lifts within the writing on the newly revealed postcards, something she would have expected to see if someone trying to copy her sister's handwriting style wrote them. Not that her amateur examination was worth much. She had taken handwriting analysis classes at Quantico, but she was no expert. If these postcards were tied to a current criminal investigation, she would have sent them to the lab for professional analysis, but she didn't have that ability, and was forced to rely upon her own meager knowledge. Yet even if she couldn't detect the hallmarks of forgery within the new postcards, she still could not reconcile the discrepancy in the way her sister signed her name.

She flicked through the old postcards; the ones kept so lovingly in the drawer of her nightstand for the past sixteen years. The last tenuous links to a sister she had given up on ever seeing again. Each of them started and ended the same way, with her sister calling her PB and signing off as Jelly. The two newly discovered postcards did neither, starting with a generic salutation and ending with Julie's given name. Even if the LAPD had not found this discrepancy worthy of further investigation, Patterson did. During her time with the FBI, she had learned that even the smallest anomalies could develop into important leads. Hairline cracks became chasms, and chasms became canyons. That awareness, coupled with her intimate knowledge of Julie's character and habits, set alarm bells ringing in her head.

Patterson touched one of the old postcards, the last one she'd received all those years ago. She picked it up. The picture on the front showed Bricktown, an entertainment district east of Oklahoma City's downtown. This was where Julie and Stacy had parted company after an argument over whether they should abandon their trip following the robbery that left the girls short of cash. The postcard must have been sent after the theft and ensuing disagreement, because the room they rented at the hotel was ransacked within hours of their arrival in the city. Julie wouldn't have had time to buy a postcard, then write and mail it. Yet the message on the back mentioned nothing of the calamity that had befallen Julie. She sounded upbeat. Happy even. Yet Patterson knew the truth. Stacy had caught a Greyhound bus back to Chicago and her sister was now alone, low on cash, and missing her only lifeline. The cell phone their parents had purchased for her because they didn't think she should travel across the country without a way to summon help if needed.

The irony was that Julie's insistence upon continuing the trip solo had put her in the very situation the lost cell phone was meant to guard against. At some point between Oklahoma City and Los Angeles trouble had found her sister. What that trouble was, Patterson did not know, but she knew that such situations rarely worked out well if the missing person was not quickly located. The FBI's National Crime Information Center released statistics every year, and while most of the 600,000 people who fell between the cracks annually were found, either alive or dead, the small percentage of missing that remained were the most likely to have met with foul play. This grim statistic, coupled with the small but significant discrepancies between the postcards prior to Las Vegas, and the final two, left Patterson with a tight knot of dread in her stomach.

She had viewed her sister's disappearance, until now, only as an emotional event in her life. A tragic yet unavoidable experience beyond her control. She was a child when it happened, and the grown-ups had taken care of it. Or so she thought. It had driven her decision to join the FBI, for sure, but she had harbored no serious ambitions to investigate her sister's disappearance. It was so long ago, after all. Even when Grant had pulled the LAPD report, it was mainly to satisfy her curiosity, and confirm that everything that could be done had been. Now, with the emergence of the new postcards, she began to wonder if the system had failed her sister. The Los Angeles Police Department, lacking any substantive evidence and having heard such pleas before, discounted her parent's claims that Julie would not have vanished of her own free will. They fell into the fatal trap of prejudging the situation based upon past experience, a mistake made countless times by lax investigators in all jurisdictions. Patterson had seen it in action during her own official investigations. Local law enforcement, state police, and even other federal agents had missed opportunities to bring criminals to justice because they jumped to conclusions. It was something she strove to guard against in her own professional life, and it broke her heart to think the detectives dealing with her sister's case had not been so diligent.

Patterson dropped the postcard back on the pile. She yawned. It was late, and she wanted to put this horrendous day behind her. She gathered up the postcards and placed them back in the drawer. All except the two her father had given her. These she propped on the nightstand, leaning against the bedside lamp. She was about to swing her legs off the bed and head to the bathroom to clean her teeth and undress when her phone rang. She glanced toward it, laying on the bed next to her. It was Grant, no doubt calling to see how she was faring. She didn't want to talk to him. Not right now. She dismissed the call and stood, then went to the bathroom. Fifteen minutes later she slipped into bed, pulled the covers up and turned the lights out, then she closed her eyes and waited for sleep.

NINE

Not going to work felt weird. Patterson had woken up at her usual time, around 6 AM. She was dressed and halfway to the kitchen to make coffee before she remembered there was nowhere to go. Patterson was on forced leave, at least for the rest of the week, after which a desk job waited. She felt the previous day's anger flicker back to life and made a conscious effort to swallow it. She sat at the kitchen counter and drank two mugs of coffee, because she couldn't see the point in going back to bed. Since joining the FBI, Patterson had taken only five days of leave. Three when she was sick with the flu, and two more to attend the funeral of a relative. She had never taken an actual vacation. She liked her job and didn't feel the need to step away. For the first three years after graduating from Quantico, Patterson got thirteen days off annually. After that it had gone up to twenty. This meant that after four years with the Bureau she had amassed more than twelve weeks of vacation and had used less than seven days, some of which counted as sick leave. Now she was, in effect, being forced to take a vacation, and she didn't like it. She spent the next few hours pacing the apartment. She turned the television on but found nothing entertaining. Daytime TV was worse than prime time, filled with babbling talk show hosts, soap operas, and game shows. At lunchtime she left and went to a Lebanese restaurant three blocks from the apartment. She ate a light meal of Tabbouleh and skewered chicken, then wandered into a used bookstore to peruse the shelves—normally one of her favorite weekend pastimes. But her mind kept returning to those two postcards. No matter how hard she tried, Patterson could not reconcile the differences between the stack of postcards she'd kept since she was a teenager, and the ones her father had given her the previous evening. She also felt bad for blanking Grant when he called the previous night. None of this was his fault, she knew. It was with these two disparate lines of thought concurrent in her mind that Patterson decided what she must do. Which was why, at seven o'clock that evening, she found herself standing outside Jonathan Grant's condo.

When he answered the door, she spoke quickly, cutting him off before he could say anything. "I know I'm probably the last person you want to see right now, but I'm here to apologize. I shouldn't have said all those mean things to you yesterday. I was out of line."

"Yes, you were," Grant replied, but his face relaxed into a soft smile, nonetheless. "Want to come in?"

"I'd like that."

Grant stepped aside to allow Patterson entry into the condo. Then he closed the door and followed her to the kitchen. He made a beeline for a tall two-zone wine cooler built into a wall of cabinets. "You look like you could use a glass of wine."

"That would be so nice." Patterson slid onto a bar stool and leaned on the island counter while Grant selected a bottle of Shiraz and uncorked it. He took down two wine glasses and placed them on the counter, then poured the wine before sliding one glass in her direction. He left the cork out of the bottle to let the remaining wine breathe.

"Cheers." He picked up his glass and clinked it against hers. He took a sip, then put the glass back down on the counter before speaking again. "Want to tell me what brought you here tonight?"

"I came to apologize," Patterson replied. "Which I've done."

"And?"

"Does there have to be another reason? You're my boyfriend after all."

"I'm fairly sure you dumped me yesterday. Unless I misheard when you said we shouldn't see each other anymore." Grant placed his hands on the counter, palms down. "And just for the record, you only said that you were here to apologize. You haven't actually done the deed yet."

"Really, Grant? I assumed contrition was inferred by my presence here," Patterson replied. "But if you actually want me to say the words out loud, then I'm sorry."

"Apology accepted." Grant was grinning now.

"You can be a real ass, you know that?"

"I've been told as much." Grant picked up his wineglass and took another sip. "Now let's get to the other reason you're here."

"How do you know there's another reason?"

"Because I can read you like a book," Grant said. "You have a horrible poker face, at least when it comes to me."

"Okay. I didn't come here just to say sorry. You're right." Patterson took a deep breath. "I've found some things out in the last twenty-four hours. About myself, and about my sister, Julie."

"What kind of things?"

"Well, for a start, her disappearance affected me more than I realized. I thought I'd put what happened to her in the past, that I'd come to terms with it."

"If the events of the raid are anything to go by, you clearly haven't."

"I know that… now. The thing is, I'd never worked on a case like that one before. The Jeffrey Dutton raid was different. It was visceral. Raw."

"Serial killers are not as plentiful as TV and books like to make out," Grant replied. "Most agents go their entire careers without ever encountering one."

"Lucky me," Patterson mused. "Don't get me wrong. I'm not whining. It's just that I wasn't prepared for the emotions that would come to the surface. When I found that girl inside the buried shipping container, I lost my objectivity, and I can't let that happen again. Not if I want to continue with my career."

"I'm glad you realize it," Grant said. "It's the first step to fixing the situation."

"But that's not all. The worst is yet to come." Patterson sipped her wine. "I saw dad last night. We met up for dinner. I really didn't want to—I was in a foul mood—but it's kind of a standing tradition and means so much to him. He's lost Julie. Mom left him. I'm the only family he has left."

"I assume he told you something."

Patterson nodded. "You could say that. It turns out my parents kept stuff from me all those years ago. There were details of my sister's disappearance they didn't share. I don't think he intended to, but dad let it slip last night. What I found out has left me questioning everything."

"Want to tell me about it?" Grant asked.

"I'll do one better. I'll show you." Patterson reached into her purse and withdrew the two sets of postcards, those she'd received when she was a teenager, and the two her father had given her the previous evening. She placed them together on the counter and pushed them toward Grant. "Look at these and tell me what you see."

Grant studied the postcards. He thumbed through them, identifying the LA and Vegas cards immediately. His brow furrowed. "There are discrepancies between these two and the others. It looks like the same handwriting, but the tone changes. In the Vegas and Los Angeles cards she doesn't refer to you specifically, and she signs her name as Julie."

"Whereas in contrast, she used our childhood nicknames for the earlier cards."

"If these came across my desk as part of a missing person's case, I would want to take a closer look," Grant said solemnly.

"Which is exactly the opposite of what the LAPD did at the time."

"So, what do you want to do about it?" Grant asked. "It's unlikely you'll get an official investigation opened after so many years. If that's what you want me to do, I'm not sure that I can."

"I don't want you to open an investigation," Patterson replied. "But I do need a favor."

"What?"

"I want to take some time off. A month. Maybe two. I have plenty of vacation days accrued. More than enough. You can approve it."

"And the purpose of that would be?"

"To do what no one else could be bothered with. To find my sister," Patterson replied in a determined voice.

TEN

There was a moment of silence as Grant processed Patterson's declaration. He stroked the stem of his wineglass and looked at her before speaking again, a note of concern in his voice. "You can't be serious. Julie's been gone for a decade and a half. What makes you think you can find her when the LAPD couldn't?"

"Because they didn't look very hard. They assumed she disappeared of her own free will. Just another naïve girl with stars in her eyes coming to Hollywood to try her luck."

"I'm sure it happens all the time."

"That's no excuse to write her off. Julie would never do that."

"I understand how you feel." Grant finished the last of his wine and reached for the bottle. He poured himself another glass and topped hers up. "But you know how hard it is to investigate cold cases. Witnesses move on. Their memories become fogged by time. Locations change or disappear entirely. Trace evidence is lost or tainted. That's assuming there was an actual criminal investigation with a verifiable chain of custody. It doesn't sound like the police did much in this instance."

"They didn't, but my parents hired a private investigator. At least until they ran out of money to pay him."

"That's something, at least. Do you know what he found, if anything?"

"He didn't turn up much at all according to my dad. Drew a blank. But it's worth following up on. I'm sure dad still has the contact details."

"Assuming nothing's changed, and the guy hasn't died or retired and moved to Florida in the years since," Grant said.

"Yes. Assuming that." Patterson nodded. "Even if his contact details are outdated, he shouldn't be hard to track down if he's still alive."

"It's worth a shot." Grant picked up the postcards, studied the one sent from Las Vegas. "But there might be a reason the private investigator turned up zilch. Your sister might not have made it to LA."

"I realize that. The last postcard that I'm sure she sent came from Oklahoma City. That was where she had an argument with her friend, Stacy, who she was traveling with. It's also where they parted company. I think it's more likely something happened between there and the West Coast. The final postcards could have been sent to cover the tracks of whoever took her."

"Throw the police off or have them looking in the wrong city."

"Especially since Sin City wasn't along her route. The original plan was to go down through Sedona and visit Phoenix before heading on to LA. Stacy had a place to stay there."

"Makes sense," Grant nodded. "But keep in mind, she no longer had accommodation in Phoenix since Stacy wasn't traveling with her anymore. It wouldn't be inconceivable that she changed her plans and went in search of a good time. That would explain the detour to Vegas too."

"True. But the Vegas card was mailed weeks after the postcard from Oklahoma City, and she didn't send postcards from anywhere between the two places, which I'm sure she would have."

"Maybe she was just having too much fun and forgot. It happens."

"Or maybe someone else forced her to write the Vegas and LA cards and sent them later."

"It's impossible to know."

"Which is why I have to start at the beginning. Everything after she parted ways with her friend is an unknown."

"That's a lot of ground to cover. Where will you start?"

"With Stacy. She's the last person who saw my sister alive. It's a long shot, but she might provide a clue."

"And after that?"

"I follow my sister's intended route. Someone out there knows the truth, even if they don't realize it."

"Do you know where Stacy lives now?"

"Not yet, but it won't be hard to find out." Patterson hesitated, then continued. "Especially with your help."

"I haven't even agreed to give you the time off yet, and you're already asking me to use Bureau resources so you can run an unofficial investigation?"

"I'm not asking you to do anything illegal. If I weren't banished from the office, I could do it myself," Patterson replied. "And I'm not running an unofficial investigation. I'm looking into the disappearance of my sister as a private citizen, which I have every right to do."

"Except you want to involve the Bureau, which brings us back to an unofficial investigation."

"Are you going to help me or not?" Patterson could feel her frustration rising.

"Take it easy. You know I'll help."

"Does that mean you'll approve the vacation time, too?"

"I don't see any reason not to. It's your vacation and you've used none of it. Ordinarily I wouldn't be happy with an agent taking so many weeks off at once, but you'll only be stuck behind a desk, anyway. Besides, the whole point of pulling you from the field was to resolve this issue with your sister. Upon your return you will still be required to undergo a psych eval at Quantico before we put you back on active duty though."

"I'm good with that," Patterson replied.

"And there's a caveat to my help," Grant said.

"What?"

"We stick to the rules. You can't use the FBI as your personal investigative tool. If I can help, I will, but if it crosses the line into an area that would require official sanction from higher up the food chain, then it's a no go."

"I understand."

"Good. You can fill out the vacation request in the morning. I'll give it the rubberstamp and push it along to HR."

"Thank you." Patterson felt a rush of relief. The new information about her sister's disappearance, the fact that her parents had hired a private investigator, and the postcards she hadn't known about, had hung over her like a black cloud for the past twenty-four hours. Now she felt the sun poking through. "You really are the best boyfriend ever."

Grant shrugged. "I do my best. Speaking of which, why don't we top up our wine glasses and head into the living room. I've had enough shop talk for one night."

"Jonathan Grant, are you trying to get me drunk so you can take advantage of me?"

"Not in the least. But I am hoping you'll stay tonight."

"You are, huh?" Patterson smiled.

"It doesn't appear I'll see you much over the next couple of months, so I'd like to spend time with you while I can."

"In that case, how could I refuse?"

"You can't. Especially since I'll be approving that vacation request in the morning."

"That sounds like blackmail to me." Patterson laughed, and it felt good.

"I prefer to think of it as an incentive not to run home once the wine runs out."

"Well, I don't need any incentive other than your company.

The only way you're getting rid of me tonight is if you kick me out and lock the door, and I'm fairly sure that's not going to happen."

"Not in a million years," Grant replied. He stepped around the counter and approached Patterson, slipping his arms around her waist, then kissed her gently on the lips.

Patterson returned the kiss, then leaned her head against his shoulder. Tomorrow she would start the search for her sister, but tonight she was right where she wanted to be.

ELEVEN

The private investigator in Los Angeles was a dead end. It was late afternoon, the day after her conversation with Grant at his condo and she was back in her apartment, sitting at the small desk in the corner of the living room upon which she kept her personal laptop. Her phone was lying next to the computer. She had called her father that morning and left a message asking him about the PI. He'd finally gotten back to her after his 4 AM to noon early shift ended and provided the man's name, the company he worked for, and a phone number, which was no longer in service. Patterson went online and looked the business up, discovering it had ceased operations almost a decade before. Worse, the PI had died in 2010. His obituary came up on the first page of results when she typed his name into the web browser. So did an article from the LA Times detailing how he'd been shot and killed by a cheating husband who mistook him for a burglar on the grounds of the mistress's West Hollywood abode.

This was a setback, but a search of the California Secretary of State's website for the defunct investigation company's registration details told her that the private investigator had a business partner. A man named Cole Underwood. It took less than ten minutes to track him down and make a call. He answered on the first ring, but alas, he was of no more help than his dead partner. The company had closed down after the shooting and Underwood was now working as a night watchman for a scrapyard. He remembered Julie because the gig was unusual. They had mostly worked domestics, gathering evidence of unfaithful spouses for divorce proceedings, and insurance fraud cases. The company's files were in a storage locker in Glendale, and the ex-private investigator was in no mood to spend hours rummaging through them. But he didn't need to, because he recalled the contemporaneous conversations about the case with his now deceased partner. The company's inquiries had gone absolutely nowhere. In the short time Patterson's father could afford to pay, they hadn't found a single speck of evidence to suggest that Julie was ever in the Los Angeles area. No one had seen her. No one recognized her photograph or name. If she'd checked into a hotel they couldn't find any evidence of it.

Even though Patterson expected to hear this, she still felt a twinge of disappointment. She had clung to a small hope that some detail, deemed insignificant by the private investigator at the time, might provide her with a thread to pull at. Which was why her spirits lifted when the phone rang, and she saw it was Grant.

"Hey." She picked up the phone and answered. "You were gone already when I woke this morning."

"Some of us still have to work." Grant chuckled.

"Wow. A bit close to the knuckle," Patterson said.

"Sorry."

"I would've liked to say goodbye."

"You looked so peaceful, sleeping. I didn't want to disturb you."

"I wouldn't have minded." Patterson walked to the kitchen where she poured a tall glass of iced tea. "Did you approve the vacation request?"

"All done. You're a free woman until the middle of next

month," Grant replied. "Did you have any luck with the private investigator?"

"No. My dad gave me the details, and I tracked the guy down online. He's dead and his old partner doesn't know anything. It's a brick wall."

"I'm sorry to hear that, but this might cheer you up. I found Julie's friend, Stacy Trafford. She's married now and goes by Stacy Jensen. After completing her bachelor's degree, she went on to law school. She's an attorney working for the Cook County Public Defender's Office."

"She's still in Chicago."

"Yes. I have her home address and number. I'll email them to you, but it sounds like she works long hours, so it might be easier to contact her at work. I'll include her work email and number too."

"Thanks. But I don't think I want to talk to her over the phone. She was the last verified person who saw Julie alive. I want to hear what she has to say face to face. I want to see her reactions when she talks about my sister."

"You're going to Chicago."

"I think that would be for the best, don't you?"

"Probably." Grant hesitated. "Listen, Patterson, I wouldn't get your hopes up. A long time has passed and if Stacy knew anything of relevance, she probably would have told your parents or the investigators at the time. This could very well be a wild goose chase just like the private investigator."

"I'm aware of that." Patterson sighed deeply. "I have to try, though. Leave no stone unturned. Whatever happened to my sister, I don't believe it happened in Los Angeles. My instincts are telling me everyone was looking in the wrong place sixteen years ago."

"I just don't want you to get your hopes up unnecessarily."

"That's sweet. But I know what I'm doing. I'm a trained FBI agent. I'm aware the deck is stacked against me on this."

"But you're going to do it, anyway."

"It's the only way I can put Julie behind me once and for all. Lay her spirit to rest."

"I understand," Grant replied. "When will you leave?"

"As soon as possible. I've got the time off and I want to make the most of it."

"Okay, then. You'll keep me appraised of the situation?"

"Naturally."

"Patterson?"

"Yes?"

"I know I probably don't need to say this, but I just want to reiterate. Everything you do in search of your sister needs to be done as a private citizen. You won't be able to use the FBI or your status as a special agent to open doors."

"I thought you said you'd help me."

"And I will. As long as we stay within the boundaries. You're already on the SAC's radar. I don't need to tell you what will happen if she thinks you've gone rogue."

"Rogue? That's a bit harsh."

"I'm just warning you to play it smart. If you need something, call. If it's within my powers, I will make it happen. If it's likely to get you in trouble, I won't."

"You don't need to worry. I'll color within the lines."

"That's all I want to hear." Grant let a moment of dead air pass before he spoke again. "Just know that I've got your back. Always."

"I never doubted it," Patterson said, and it was true. Despite their disagreement earlier in the week, she trusted Grant more than anyone else in her life, save for her father. Which was why her voice cracked when she next spoke. "I'll miss you, Jonathan."

"Me too," Grant replied. "Take care of yourself out there, Patterson. Come back soon."

"I will." Patterson hung up and stared at the phone's screen for a long minute. Then she placed it on the desk and turned her attention back to the laptop. She went to Expedia and typed in her flight requirements. Fifteen minutes later, she had what she needed. An early morning direct out of JFK. She would be in Chicago by noon the next day. As she stood and headed to the kitchen to grab a late lunch, she couldn't help but wonder what fresh revelations were waiting there.

TWELVE

Patterson arrived at the airport early the next morning. She had packed light, bringing only a roll-on. Having traveled extensively over the past five years in the course of her employment, she had discovered that waiting for checked baggage was an unnecessary inconvenience. She proceeded straight to the pre-check line and identified herself as a federal agent. Her Bureau-issued handgun, a 9mm Glock 19M Gen 5, sat snug to the left side of her body in a tactical shoulder holster, over which she wore a heavy concealing jacket. The FBI encouraged its agents, whether on duty or not, to carry their service weapons whenever possible. That included on flights. Patterson was not officially suspended or removed from duty and had therefore decided to keep her firearm rather than check it.

Once the TSA agent had confirmed her credentials, Patterson made her way to the gate and once again identified herself as an armed federal agent. She pre-boarded the flight and settled in for the two hours and forty-five-minute journey.

It was 11 AM when she landed at O'Hare. Patterson proceeded straight to ground transportation and picked up an Uber, which took her to a Holiday Inn downtown. She had booked this for two nights, figuring she could extend her stay if necessary, although she thought that would be unlikely. She checked in and went to her room, shedding the heavy jacket with relief. She hadn't removed it during the flight, mainly because the sight of a federal agent openly carrying on a commercial flight would spook the other passengers, and firearms were not allowed in the overhead lockers.

Grabbing a lighter jacket, Patterson left her room and rode the elevator down to street level. She crossed the lobby and stopped at the concierge desk, then exited the hotel and followed the concierge's directions three blocks north to a Chipotle Mexican Grill. She'd eaten a light breakfast before leaving the apartment back in Queens, but now, many hours later, she was hungry again. After ordering a burrito along with a side of chips and salsa, she found a seat and took out her phone.

Grant had emailed everything he'd found out about Stacy Jensen, née Trafford. She worked in the Felony Trial Division of the Public Defender's Office in the South Lawndale area of the city five miles from the hotel. Patterson would have preferred to be closer, but most of the decent hotels were clustered downtown, and she figured that any accommodation near the Public Defender's Office would be little more than a fleabag. Especially since the Cook County jail was located a stone's throw away.

Patterson ate a few bites of her burrito, munched some chips, and then called Stacy's office number. When the receptionist came on the line, she identified herself as a federal agent and asked to be put through. There was a click on the other end of the line and a few minutes of hold music—a sixties song that she vaguely recognized—before a fresh voice said, "Hello? How can I help you?"

"Stacy Jensen?"

"That's me," the voice replied. "The desk said you're a federal agent. Is this to do with a case?"

"In a roundabout way," Patterson replied. "I'm conducting a missing persons investigation, and I think you might be of help."

"I don't see how. There's nothing like that in my caseload."

"I'd still like to talk. In person if possible. Can we meet up?"

"I suppose." Stacy sounded unsure. "I'm sorry, but I didn't catch your name."

"Patterson. I'm a special agent with the FBI out of the New York Field Office."

"I see." There was still a measure of apprehension in Stacy's voice. "I'm in court this afternoon. Drug trafficking case. I was about to leave for the courthouse so it's lucky you caught me. If it's an urgent matter, I can push my schedule back and ask for an adjournment until morning."

"That won't be necessary," Patterson replied. "But if you have some free time tomorrow, it's really important I talk with you."

"I have hearings until noon, but I've a couple of hours free after that."

"That will be just fine," Patterson said.

"Where are you staying while you're in town?" Stacy asked.

"The Holiday Inn downtown. It's on Harrison Street."

"I know where it is. Why don't we meet for lunch."

"Lunch will be just fine."

"Perfect. There's a hot dog place about six blocks south of your location. Portillo's. Why don't we get together there at one o'clock? I assume you like hot dogs?"

"I'm from New York, so what do you think?"

"Yeah. These are better than those New York dogs. Up here we do 'em right."

"We'll see about that," Patterson said with a smile. She understood why her sister had liked Stacy. The woman might spend her days defending drug dealers, pimps, and all manner of other lowlifes, but she had a snarky yet playful attitude. It would've been even more pronounced back then. Patterson felt a tug of wistful sorrow in her gut. This was the closest she'd been to Julie in a long time. "How will I recognize you?"

"Oh, you'll know who I am. I'll be the only person who looks like their hair was dunked in a can of red paint."

"That should be easy, then," Patterson replied. "I'll see you tomorrow at one."

"You've got it." Stacy said.

Patterson said goodbye and ended the call, then turned her attention back to the burrito. It appeared she had the rest of the day to herself. Julie's postcards were tucked into the front pocket of her carry-on bag, along with a copy of the LAPD police report on Julie's disappearance that Grant had requested shortly after Patterson joined the Bureau. When she was done eating, she would head back to the hotel and go over everything one more time. Patterson didn't expect to uncover any new information, but it would take her mind off the fact that she had to wait until the next day to interview Stacy. She was eager to hear what Julie's old friend had to say for herself. Whatever happened, tomorrow would be interesting.

THIRTEEN

The next day at half-past twelve in the afternoon, Patterson left the hotel and made her way south toward Portillo's. The restaurant occupied a standalone brick building set back from the street and surrounded by a wraparound parking lot. A metal awning covered an outside seating area. It was here that Patterson saw Stacy Jensen, sitting alone at a table near the iron railings that separated the parking lot from the eating area. The woman had not exaggerated her hair. It cascaded down over her shoulders in a fiery red waterfall of curly abandon and left no doubt regarding who she was.

Patterson crossed the parking lot and entered the patio area. As she approached, Stacy stood to reveal neatly groomed business attire that looked out of place beneath the shock of unruly hair.

"You must be the FBI agent," she said as Patterson reached the table. "I must admit, I've been intrigued ever since your call yesterday. I can't for the life of me think how I could help with a missing person's case. It's hardly within my usual scope of expertise."

"I'm hoping you can help with this one anyway," Patterson said.

"I'll do my best." Stacy nodded toward the dining room. "But first things first, we should take care of the food."

"Sounds good." Patterson nodded and followed Stacy to the service counter, where they both ordered hotdogs with the works and a side of fries.

After collecting the food, they went back outside where Stacy retook her seat. "Have you visited Chicago before?" She asked.

Patterson pulled out a chair and settled opposite her. "No. I've travelled with my job, but this is my first time here."

"Well then, we couldn't have picked a better place to introduce you to real Chicago chow. You're going to love it."

"I hope so," Patterson replied, tearing open a ketchup packet and squeezing red sauce over her fries.

"So tell me, what does the FBI need from a lowly public defender?"

"Actually, I'm not here in my official capacity as a federal agent," Patterson admitted. "The investigation I'm conducting is personal."

"Oh?" A look of bewilderment flashed across Stacy's face. "I guess that would explain why your agency didn't reach out ahead of time to make an appointment through regular channels."

"I do have the blessing of my direct supervisor on this," Patterson said quickly. "My inquiries are personal, but they relate to an existing case and the New York Field Office are aware of the situation."

"I see." Stacy picked up her hot dog and bit into it. "You'd better tell me what this is about. And while you're at it, exactly who I'm speaking to. You only gave me your first name."

"I'm sorry about that, but there was a reason. I want to analyze your responses in real time."

"Or to put it another way, you didn't want to give me the ability to think on it before we met up and prepare my answers." The look on Stacy's face turned to one of irritation. "I might only be a lowly public defender, but I've done my fair share of cross examinations. People are more apt to let slip when they're put on the spot."

"Precisely. Although in this case I'm not looking to trip you up. I just want to find the truth."

"Since we're talking about truth, how about we start with who you are and the real reason you're here," Stacy said. She wasn't eating her hotdog now, apparently having lost her appetite.

"That seems fair. My name is Patterson Blake."

"Blake?" Stacy recoiled as if someone had slapped her in the face. "Of course. It makes sense now. You're Julie's sister."

"That's right." Patterson reached into her pocket and removed her credentials and FBI shield. She flipped the slim black wallet open and placed it on the table in front of Stacy so she could see the ID card. "But I'm also a real special agent with the FBI. Everything I told you is true. I just omitted to mention my surname."

"You're searching for your sister."

"Yes."

"Why now? You must have been a kid when she disappeared. It's been sixteen years."

"Because new information came to light, and it didn't sit well with me."

"You realize the police searched for her at the time and they found nothing, right?" Stacy was regaining her composure. She finally picked up a fry and popped it into her mouth. "The LAPD had a local cop drop by the university and take a statement. There was some discussion of a homicide detective coming from California to interview me in person, but no one ever showed up."

"The police didn't take it seriously," Patterson replied. "And besides, I don't think they were even looking in the right place."

"That was my thought at the time." Stacy said. "I never believed she would decide to stay in Los Angeles instead of coming back to college. She was always so studious. Much more so than me. Sometimes I wonder how I ever got through my degree course and then four years of law school. To be honest, I think Julie had something to do with it. After she vanished, I started taking life more seriously. Don't get me wrong, I wasn't a saint—I'm still not—but it made me realize how precious our lives are. Julie never got to finish school, and I felt like it was my duty not to squander the opportunity I'd been given."

"Would you mind telling me what happened in Oklahoma City?" Patterson asked. "I know it's been a long time, but anything you can remember would be a great help."

"It *has* been a long time," Stacy agreed. "But believe me, I haven't forgotten a moment of it. I've carried the guilt of leaving her there ever since that day that I went to the Greyhound station and caught a bus back to Chicago. Honestly, I believed she'd come to her senses and go home too once I was gone. I'm not making excuses for my actions. I'm just telling you how it was."

"I know." Patterson nodded. "But we're getting ahead of ourselves. Let's start from the beginning."

FOURTEEN

The trip was Julie's idea." Stacy Jensen smiled as if she were recalling some long-forgotten nugget that had only now surfaced within her mind. "It was about a month before the end of spring semester. We were roommates. Her bed was on the left side of the room and mine was on the right. It was late at night and I think we'd been drinking. Actually, I'm sure we had. It was probably a Saturday. She was sitting with her head propped against the headboard and a bottle of water wedged between her knees. She always drank water when we got back to our room after a night out, especially if we'd sunk a few. We were talking about the places we'd visited, or rather all the places I'd visited. She said she'd never really traveled much, outside of New York City and Chicago, that was. Next thing, she had this idea that we should go on a road trip over the summer. Go all the way to the west coast. Los Angeles. Maybe even San Francisco after that. I told her about a friend from high school who was living down in Phoenix. She'd moved there to be close to her boyfriend. I suggested we head in that direction and spend a week at my friend's place, then cut across to California from there. That's how the plan came together. Chicago to LA and all the places in-between. It was some stupid romantic notion. But it stuck in our heads."

"And that's what you did." Patterson picked up her hot dog and took a bite. She didn't care for it as much as a New York street dog, but it was still good.

"Yes. We left about a week after finals. Her parents—sorry, your parents too—were not happy. I know because we were staying in the halls of residence and there was a pay phone in the corridor right next to our room. We could hear the conversations of every student on our floor, or at least their half of it. Julie spent an hour on that phone convincing your parents to let her go on the trip. They finally agreed, but on the condition she took a cell phone with her. Just for safety. Neither of us had a phone, even though they were becoming commonplace by then. She went down to the wireless store and your dad paid for it because I don't think she had good enough credit to get one on her own."

"I know about the cell phone," Patterson said. "I'm more interested in what happened once you got on the road."

"My family lives just outside Chicago, so we moved out of our room at the college and stashed our belongings in my parent's garage before leaving."

"Your folks didn't mind you taking off on a road trip like that?"

"Nah. They're pretty free-spirited. They travelled in Europe when they were young and thought it would build my character. We even stayed at the house a few days before taking off and they helped us plan our stops. They're pretty cool people."

"What happened after you got on the road?"

"For the first couple of weeks, it was great. Neither of us had a car so we rode the bus most of the way, but at one point we hitchhiked." Stacy shook her head. "God, if I knew then what I know now I'd never have done something so reckless."

"So you left Chicago and made your way south, finally ending up in Oklahoma City."

"Yes." Stacy nodded.

"Did you meet anyone during the trip? Were there any incidents that stood out?"

"Not really. We met a couple of cute boys in St. Louis. We stayed in the city for a bunch of nights. I can't remember how many, but it must've been five or six."

"Where did you meet the boys?"

"In a nightclub toward the end of our stay. I was more into them than she was. We hung out the day after, and they showed us the sights. It must've been a Saturday. Then we carried on our way and never saw them again."

"Anything else?"

"Nope." Stacy shook her head. "We stopped in Springfield, Missouri. We weren't exactly flush with cash, so we decided to earn some money. We spent three days at a strawberry farm, picking fruit. It was backbreaking work and wasn't much fun. The pay was lousy too, but it replenished the coffers. When we left there, we went to Joplin, then spent a couple of days in Tulsa, and finally Oklahoma City."

"Which is where you got robbed and went your separate ways."

"U-huh. We hadn't even been there for three hours. The money was getting low again, so we checked into a cheap hotel that Julie had found on the internet. It was above a bar and we had to share the toilet and shower with the rest of the rooms on our floor, but it was twenty bucks a night, which we thought was fantastic. We checked in and dropped our bags in the room, then decided to find something to eat. It was a pretty seedy area of town and we didn't want to take our wallets, so we left them in our bags and just took cash. That was our big mistake."

"Someone broke into the room while you were out," Patterson said.

"Yup. They went through our bags. Took everything of value. Including the cell phone, which Julie had hidden in the bottom of her bag. They even took some of our clothes. I had a couple of travel bags. One big and another smaller one with my toiletries and things. They emptied the small bag and used it to carry the stuff they took. Dumped my makeup and stuff all over the floor."

"The thief took clothes?" Patterson said, surprised.

"Yes. A couple pairs of jeans, including my favorite ones. A summer dress of Julie's. Even our bras and panties. All of them, even the dirty ones. It was weird, and frankly disturbing."

"What did you do about it?"

"We called the police. Filed a report. They didn't sound confident about recovering any of it."

"Did anyone at the hotel see or hear anything?"

"No. Nothing. Or at least, that's what they claimed. The place didn't have surveillance cameras, and there was a seedy bar on the ground floor next to the lobby. Anyone could have wandered up to the rooms above," Stacy said. "After that, the evening went to shit. Julie had the room key, and I accused her of leaving the door unlocked because there was no sign of forced entry. In hindsight, it was probably one of the workers at the hotel, because I remember watching her lock the door. But I wasn't thinking straight. I was so mad that our stuff was gone."

"So you argued?"

"Did we ever. We were screaming at each other. I told Julie I wanted to go back to Chicago. I was done. There was no point continuing. Our wallets were gone. We had no identification. No cell phone. All we had were our clothes—those the thief had left behind—and whatever money we'd taken with us when we went for food. I left her in the room and stormed out. There was a pay phone in the lobby. I called my dad collect, told him what had happened. He agreed to buy me a bus ticket home. School was closed for the summer and we'd already moved out of our room so I couldn't go back there."

"When did you leave to go back?" Patterson asked.

"The next morning, as soon as my dad arranged the ticket. By the time I got back to the room that night, I'd simmered down a bit. We made up. Sort of. I told Julie I was going home, which didn't please her. Until then, we'd been having so much fun. I did my best to convince her to catch a bus home. Go spend the rest of the summer with her parents but she refused. She was determined to keep going, although I have no clue why. Maybe it's because she'd never traveled before and didn't want her first trip to end that way. She'd been looking forward to seeing California so much. It was awful. I didn't want to leave her there alone. But I didn't want to stay there either. I thought it was unsafe. The underwear being taken was the worst. I felt so violated. She accompanied me to the bus station and saw me off. I made one last attempt to talk her out of continuing on, but her mind was made up. I told her to call her dad, at least. But she wouldn't do that either. She was afraid he'd be mad because of the stolen cell phone."

"Julie could be stubborn."

"Tell me about it," Stacy replied, a grim look passing across her face. "I gave her all the money I had left and told her to use it for a bus ticket home. I kind of figured she'd come to her senses when she realized I was really gone. But she didn't. The last time I saw your sister, she was standing on the curb by the side of the bus as it pulled off. I waved to her out the window and she waved back. I think she was crying. At the very least, she wiped her eyes. I was crying too. It was a miserable ride home all alone. Second guessing my decision. Wondering if I should have forced myself to stay."

"Apart from the break-in, did you notice anything suspicious in Oklahoma City?"

"No. Nothing."

"And you didn't meet up with anyone there?"

"Never had time. We'd only been in town a couple of hours when we got robbed."

"There was absolutely nothing unusual about the last days you spent with Julie?"

"Nothing I didn't tell the police after she went missing, and that I've told you, right now."

"I see." Patterson felt a thud of disappointment. Even though it was a long shot, she'd hoped Julie would mention something that had been previously overlooked. "It appears I wasted your time."

"Not at all." Stacy smiled. "You look so much like Julie. Same eyes. Same hair. It feels like you brought her into my life again. It's a strange feeling."

"My dad tells me I look like her all the time."

"He's right." Stacy lapsed into silence for a moment, her eyes drifting away into the parking lot before returning to meet Patterson's gaze. "If Julie were here right now, I bet the two of you would almost look like twins."

"I know," Patterson said, her mind churning over the new information Stacy had provided. Some of the girl's clothes had been stolen including their underwear. Odd items that didn't make sense. This wasn't in the LAPD report. Patterson felt like it should be important but could not make the connection. She felt a surge of disappointment. She was no closer to discovering what happened to Julie. The trip to Chicago was another dead end, just like the private investigator.

FIFTEEN

When lunch was over, Stacy offered to give Patterson a ride back to the hotel. She was apologetic because she couldn't provide more information and appeared genuinely pleased to have connected with the sister of her old friend.

When they reached the Holiday Inn, Stacy reached into the car's backseat, found her purse, and opened it. She removed a business card and handed it to Patterson.

"If you have any more questions, call me," Stacy said. "Don't bother going through the office. Just call me directly on my cell number. It's on the card."

"I will, thank you." Patterson reached into her pocket and pulled out a business card of her own, with the FBI crest on one side and her contact details printed on the other. "And if you think of anything else, no matter how small, please let me know."

"I will," Stacy promised. She waited at the curb, engine idling, while Patterson climbed out and closed the passenger door. Then she rolled the passenger side window down and leaned to look up at the FBI agent through the window. "I know it's been a long time, but I hope you'll find out what happened to Julie."

"Me too," Patterson replied. "If I do, I'll tell you."

"I'd appreciate that, thanks." A thin smile touched Stacy's lips.

Patterson said goodbye and took a step back just as a yellow cab swooped in behind Stacy's vehicle. The taxi driver leaned on his horn and shouted something unintelligible because he couldn't get six feet closer to the hotel doors with his fare. Patterson considered whipping out her FBI badge and slapping it against his window, making him exit the car and explain himself. But she didn't. The last thing she needed was Grant yelling at her for harassing some lowlife cabbie and getting a complaint filed against her. Instead, she ignored the obnoxious driver and watched Stacy pull away and edge back into the downtown traffic. Then she entered the hotel and went straight to her room.

With a do not disturb sign hung on the outside door handle and the security bolt pulled across, Patterson took off her jacket and unstrapped her shoulder holster. She placed the gun on one of the two queen beds along with her jacket and slipped out of her shoes.

She was tired.

She'd risen before dawn the day before to catch the flight from New York to Chicago. She hadn't slept well the previous night, either. Her mind had refused to shut off. All she could think about was her sister, and even when she did finally doze off, Julie had been waiting in her dreams, crying out for help that would never come.

Patterson glanced toward the bed. It was only three in the afternoon, but she had nothing to do for the rest of the day. She also had to figure out her next move. But that could wait. She undressed and placed her clothes in a neat pile on the bed next to the holster and jacket, then went to the bathroom and ran a shower. She stood under the tumbling water for a long while, thinking over her conversation with Stacy and hoping inspiration would strike. But it didn't. No matter how much she wanted to find a hitherto undiscovered clue in the story of how Julie and her friend parted ways, a piece of information that would set her in the right direction, she couldn't.

Frustrated, Patterson stepped from the shower and dried off. She returned to the bedroom and pulled the room darkening shades across the window, then climbed into the bed furthest from the door and pulled the covers up over her shoulders. She closed her eyes, and despite it being the middle of the afternoon, was soon asleep.

————

The ringing phone jolted Patterson awake.

She opened her eyes and was surprised to find the room swathed in blackness. She had slept right through the rest of the afternoon and into the evening. The sun had set.

She pushed the covers back and slipped from the bed, searching the nightstand for her cell phone before she remembered it was on the other queen bed, along with her gun and clothes.

She reached for the bedside lamp and fumbled underneath the shade until her fingers found the round switch that activated the light. Able to see now, she hurried to the other bed and picked up her phone just as it stopped ringing.

The screen informed her that the missed call was from Grant. She had intended to call him this evening, but he'd beat her to it. Except she hadn't answered.

Patterson unlocked the phone's screen and returned the call.

Grant answered on the third ring.

"I was beginning to think you were ignoring me," he said. "I've called three times, and you didn't answer."

"I'm so sorry," Patterson replied. She must've slept right through his first two calls. "I was exhausted. Catching up on sleep."

"Have you spoken to Stacy Jensen yet?" Grant asked.

"I met her for lunch today," Patterson replied. "It didn't get me far, though."

"I'm sorry to hear that."

"At least I confirmed what happened in Oklahoma City. I've only ever heard it second-hand before, but now I know exactly what transpired."

"Must've been weird," Grant said. "Coming face to face with your sister's friend like that. Someone who played such a pivotal role in Julie's disappearance."

"I'm not sure how it felt," Patterson admitted. "She told me I looked like Julie. I think she was taken aback by the resemblance between us. It must've opened up old wounds for her."

"I'm more worried about you. What are you going to do next?"

"This doesn't change anything," Patterson said. "I knew that talking to Stacy was a long shot. But it was worth a try. I guess now I follow my sister's trail. Walk a mile in her shoes, so to speak."

"Which means?"

"It means that my next stop is Oklahoma City. Maybe I'll have more luck there."

"Sounds reasonable. Have you booked a flight yet?"

"No. I'm not going to fly," Patterson said. "I want to follow the same route as Julie. Give myself the time to get in her head. I think I'm going to drive."

SIXTEEN

There was a long silence on the other end of the line. Patterson wondered if they had gotten disconnected. "Grant, you still there?"

"I'm here. Just letting what you said sink in." He cleared his throat. "Not sure I want you out on the road all alone like that."

"Why? Because I'm a woman?"

"No. Because it's not safe. That's how your sister ended up missing."

Now it was Patterson's turn to say nothing because she wasn't sure how to respond to his comment.

Finally, Grant spoke again. "I'm sorry. That was below the belt."

"Yes, it was." Patterson drew in a long breath. Calmed herself. She knew he was just worried about her. "Do I need to remind you I'm an FBI agent? I have a gun strapped to me at all times. Anyone trying it on is going to get a short sharp shock."

"I know you can take care of yourself."

"Damn right."

"I also know that I can't stop you doing this if you've made up your mind."

"For someone who just said a dumb thing, you're a pretty smart man."

"Thank you. I think. I might regret asking this, but how do you actually plan to get between Chicago and Oklahoma City?"

"I figure I'll hitch," Patterson said, smirking. "I've got a pair of short-shorts and a crop top in my bag. That should get me some rides, don't you think?"

"Very funny."

"You deserve it." Patterson was all business again now. "Seriously though, I'll need to rent a car. If Oklahoma City doesn't pan out, then I'll keep pressing on. Someone, somewhere must know something."

"Do me a favor. Don't rent that car just yet," Grant said thoughtfully.

"Why?"

"Just give me an hour or two. I'll call you back."

"What are you up to?"

"Let me make a few calls, okay?" Grant was being frustratingly enigmatic. "I might be able to help you out on this one."

"Fine. You've got an hour. But then I'm going to make my arrangements. I have to be out of here tomorrow."

"I know that," Grant replied. "I'll call you back soon. Promise. Love you."

"Love you, too," Patterson replied, a moment before the line went dead.

She dropped the phone back on the bed and got dressed. She hadn't meant to sleep so long but was glad anyway. She felt refreshed now. Ready for whatever awaited her down the road in Oklahoma City. First, though, she would need to get some dinner. A hot dog and fries were not enough to sustain her all day.

She went to the queen bed nearest the door—the one she wasn't sleeping in—and slipped her gun from its holster. There was a wall safe with a digital lock on the wall inside the room's closet. It wasn't big enough to fit both the gun and holster, but it would keep her weapon secure while she was out of the room. She released the magazine before stowing the gun and closing the safe door, then typed a four-digit code into the safe's keypad and hit the pound key. She waited for the code to flash momentarily on the screen to confirm it was correct before turning and heading for the door.

She didn't feel like visiting Chipotle again, and there was little else to eat within walking distance of the hotel besides the hot dog place where she'd met Stacy earlier in the day. Patterson didn't feel like catching an Uber further afield, but there was a bar and grill off the lobby.

She entered and approached the bar, sliding onto a stool and picking up a menu. When the bartender approached, she asked for a Heineken. From the menu she ordered fish tacos with red snapper, and a side salad. The bar was mostly empty, and the food soon arrived. Twenty minutes later she was on her way back to the room.

It would be another three quarters of an hour before Grant called back. When she answered, he sounded pleased with himself.

"All taken care of," he said. "I found you a ride."

"Really?" Patterson was surprised. "What kind of ride?"

"A seized vehicle. It's yours for as long as you need it."

"How did you manage that?"

"I called in a favor with a buddy of mine at the Chicago Field Office. We were at the Academy together. He's the Special Agent in Charge out there now. You can head on over to the office in the morning and ask for Bill Walters. He'll take care of it from there."

"Thank you. You didn't have to do that."

"There is a condition attached," Grant said. "You're probably not going to like it."

"What condition?" Patterson asked, warily.

"I want you to check in with the field office when you reach Oklahoma City. Let them know you're in town."

"Why? I'm on my own time."

"That's true. But you'll be driving an official FBI vehicle. Federal plates. You'll also be asking questions around town, no doubt. It's only fair that you appraise them of your activities while you're there. As a courtesy."

"I still don't see why—"

"It's not a request, Patterson. If you want the car, then you'll do this one thing for me. I'm not stupid. I know you'll be flashing your badge when you're down there. The last thing I need is a complaint that one of my team is running around conducting an off-the-books investigation and using FBI clout to do it. Or worse, you get arrested for impersonating a federal agent."

"No one is going to arrest me. I'm a real federal agent."

"Which is precisely why I want you to check in. And not just in Oklahoma City. Every place you stop. Doesn't matter whether it's a field office, a resident agency, or the local county sheriff. You appraise them of your presence."

"All right, fine." Patterson felt a rush of frustration. Was this Grant's way of keeping tabs on her? "I'll go tell the locals I'm in town. Happy?"

"You don't have to sound so irritated," Grant replied. "This actually works in your favor. If you go it alone, you'll be out in the cold. If you do as I ask, you'll generate goodwill. You might even be able to use some of the local resources. Apart from anything else, it's just polite to say hello when you're playing in someone else's sandbox."

"Okay. I already said I'd play nice." Despite her annoyance, Patterson had to admit that Grant had a point. It might be beneficial to have contacts at the local field office. And she wanted that car. A rental was fine, but the federal vehicle was better. Those government issued plates were worth far more than the money she would save on the rental contract. They would get her into places she would not otherwise be able to go. They would allow her to park in restricted areas. They would also give her credibility. While she was sure that Grant wanted to track her progress across the country, he was also trying to help. She took a deep breath. "Thank you. I know you have my back. I do appreciate it, even if I don't show it all the time."

"I know," Grant said. "And I understand how you feel. You've gone through a lot in the past few days, and it isn't easy dating a coworker, especially when they're your boss."

"I'm sure it's not easy being that boss either," Patterson conceded. "I can be hardheaded. I know that. And we always knew there might come a time when our personal lives would clash with our professional lives. I'll try harder to see things from your perspective in the future."

"I'd appreciate that." Grant sounded relieved.

"I don't want to lose you."

"You won't," Grant said. "Just get this thing with your sister taken care of. Work it out and hurry home. I miss you."

"Miss you, too," Patterson replied, feeling the miles between them all of a sudden. Any remaining irritation faded to be replaced by longing. "I wish you were here with me."

"Me too," Grant said in a soft voice. "Me too."

SEVENTEEN

By the time Grant hung up the phone, it was almost eleven. Patterson was not a night owl, preferring to go to bed at a reasonable time and get up early. Under normal circumstances this was a good thing, because she had to be up before 6 AM to make it into Lower Manhattan by eight, when her workday began. Even on weekends she did not change this habit, her circadian rhythm having been immutably programmed ever since the academy. Not that her job didn't come with the occasional late night or two. She had spent more than one evening on stakeout watching a subject or working some emergency or other. But she did not prefer this, and relied on copious amounts of caffeine to get through.

She turned on the TV and browsed to a news channel, as she often did in the evening before bed. She liked to stay informed. Sometimes today's news would end up as tomorrow's work. Local cops working a homicide might call the FBI in to assist, for example.

Listening to the news anchor, she made her way to the bathroom to clean her teeth. She barely got halfway when a new sound drew her attention. The phone was ringing again. She changed course and went to the nightstand, where she'd left it after her conversation with Grant. She expected it to be him calling back, but when she looked at the screen, she was surprised to see a different name displayed. One she had only entered into her contacts that afternoon.

Stacy Jensen.

When she answered, her sister's old friend sounded apologetic.

"Hope you don't mind me calling so late," Stacy said. "I wasn't sure if I should wait until morning, but I didn't want to miss you since you're checking out tomorrow."

"Another ten minutes and I would've hit the sack already," Patterson replied. She picked up the remote and pointed it at the TV, shutting it off. "But I'm still up right now."

"Oh, good." Stacy sounded relieved. "I'm glad to hear it."

"What's on your mind?" Patterson asked. "Did you remember something else about the trip?"

"In a roundabout way. This is better. I have something for you."

"What is it?" Patterson felt her heart leap. Any thought of sleep faded.

"Why don't you meet me in the lobby, and I'll show you," Stacy said. "I'm on my way to the hotel right now. There's barely any traffic downtown at this time of night. The GPS says I'll be there in less than ten minutes. Give me another five to park."

"Fifteen minutes. Got it." Patterson was burning with curiosity. "There's a bar and restaurant in the lobby. I think they close at twelve. Why don't we meet there instead?"

"I know the place. I've been there before."

"Great, see you then." Patterson hung up the phone.

When she arrived at the bar, Stacy wasn't there yet. There were few other customers at this late hour. Two men in business suits were shooting pool and drinking tumblers of whiskey. A couple in their sixties sat at the bar, their heads bent low in conversation.

When she approached, the bartender nodded, recognizing her from earlier in the evening. She ordered another Heineken and sat nursing it until she saw Stacy enter.

The public defender waved and started toward her.

Patterson noticed she was carrying a large manila envelope and wondered what was inside that had prompted Julie's old friend to make the trip across town when most people were thinking about climbing into bed.

"I'm so glad I didn't catch you in bed when I called," Stacy said, sliding up onto a stool next to Patterson. She turned to motion the bartender, ordering a glass of house Merlot.

"I'll get that," Patterson said, asking the bartender to put it on her room. "It's the least I can do since you raced here to meet me like this."

"It's nothing. Really. Julie was my best friend. I'd do anything to know what happened to her." She placed the manila envelope on the bar. "You're probably wondering what all this is about."

"I'm more than a little intrigued," Patterson admitted. She picked up her beer mug and took a swig just as Stacy's wine arrived. "I figured you told me everything you knew at lunch."

"I did." Stacy sipped her wine. "But after we talked, I couldn't help thinking about Julie. She was on my mind all afternoon and evening. Meeting you really brought it all back. The shock of her disappearance. Talking to the police. Waiting for years, hoping there would be news of her. I wished there were something more I could do to help you."

"Just talking to you today, hearing firsthand what happened in Oklahoma City, was a big help," Patterson said. "To be honest, I feel closer to Julie for having met you."

"That's kind of you to say." Stacy tapped on the manila envelope. "But I'm hoping that what I have here will be of even more help."

"What is it?" Patterson asked.

"Look for yourself." Stacy pushed the envelope along the bar. Patterson picked it up and opened the flap. She reached in and withdrew a folded roadmap with dogeared corners and a crease running through it. "A map?"

"Not just any map. This is the one that Julie and I planned our trip on. I bought it at the Borders bookstore near the university campus. We marked all the cities we wanted to visit on it, worked out where we were going to go. I didn't realize I still had it in my bag when I took the bus back to Chicago."

Patterson listened with growing excitement. "This is the actual map you and Julie used on the trip?"

Stacy nodded. "At least until we got to Oklahoma City. It's been in a shoebox at the back of my closet all these years. I'd pretty much forgotten about it until tonight. Tore my whole spare bedroom apart, looking for it. I wanted to give it to you before you left. I figured it might be useful."

"I don't know what to say." Patterson felt tears welling in her eyes. Her sister had used this map. Studied it. Written on it. She felt a visceral connection to Julie when she held it. She wanted to open the map and lay it out, see what lay within its folds. But not here, in the bar. It could get wet, or beer stained. That would ruin it. Patterson couldn't take the chance. "Are you sure you want to part with this?"

"If it were anyone else, I wouldn't. But you're Julie's sister. Not only that, but you might find the answers I've wanted for so long. Please, take it. I insist."

"Thank you." Patterson slipped the map back into its protective envelope. "You don't know how much this means to me."

"I have a fair idea." Stacy finished the last of her wine. "I've kept you long enough. Besides, it's late and I have court in the morning. If you have more questions, just call me."

"I will." Patterson nodded.

Stacy climbed down from the stool and removed a set of car keys from her pocket. She met Patterson's gaze. "Good luck out there. Stay safe."

Again, Patterson nodded, her eyes drifting back to the envelope containing the map. When she looked around, Stacy was already on her way toward the door. Patterson swallowed the last of her beer, picked up the envelope, and followed.

EIGHTEEN

With trembling hands, Patterson gently unfolded the map and spread it out in front of her on the queen bed closest to the hotel room door. The bed she wasn't sleeping in. Moments before, she had swept her clothes and the gun holster from atop the comforter to make space.

She could hardly believe it. This was the actual map Stacy and Julie had used to plan their trip from Chicago to Los Angeles all those years ago. It was an unbelievable find and made her trip to the Windy City more than worthwhile. Now she had solid evidence of the places her sister visited and had planned to go. The map was of the entire United States. Either Stacy or Julie had drawn their route using a black marker. The ink was now faded to a dark brown, but the meandering hand-drawn line from the top of the country to the West Coast was still visible. Several cities and towns were circled, too. Next to these were notes, some of which were written in a handwriting that Patterson recognized as Julie's. One notation, next to St. Louis, read *we should stay here a few days*. Another, written in red ink, said *always wanted to visit here*. This was next to Sedona, a town between Flagstaff and Phoenix in Arizona. Surrounded by red colored rocky buttes and forests of Pine, the desert town was a vibrant New Age center. It was also home to canyons and trails that offered some of the best hiking in the state. That Julie wanted to visit this place was no surprise. She had always possessed a free spirit and loved the outdoors.

Had her sister still followed that route anyway, or had she amended her journey after she found herself alone on the trip? Patterson knew she hadn't stayed with Stacy's friend—the private investigator in Los Angeles had confirmed that—but she could have found alternate lodgings.

Patterson stood and went to her travel bag. She removed the stack of postcards and returned to the map, placing the bottom one over Chicago, the start of her sister's journey. Julie had sent this postcard before the two friends left and had written a gushing message on the back, proclaiming her excitement for the adventure ahead. Just like all the postcards before Vegas, this one was addressed to PB. It was signed Jelly–her sister's childhood nickname. The postcard was full of hope. Promise. That trend continued until Julie and Stacy parted ways.

Patterson placed more postcards on the map. St. Louis. Joplin. Tulsa. She kept going all the way to Oklahoma City, which she thought, until recently, to be the last postcard sent.

Patterson placed the two new postcards on the map, one over Las Vegas, and the other next to Los Angeles. She stood and looked at her handiwork. The brightly colored rectangles of cardboard formed a snaking montage across the surface of the map. They overlapped each other, the top postcard obscuring the picture of the one beneath. All except the final two. The pair of postcards her father had finally admitted to keeping from Patterson. Even on the map they were an anomaly, spread too far from the rest.

Patterson felt a lump rise in her throat. She was looking at a graphic representation of her sister's last known movements. The final days of normality before the darkness had descended upon Patterson's family, tearing them apart forever. Her gaze lingered on the space between Oklahoma City and Las Vegas.

Somewhere within those few inches of creased map, her sister had fallen off the face of the planet.

"What happened to you, Jelly?" she whispered to the silent room. "Where did you go?"

But she received no answer.

Patterson's eyes moistened with tears. She took a deep breath and fought back the sorrow. Then she gathered up the postcards and returned them to the front pouch of her bag. Turning back to the opened map, Patterson studied the hand-drawn route and the excited comments the two friends had scribbled so many years ago. One stood out. It was not in Julie's hand, which meant Stacy had added it, possibly before they ever even left Chicago. She had circled Los Angeles in red pen and written four small words next to it in blocky capitals.

END OF THE ROAD.

The comment was almost prophetic, except the end of the road came much sooner for both girls. Stacy in Oklahoma City. Her sister sometime afterward. Because try as she might, Patterson could not accept that Julie mailed the final two oddly worded postcards. At least, not willingly. If her sister had ever even made it to Los Angeles, she was already in trouble.

Another thought occurred to Patterson, one that she had so far refused to entertain. Julie was already dead when the postcards were mailed.

Patterson didn't want to think about that. She pushed the dreadful thought from her mind and focused instead on the task at hand. Tomorrow she would leave Chicago and head south, following her sister's trail. She studied the map a moment longer, then folded and returned it to the manila envelope, which she placed in the front pocket of her travel bag alongside the postcards.

It was after midnight now. The hotel was quiet, most of the other guests already sleeping. Patterson had a long journey ahead of her and didn't want to be tired in the morning. She undressed and slipped on the oversized Yankees T-shirt she wore to bed, because she hated her shoulders being cold at night. Then she cleaned her teeth and climbed beneath the covers before turning out the light. And as sleep crept upon her, Patterson said a silent prayer to whatever force controlled the universe, that she would find Julie alive and well, and if not, that her sister hadn't suffered.

NINETEEN

Patterson checked out of the hotel first thing the next morning and summoned an Uber. When it arrived, she told the driver to take her to the FBI's field office on Roosevelt Road. Three miles and ten minutes later, they arrived at her destination.

The FBI offices occupied a modern concrete and glass building that rose ten stories into the air. It was surrounded by black metal railings that were probably not as flimsy as they looked. The only access was through a turnstile next to a squat free-standing guardhouse. Nearby, a flagpole flew the United States flag at half-mast. There had been two mass shootings in the previous month and at least nine so far since the beginning of the year. And that was just those the national media reported. Many more slipped by without such widespread attention. Lowered flags were becoming the norm, a trend which worried Patterson.

She approached the guardhouse window and displayed her FBI credentials. When the guard asked about her business inside the building, she informed him she was there to meet the Special Agent in Charge, Bill Walters. The guard picked up the handset, conversed for a few seconds, then pushed the visitor sign-in sheet her away before releasing the turnstile to allow her entry into the courtyard fronting the building proper.

Special Agent in Charge Bill Walters was already waiting in the lobby when she entered. He was a large man with thinning brown hair and black-rimmed glasses. As she approached, a wide grin broke out on his face.

"You must be Patterson Blake," he said. "I've heard so much about you from Grant. I'm happy we finally get a chance to meet."

"Me too," Patterson replied, not mentioning that until twelve hours ago she had never heard of Bill Walters. Grant was obviously more forthcoming with his old friend than he had been with her. She wondered how often the pair talked. "I've been told you have a car for me."

Bill pushed a hand into his pocket and took out a set of keys, which he held out between two fingers. "I do, indeed. Although I have to warn you, it isn't the most luxurious ride."

"As long as it gets me from A to B, I'll be happy." Patterson accepted the keys. "Grant told you what I need the car for, right? You know I'll be driving it out of state?"

"He let me know the situation. I wouldn't usually release a vehicle to an off-duty agent for personal business, but Grant is an old friend. I owe him. Besides, I figure you're investigating a cold case that crosses state lines. If you find anything it may very well shift from a personal quest to an active investigation. Given the circumstances, I think a little bending of the rules is within my purview."

"I appreciate it," Patterson replied. She wondered what the Chicago Field Office SAC was indebted to her boyfriend for, but she didn't ask. "I really do."

"You might want to refrain from thanking me until you've seen the car."

"It's that bad?" Patterson wondered what Grant had saddled her with. It was, after all, a seized asset. An image flashed through her mind of a tricked-out Camaro with fat tires, lowered suspension, and a pair of dice hanging from the rearview mirror.

"Why don't you come see for yourself." Bill turned and motioned for her to follow him through a set of doors on the far side of the lobby. These led into a multistory parking garage attached to the rear of the building. Sitting in a bay in the first row was a Toyota Corolla with faded lime green paint, oversized rims, and low-profile tires, to which Bill instantly veered.

"This is the car?" Patterson stared at the vehicle in disbelief. "It's so…"

"Gaudy?"

"That isn't quite the word I was searching for, but it will do," Patterson replied. It was not the Camaro she'd imagined, but the Toyota was close enough.

"Hey, beggars can't be choosers. Am I right?" Bill chuckled, obviously amused at the thought of her driving across the country in a car that looked like it had been plucked from the set of a low budget street racer movie.

"Why do you even have this?" Patterson asked.

"It's a forfeiture that came our way a couple of years ago. Instead of sending it to the GSA auction, we kept it as an undercover vehicle. Came in pretty useful for a while, until the local lowlifes started recognizing it. We haven't used it for six months. I was about to send it over to the auction, get rid of the damn thing."

"I see." Patterson wondered if it was too late to change her mind and rent something instead.

"Now that you've come along, I don't need to. At least for a while. Saves me some paperwork."

"Glad I could be of help," Patterson said.

"Grant said you need it for a month, maybe longer."

"That's right." Patterson nodded.

"One thing, which I'm sure Grant already mentioned. We had regular state plates on this when we were using it in the field, but it has federal plates now. The plates are assigned to the

Chicago Field Office, so keep out of trouble. I don't want to be paying any speeding tickets or answering unnecessary questions about why you're driving around the country in this. Got it?"

"Understood." Patterson nodded. "I'll bring it back when I'm done."

"That would be appreciated."

Patterson went to the rear of the vehicle and opened the trunk. She placed her travel bag inside, then slammed it shut before climbing into the driver's seat.

Bill leaned down and spoke through the open door. "Tell Grant he owes me a steak dinner and a couple of beers next time I'm in the Big Apple."

"I'll make sure he's aware of his responsibilities," Patterson said with a smile, then pulled the door closed.

She pushed the key into the ignition and started the car. The engine sputtered for a moment, then caught. She glanced down at the dials. There was half a tank of gas. Enough to get her far from Chicago.

She eased out of the parking space and turned in the direction of the exit. Bill Walters was standing near the vacated parking space, watching her leave. She steered left and pulled up to the parking garage's barrier gate. Fifteen minutes later she was on the highway and heading out of the city.

TWENTY

Patterson left the city behind and drove out through the suburbs, passing through Cicero, the village of Lyons, then McCook, and finally Burr Ridge, which was where she picked up I-55.

The trip to Oklahoma City was almost eight hundred miles. The car did not have a built-in GPS, but there was one on her phone. Without accounting for traffic, bathroom breaks, or stopping to eat, the journey would take approximately twelve hours. This was lengthened to fifteen when current road conditions were taken into account. There was the potential for even longer delays if she hit the larger cities and towns along the way during the morning or evening commutes. All things considered, she would be lucky to make it in less than twenty hours. This meant an overnight stop, either in St. Louis, which was less than half the distance to Oklahoma City, or Springfield, Missouri, over an hour past the halfway point. Either way, one day's drive would be longer than the other. It was already 11 AM, and she hadn't eaten yet, having skipped breakfast. She would need to stop soon and find food. This meant she would arrive in St. Louis right about the time evening rush hour was kicking off. Rather than fight through gridlocked traffic, she decided that St. Louis made the most sense for a layover.

She pushed on for the next hour, content to put Chicago far behind her before looking for a place to stop and eat lunch, which ended up being a diner in Bloomington, Illinois. The place sat on the outskirts of town near the highway. A one-story building built to look like an old railway dining car. It served a mean corned beef hash, which Patterson ate with gusto. With her appetite sated, she drank coffee and used her phone to book a room at the Hyatt Regency Downtown. She could have found a cheap motel off the highway, but Patterson couldn't see the point. It would shave half an hour off her travel time, but at the expense of a clean room and comfortable bed. Besides, Julie had spent time in St. Louis and even though Patterson did not need to investigate in the city, she felt closer to her sister by staying in the heart of it all.

After finishing her third cup of joe and checking the hotel's confirmation email, Patterson hit the road again and drove for the next three hours, arriving at her stopover in the late afternoon. She checked into the hotel and went to her room, which was on the third floor near the elevators. The desk clerk was a chatty man in his late twenties who took a shine to her and thus provided Patterson with a view of Gateway Arch National Park and the Mississippi River beyond.

She took a shower and went for a walk, heading for the arch, and then strolling along the riverbank for an hour. Afterward, she found an Italian restaurant downtown and ate a wood-fired pizza, washed down with an iced tea before returning to her room for the night. The next morning, she woke early and pushed on after a light breakfast, determined to reach Oklahoma City as quickly as possible. Ten hours later, weary from the road, she entered the city and drove directly to the accommodation where Julie had stayed sixteen years before.

TWENTY-ONE

The Welcome Inn sat in the Uptown district of Oklahoma City nestled between a neighborhood grocery store and a nail salon. It was an older brick building with a tavern occupying the ground floor. Patterson turned into the side parking lot and made her way to the lobby, which was accessed through a door to the right of the tavern.

The neighborhood didn't seem too bad compared to some of the worst areas of New York City, but it wasn't trendy chic either. Patterson had decided during the drive south that she would book a room at the same accommodation Julie had all those years before, but now she hesitated. There were nicer accommodations down the road in hip areas like Bricktown, which Patterson intended to explore, if only because the postcard Julie sent was from there. But there was a reason Patterson decided to stay at the Welcome Inn. She wanted to get a feel for the situation Julie found herself in all those years ago. She also wanted to check out the neighborhood. From here on out, Julie's movements were an unknown. Patterson didn't know how long her sister had stayed in Oklahoma City, or where she'd gone while she was here, but hoped to find out. Making up her mind, Patterson pushed the door open and stepped inside.

The Welcome Inn's lobby smelled like a mix of cigarette smoke and mold. It was a small space containing only a couple of hard plastic chairs against one wall, a mostly empty brochure rack with a sign above it that read, *Discover OKC*, and a coffeemaker sitting on a worn wooden table next to a tub of creamers and sugar packets. There were no cups and the coffee in the half empty carafe looked stewed. The coffee maker's plug was out of the wall socket, which meant the brew was also stone cold. There was an opening on the far wall through which Patterson could see a staircase ascending into gloom, no doubt leading to the guest rooms above. The lobby's only other feature was a registration window cut into the wall to her right.

The desk clerk looked up at Patterson's approach. He was an older man with a gut and a ring of patchy gray hair surrounding the dome of his bald head. He wore a pair of glasses with thick brown frames. A cigarette smoldered in an ashtray on his desk despite a no smoking sign screwed to the wall. Beneath this was another sign informing guests that visitors were not allowed in the rooms after 10 PM.

"Can I help you, sweetie?" The man asked in a gravelly voice.

"I'll take a room," Patterson replied. "Second floor if you have it."

"I think we can accommodate that," the desk clerk replied, tapping away at a keyboard connected to an older model desktop computer. "I have a room with two twins. No queen beds. No en suite either. There's a bathroom on both floors so you have to share."

"How many rooms are there on each floor?" Patterson asked. She would have more questions later, but she wanted to see the room first.

"Ten." The man coughed, clearing phlegm from his throat. "Most are taken by long-term residents who pay by the month."

"Really? Has that always been the case?"

"As long as I've worked here."

"And how long is that?"

"Eighteen years, give or take. I've pretty much run the place single-handed for the past six. The guy who owns the building lives down in Florida these days. Miami. He put me in charge when he left. Except for the tavern, that is. His son runs that."

"I see." Patterson wondered if the owner's son had also been running the bar when Julie stayed. It might be worth talking to him. She also wondered if there had been any long-term residents back then. "How long has your oldest resident been living here?"

The man shrugged. "A couple years. Most folks don't stay too long. It ain't exactly the Ritz." He looked up at her with watery eyes. "So, you want a room, or not?"

"Yes." Patterson nodded.

"Okey-doke. It's fifty bucks a night. Weekly rate is three hundred and if you book by the month, you get an extra ten percent off on top."

"Two nights will be fine for now," Patterson replied. She wondered who would pay over a thousand dollars a month to stay in a dive that didn't even provide private bathrooms. "If I need longer, I'll come back and see you."

The desk clerk sighed and tapped at his computer again, then reached behind to a pegboard and plucked a key on a fat red fob. No modern electronic locks here. He placed the key on the counter and pushed it toward her. "Room 201. Go up the stairs and turn left, then follow the corridor all the way to the end. It'll be the last door on your right."

"Thank you." Patterson took the key. "One more thing…"

"Yes?"

"My sister rented a room here several years ago. If I wanted to find out how many nights she stayed, would you be able to tell me?"

"Depends." The man rubbed his chin. "How long ago?"

"Sixteen years."

"Holy cow, lady. We didn't even have a computer back then.

Did everything with handwritten registration cards." He nodded toward the machine sitting on his desk. "I only got this after the owner made me manager of the place. He was old-school. Pen and paper and all that jazz."

"You still have the registration cards?"

"Sure. There are boxes of 'em in the storage closet under the stairs. Can't say I'm inclined to paw through them. Why don't you just ask your sister if it's so important to you?"

"We don't keep in touch anymore," Patterson replied without elaborating. She didn't want to discuss her reason for being in town with a stranger. Especially one who was working at the place during the time Julie was staying there. For all Patterson knew, the hotel manager was involved in her disappearance—although she thought it unlikely. "I could make it worth your while."

The manager's eyes grew brighter. He licked his lips. "What did you have in mind?"

"Fifty bucks, cash," Patterson replied, wondering if the man had jumped to the wrong conclusion. "Will that do it?"

"I don't know. It's an awful lot of work."

"How much do you want?" Patterson asked. She briefly toyed with the idea of flashing her credentials but thought better of it. If he clammed up, she would never find out how long her sister had stayed in the city. Not only that, but he might not enjoy having a federal agent on the property. She could find herself kicked out before she got any information.

"Make it a Benny and I'll see what I can do."

"A hundred dollars just to look through some old registration cards?"

"You want me to take a look, or don't you?"

"Fine. How long will it take?"

"Give me twenty-four hours." The manager picked up a pen. "I'll need the approximate date your sister stayed here and her name."

"It would have been June 2005. Julie Blake. She was traveling with a friend, Stacy Trafford," Patterson replied, giving Stacy's maiden name.

The man scribbled the information down and nodded. "Got it."

"Great." Patterson picked up her travel bag and turned toward the stairs. But before she could take a step, the manager spoke again.

"I'll need the money up front."

"That isn't going to happen," Patterson replied, setting her bag down once more. She opened it and removed her purse—careful not to let her jacket fall open to reveal the Glock handgun concealed in its holster beneath—and took out a fifty-dollar bill which she slapped down on the counter. "You can make do with this for now. I'll pay the rest when you have the information I need."

"There's no guarantee I can find anything," the manager said, scooping up the cash and pushing into his shirt pocket. "Nobody's looked at those old cards in over a decade. I was thinking about trashing the lot of them, to tell the truth. There's no reason to keep them. Who knows, some might've already gotten dumped."

"Just do your best," Patterson replied, irritated. Then she hoisted her bag and started toward the stairs, resisting the urge to blow her cover and arrest him for being an obnoxious dick.

TWENTY-TWO

I t was 7 PM by the time Patterson entered her room, and it was every bit as bad as she had imagined. There were two twin beds, one pushed up against each wall with a shared nightstand between them. A tall brown dresser stood opposite the beds, one drawer coming off its rails and sitting at an angle. The room was painted an off-white color that did nothing to hide the grime. A thin rug covered the wood floor between the two beds, its pattern long since faded. A single window with security bars affixed to the outside frame—which was surely not up to code—cast a patch of weak light into the dim space. The room reminded her of a prison cell. She wondered how people could live long term in such a place.

Patterson sat on the bed closest to the door, noting how thin the mattress was. She closed her eyes and tried to imagine Julie here. There was no way for Patterson to know which room had been Julie's, but with any luck she would soon find out how long Julie had spent in Oklahoma City when the desk clerk retrieved her sister's registration card.

She would also need to visit the FBI office first thing in the morning and notify them of her presence in town, as per her agreement with Grant.

Speaking of which, she hadn't spoken to him since leaving Chicago. He was trying to give her space, which was nice, but she missed hearing his voice. She took out her phone and called him but was disappointed when it went to voicemail. Deflated, Patterson decided to head across the road to a hamburger joint she'd noticed when she pulled into the parking lot. It was the only eatery within two blocks and therefore must have been the place Julie and Stacy dined on that fateful night when their room was broken into. It would not provide any clues regarding her sister's disappearance, but it would be another glimpse into the reality of Julie's last known movements.

Patterson stood and moved her travel bag from the bed to the floor, sliding it under the bed frame and pushing as far back as she could. Julie had thought she was safe leaving her luggage here, and even though it was a decade and a half later, Patterson wanted to take no chances.

With her bag safely hidden, she left the room and made her way down the dingy hallway to the stairs. When she passed through the lobby, the manager looked up, his beady eyes trailing her to the door.

It was at that moment that her phone rang.

It was Grant calling back.

"Hey," Patterson said, accepting the call. "I was just about to go find something to eat. I figured you might have gotten held up at work and couldn't answer your phone."

"Sorry. It wasn't that. I was driving. I'm home now."

Grant's voice sounded strained. Patterson wondered if he was struggling with her decision to investigate Julie's disappearance, or if something else was on his mind.

"Whatever. I'm glad you called," she said. "I just arrived in Oklahoma City and checked into the same hotel Julie was staying at."

"You mean that dingy hotel?" Grant sounded surprised and a little worried.

"I want to have the same experience she did. Get inside her

head. And anyway, I need information from them, and I figured that throwing some business their way might grease the wheels." She didn't mention the hundred dollars promised to the hotel manager if he located Julie's registration card.

"Or you could find another way to grease the wheels and stay somewhere safe. A decent hotel in a better part of town."

"I'm staying at the hotel," Patterson replied. "It's not up for discussion."

"Hey, I'm just worried about you," Grant said. "I know how much this means to you, but please be careful."

"I'm always careful," Patterson replied. "You know that."

"All I'm saying is don't get carried away with this and lose your objectivity."

"I'm not going to. And you need to stop worrying."

"Not going to happen," Grant replied. "Have you checked in with the local field office yet?"

"I've only just gotten here," Patterson said. She was standing outside of the burger place and peering in through the window. The interior looked new. Clean. The tables and chairs were modern. The sign above the door had a date painted on it next to the restaurant's name. *Est. 2014.* This might be the right building, but it was not the restaurant Julie and Stacy had visited on the night they got robbed. It was a reminder of how many years had passed and how quickly things changed. It also highlighted the difficulty of tracking her sister and uncovering fresh leads after so much time. She looked around, tried to imagine her sister on this same street, felt the gulf of years between them.

"Patterson?"

With a jolt, she realized Grant was still talking, and she wasn't paying attention. He paused, apparently expecting her to reply. Instead, she was forced to admit that she had not been listening. "I'm sorry, I got distracted. What were you saying?"

"I was asking when you intend to make the locals aware of your presence."

"I'll go to the field office first thing tomorrow."

"Good. Make sure that you do."

"Yes, sir," Patterson replied sarcastically.

"I am still your boss, you know."

"And right now, I'm officially on vacation, which makes you my boyfriend first and my boss second."

"Fair enough," Grant admitted. "Have you figured out the next move yet?"

"No. I'm hoping the hotel can tell me how long Julie stayed there, and if they have a record of her checking out, but beyond that I'm stumped."

"You realize it might be impossible to confirm her movements once she parted ways with her friend, right? The trail went cold so many years ago. Even with the full resources of the FBI behind you it would be a gargantuan task, and you're out there all on your own."

"I'm aware of that," Patterson said, looking back through the window into the restaurant again. She could almost imagine her sister and Stacy sitting there all those years ago while across the street someone was breaking into their room and setting off a chain of events that would alter her family's life forever. A lump formed in her throat. When she spoke again, it was all she could do to keep the tremble from her voice. "But what other choice do I have? Something happened to my sister, Grant. Something really bad, and I need to find out what that was. Because if I don't look for her, no one else will."

TWENTY-THREE

At ten in the morning Patterson Blake stood in the lobby of the Oklahoma City FBI building, with her damp hair matted to her scalp, wishing she'd possessed the forethought to bring an umbrella with her. It was raining outside, the sky a sheet of dull gray. The weather had rolled in during the early morning hours with a thunderstorm that rattled across the city, rousing her from slumber. After that Patterson found it impossible to fall back to sleep, and lay counting off the hours, tossing and turning to find a comfortable spot on the hotel's thin and lumpy mattress.

She stretched to relieve a kink in her back, a lingering hangover of her restless night. She reached up and rubbed the nape of her neck, kneading the tense muscles with a satisfied grunt. When she heard footsteps ringing on the lobby's tiled floor, Patterson dropped her arm and turned.

"You must be Patterson Blake," said the woman who was striding toward her. She was older than Patterson by at least a decade. Her shoulder-length dusty blonde hair was pulled tight to the back of her head. She wore a white blouse and black pants, with her FBI shield clipped to the belt. "I'm Supervisory Special

Agent Mary Quinn. The New York office said you'd be checking in with us."

"And here I am," Patterson said. "Dripping all over your floor."

"Yeah. You wouldn't be the first person. Oklahoma weather. June is the wettest month."

"Guess I picked the right time to visit, then." Patterson made a mental note to hunt down an umbrella if she was going to spend any significant time in the city.

"At least it's not too hot yet. A few more weeks and it'll be like an oven." Quinn motioned for Patterson to follow her. "Come on, let's find somewhere more comfortable to talk."

Quinn turned to a door marked *no public access*. She produced a key card, which she swiped to allow them through. After holding the door open for Patterson, Quinn led her along a corridor to a small office containing a desk, bookshelf, and three chairs-one on the business side of the desk and the other two arranged for visitors.

"Take the weight off," Quinn said, rounding the desk and sitting down.

"Thanks." Patterson settled opposite Quinn and looked at her across the desk. "Sorry I'm wasting your day with this unnecessary meet and greet."

"Don't be. You're saving me from a mound of paperwork. We had a little excitement yesterday. Some fool waving a water pistol walked into Plains Trust Bank and demanded three grand in small bills. Almost got himself shot before we realized his gun wasn't real. Idiot." Quinn leaned back in her chair. "But enough of that. Let's talk about the reason for this little face-to-face. You're in town pursuing a cold case with a personal connection, I believe."

"That's right. My older sister, Julie." Patterson nodded. "Her last confirmed whereabouts was here sixteen years ago. She was in the middle of a cross-country road trip."

"I've read the file. Your boss, Jonathan Grant, sent it over. She was traveling with a friend, but they had a falling out and parted ways. No one's seen your sister since." Quinn folded her arms. "It's tragic, for sure. But what makes you think there's anything worth investigating after so many years?"

"Because new information has come to light—at least new to me. Everyone assumed she made it to LA and then vanished. I think something happened to her much earlier in her trip."

"Did the FBI get involved at the time?"

"No. The LAPD handled the investigation, and not very well, I might add."

"And they came up empty, I assume."

"Correct."

"I don't need to tell you the chances of your sister still being alive are slim to none." A look of sympathy flashed across Quinn's face. "As are the chances of you finding her."

"I'm aware of the odds. I know Julie didn't go missing of her own accord—that wasn't who she was—which leaves only one logical conclusion."

"Someone took her," Quinn replied.

"Yes."

"Which means you are most likely following the trail of a murder victim." Quinn drew in a sharp breath. "Odds are your sister has been dead since not long after she vanished. I'm sorry to be blunt, but I can't see the point in sugarcoating it. You are an FBI agent, after all. You more than most people know the evil that lurks in this world."

"I'm prepared for the uncomfortable reality of what I might discover," Patterson said. "But the truth is, my sister's disappearance tore my family apart. It was awful. As a teenager, I had to watch my parents fighting day and night. At least until my mother left us. He doesn't speak of it often, but I know my father still wonders. Not knowing what happened to her still eats at him. I'd like to give him closure."

"And give yourself closure, too."

Patterson nodded.

"Where are you staying while you're in town?"

"The Welcome Inn."

"That rathole? It's barely more than a flophouse."

"It's also where my sister stayed sixteen years ago. I figured I might find something there."

"I'm sure you will, but it's more likely to be bedbugs than anything related to your sister's case."

"It isn't the most comfortable place I've ever stayed," Patterson admitted.

"There are plenty of better hotels in the city. If I were you, I'd go to one of those. It isn't safe where you're staying."

"Now you sound like Jonathan. Did he put you up to this?"

"No. I just hate to think of a fellow agent laying their head in a place like that. But it's your choice."

"I appreciate the concern," Patterson said. "I'll be careful."

"Make sure that you are. Is there a way I can contact you, should I need to?"

"Here." Patterson reached into her coat pocket and removed an FBI business card. She handed it to Quinn. "My cell number is on there."

Quinn handed her a card in return. "Keep this handy. If you need anything while you're in town, just call."

"Thank you, I will." Patterson stood up. "I think I've taken enough of your time."

"Not at all. It's always a pleasure to meet another female agent. There aren't enough of us, that's for sure." Quinn rose to her feet. "I'll walk you out."

TWENTY-FOUR

I t was still raining when Patterson drove back across town to the hotel. After making her presence known to the local FBI field office, she was at a loose end with no firm leads to chase. She wondered if the manager had found Julie's registration card yet. Knowing how long her sister had stayed in town would give Patterson a better idea of how much time to invest in searching Oklahoma City before moving further along the route marked on the map Stacy had given her.

When she thought about what had happened to her sister and Stacy all those years ago at the hotel, one detail still nagged at the back of her mind. She could understand why someone would break into their room and steal money, purses, and a cell phone. These things were valuable. Less clear was why a thief would take articles of clothing, including underwear.

Maybe it was a woman who stole the clothes.

Patterson considered this for a moment but thought it unlikely. The thief would need to be the same size as the girls in order to wear the clothes. And stealing the bras and panties made even less sense. It was unlikely that Julie and Stacy were the same cup size, let alone the person who took the garments. Besides, who would want to wear someone else's dirty undies?

This led Patterson to a more troubling conclusion. The items of clothing had been taken not because the perpetrator wanted to wear them, but rather to satisfy some sick fetish.

If that were true, then it painted the robbery in a whole new light. It also provided a valid line of inquiry. Was the thief satisfied by a few pairs of used panties or was there a darker urge propelling them forward. One that might lead to an even more nefarious act?

This grim thought sent a cold chill racing up Patterson's spine.

She pulled into the side lot next to the hotel and parked, then hurried inside with her head bent low against the driving rain.

When she approached the registration counter the manager didn't look up. His attention remained focused on his aging desktop computer. She stood for a moment watching him through the square hatch cut in the wall, then cleared her throat to alert him of her presence.

He looked up with a barely concealed scowl. "If you're here to ask about the registration card, I haven't had time to look for it yet."

"I can see that," Patterson said, her eyes roving the empty lobby before returning to the manager.

"Look, lady, just because there ain't a line of people squabbling over the bridal suite, doesn't mean I've been sitting on my ass all morning. The moron in 305 managed to block the third floor toilet and then kept flushing even though he could clearly see nothing was going down. Not only did I have to snake the pipes, but I spent the good part of an hour mopping shit off the bathroom floor. After that, I took a shower before swapping out a broken TV. Honestly, if the cheapskate that owns this place would spend a dime on sprucing it up instead of blowing it all on margaritas in Florida, we might be able to afford a maintenance man. Until that happens, you're looking at him."

"Hey, I just wanted to ask you a question." Patterson didn't like being called *lady*. It made her feel old. But that was a fight for another day. "When my sister was staying here, someone broke into her room. I was hoping you'd remember it."

"Didn't you say it was sixteen years ago?"

Patterson nodded. "That's right."

"Hell. What do you think I have, one of those photogenic memories?"

"Actually, you mean a photographic memory. But that's just being able to accurately recall images. What you're really referring to is hyperthymesia. The ability to recollect all the events of your life in great detail."

"Well, pardon me. I'll try to remember that," the manager replied without a hint of irony.

"Do you recall the incident, or not?" Patterson was growing weary of the manager's surly attitude. "It's possible there were other thefts around the same time. It might have been an employee because there was no sign of forced entry."

"Look, I don't know about any rooms being broken into. Certainly not by anyone that ever worked here. We run stringent background checks on all our employees."

"That's good to hear," Patterson replied, although she didn't believe for one second the hotel was spending the money to screen its workers, either back then or now.

"Is there anything else?"

"Not at the moment." Patterson knew she wasn't going to get anywhere with the hotel manager. Even if he remembered the break-in, he wasn't in any mood to tell her. "I'll let you get back to your day, then."

"Thank heaven for small mercies."

"If you remember anything after you've had time to think on it, let me know. Okay?"

"I'll make it my first priority," the manager replied, turning his attention back to the computer screen.

Patterson turned and headed for the stairs. As she reached the bottom step she heard him mutter, "Have a nice day now."

TWENTY-FIVE

Patterson returned to her room and hung her wet coat on a hook behind the door. She unclipped her holster and laid it on the bed, then found dry clothes in her travel bag. Grabbing a towel, she made her way along the corridor to the shared shower and locked the door behind her.

The shower room was small with a narrow window of frosted glass letting in so little illumination she had to click on the overhead light, even though it was still daylight. Square brown tiles with dirty grout lines covered the floor, some of them cracked. A plastic shower curtain printed in a faded yellow flower design hung limply from a rusting rod. Patterson pulled it back to reveal a cramped shower stall with outdated fixtures and a shower head caked with mineral deposits.

She forced her gaze away and turned the valve, then peeled off her damp clothing and waited for the shower to heat, listening to the pipes in the walls knock with the sudden pressure of water moving through them.

It took another minute before she could comfortably stand under the stream, and even then, the water wasn't as hot as she would have liked.

Patterson washed herself quickly, grossed out by her

surroundings. After rinsing the shampoo from her hair she applied conditioner, forced herself to stay in the cubicle long enough for it to work before finishing up and stepping out onto a towel she had placed on the floor. A couple of minutes later, dressed in dry, clean clothes, Patterson returned to her room.

Patterson took out her laptop and climbed onto the bed with her back against the wall, because there was no desk or chair. She propped a pillow behind her head for comfort and lifted the computer's screen, then logged on to the hotel's weak Wi-Fi.

The hotel manager's claim not to remember the theft from her sister's room sixteen years ago still irritated Patterson. She didn't believe him. But there might be something online if others had encountered the same situation. A newspaper article, or even hotel reviews that mentioned items being stolen from guest rooms.

She brought a browser window and went to Google, typing her query into the search bar.

Welcome Inn, Oklahoma City, hotel room thefts.

There were plenty of negative reviews for the hotel, sprinkled across a handful of online booking sites. Most dealt with the condition of the rooms. Dirty carpets. Uncomfortable beds. Cockroaches in the hallways. A handful mentioned loud music coming from the bar on weekends, and drunks hanging around on the sidewalk outside.

Patterson began to think that Special Agent Quinn was correct. She should move to a better hotel. But she was sure the manager knew more than he was letting on and would have more luck convincing him to talk as a paying guest, and therefore a constant thorn in his side.

She kept going, scrolling through progressively older reviews. She found the first mention of a room theft on page three. A review dated August 2008 that mentioned the loss of a wristwatch and silver chain. The guest, dissatisfied with the hotel's lackluster response, had threatened to call the police, although the review did not mention whether they had actually done so.

Then, several reviews earlier, from January of the year before, another mention of something being taken. This time it was a winter coat. But what caught Patterson's eye was the fact that some underwear had also gone missing. This was too specific to be coincidence. The break in that prompted the argument between Julie and Stacy was part of a larger pattern. This made the manager's claim that he didn't remember any room thefts, even less likely. It also gave Patterson ammunition to challenge his amnesia.

She browsed through another page of reviews but found no further mentions of items being stolen. She bookmarked the pair of damning reviews and closed the laptop screen.

At that moment, her cell phone rang.

Patterson placed the laptop on the bed and picked up her phone from the nightstand. It was a number she didn't recognize, with a 405 area code. There was only one person in Oklahoma City to whom she'd given her number.

"Hello?" she said, answering the call.

"Special Agent Blake?" a female voice asked. "This is Mary Quinn. We met this morning."

"I remember. How can I help you, Agent Quinn?"

"It's actually more how I can help you," Quinn replied. "After you left, I couldn't help thinking about the circumstances of your sister's disappearance, so I took another look over her file, and what I read got me wondering. Which is why I'd like to meet with you again. I have some information you might find interesting."

"Really?" Patterson replied, her curiosity piqued. "I need to hunt down lunch, anyway. It was raining so hard when I returned to the hotel, I didn't want to bother. I'll do that and then stop by the field office later this afternoon if that works for you."

"Actually, I'd rather meet in a less formal setting. There's a brewpub in the Bricktown District. Canalside Beerworks. It's a bit of a cop hangout. They have some great seasonal IPAs. We can grab a bite to eat, too. The burgers are good, and the brick oven pizza is excellent. Much better than anything you'll find around the Welcome Inn. How does 7 PM sound?"

"Works for me," Patterson said. "I'll find a snack to keep me going and meet you there."

"Perfect. I've got to run but I'll text you the address."

"Great. See you later," Patterson replied before hanging up. She put the phone down next to her laptop and leaned back with her head against the pillow. It was a little after two in the afternoon. That meant she had five hours before learning the reason why Quinn wanted to talk. Patterson had a hunch it was going to pass slowly.

TWENTY-SIX

A t a minute to seven that night, Patterson arrived at the Canalside Beerworks brewpub. As the name suggested, the brewpub sat next to the Bricktown Canal, occupying a unit spanning the bottom two floors of a five-story warehouse converted into upscale water view condos. The patio area fronted a walkway that ran the length of the tree-lined serpentine waterway. Pedestrians wandered past as she approached the building and entered via the patio, walking under strings of café lights. She could imagine how this would look once darkness fell, with hundreds of bulbs casting warm pools of light across the outside eating area while patrons drank craft beer beneath.

Mary Quinn was already waiting when Patterson entered. She sat perched at the bar with a pint of dark beer, eyes glued to her phone screen.

When Patterson approached, she put the phone down and looked up with a smile. "Hey there. Right on time. Guess you found the place okay."

Patterson nodded and took a stool, hanging her purse from a hook under the bar. She wanted to keep it close. She was intending to have a beer and avoided drinking when she was strapped, so her Glock was inside with the magazine removed.

She would have preferred to leave the gun back at the hotel, but since there was no room safe, she didn't feel comfortable doing that.

She looked up at the chalkboard above the bar containing the current beer menu. "What's good?"

"If you like IPA, try the Bricktown Pale. If you're in the mood for something darker, the OKC Stout can't be beat."

"The Bricktown sounds great," Patterson said, ordering the IPA. After the beer came, she turned to Quinn and got right to the point. "You wanted to talk. Do you have information about my sister's disappearance?"

"Not exactly that." Quinn shook her head. "More an avenue of investigation for you to explore."

"Go on," Patterson replied. "I'm listening."

"Your sister disappeared sixteen years ago, and the last person confirmed to see her alive was in Oklahoma City around the month of June."

"That's correct. There were postcards mailed from Las Vegas and Los Angeles, but they were sent later and there are questions regarding their authenticity, at least as far as I'm concerned. But you already know that. It was all in the report sent over from the New York Field Office. We discussed it this morning."

"I'm aware of that." Quinn paused, as if gathering her thoughts. She glanced around to check no one was paying them any attention, then spoke again, her voice low. "My office has been assisting in a murder investigation that spans at least a couple of decades. A serial killer with a gruesome MO."

Patterson's blood ran cold. "And you think my sister might be one of his victims?"

"I don't know. But the timeframe fits." Quinn took a drink of her beer before continuing. "Look, I probably shouldn't be telling you any of this. It's an ongoing investigation, and we have released none of this information to the public. Hell, the press hasn't even gotten wind of it yet and we'd like to keep it that way."

"That means the killer must still be active," Patterson guessed. "You don't want to alert them to your investigation."

"That's correct. Everything I tell you must remain in the strictest confidence. Honestly, if you were not a fellow agent, we wouldn't even be having this conversation."

"Understood." Patterson was letting this new information sink in. A serial murderer operating in Oklahoma City at the same time her sister went missing. Part of her hoped this would provide the answers she was looking for. A bigger part of her hoped it wouldn't, because although Patterson hadn't heard the gory details yet, she was sure they wouldn't be good. "Two decades is a long time for a killer to ply their trade without getting caught."

"But not uncommon. The BTK killer, Dennis Rader, kept going for seventeen years. He stopped killing in 1991 after finding another outlet for his horrific urges and evaded the authorities for a further fourteen years before being captured. In your own neck of the woods there's the Long Island Serial Killer."

"Otherwise known as LISK. I'm aware of that case. They found sixteen victims along Ocean Parkway near Gilgo Beach. They unearthed the first remains in 2010, but the killings date back to at least 1996. The Nassau County police reached out to our office for help, but despite investigating several persons of interest, the case is still active." Patterson glanced at her beer but didn't imbibe. She wasn't in a drinking mood suddenly. "You want to tell me why you think my sister might be a victim of the killer you asked me here to talk about?"

"I want to stress again. I'm not saying that Julie crossed paths with this killer, only that the circumstances fit."

"I understand."

"As of this moment, we have fourteen victims. All young women, and all killed in the same manner. We've identified at least four of them, including what we believe to be one of the first, who went missing in December 2000. We believe the killer kept them alive for a period, up to a year or more, before growing tired of them and moving on."

Patterson pondered the unspoken implications of that statement. "How did they die?" She asked, ignoring the knot of dread that churned in her stomach.

"Slowly," replied Quinn. "I don't know if you are aware of this, but Oklahoma has more man-made lakes than any other state in the USA. A lot of those reservoirs are in or around Oklahoma City."

"I didn't realize that," Patterson replied. "Why is it relevant?"

"Because our killer was using one of them as his dumping ground. Lake Calhoun. Three miles wide and twelve miles long. More accurately, a sliver of dry land in the middle of the lake. Bracken Island. It's a wildlife sanctuary, off-limits to the public. The island is overgrown and densely forested, which is why the bodies remained hidden for so long."

"You mentioned that the victims died slowly. What does that mean?" Patterson asked.

"It means our killer was not exactly hands on." Quinn stared down into her drink as if she didn't want to make eye contact with Patterson. "The island used to be part of a farm before the government bought the land in the 1970s under eminent domain laws for the reservoir's construction. After they dammed a tributary of the Canadian River, the surrounding land flooded, but the island remained as a high point. The farmer had several cars on his property. At least eight, most of which were still there after the lake's construction, along with the remains of the farmhouse, because the government couldn't be bothered to remove them. The killer used these rusting vehicles to his advantage. He took his victims to the island, still alive, and shackled them inside the cars."

"He left them there to die?" Patterson was horrified.

"That's right. The cars are located in the center of the island, which is normally off-limits. The victims might still be undiscovered if it wasn't for a Fish and Wildlife employee checking on whooping cranes last month."

"Whooping cranes?"

"Endangered birds that use the marshy areas around the island's periphery to nest. They've been monitoring them for years but don't normally have cause to venture beyond the shoreline. The employee heard what she thought was an injured bird that had somehow wandered into the island's interior and went to investigate."

"And she found bodies instead."

"Yes. Three of them, chained inside a rusting 1955 Ford Fairlane. Two in the back, one in the driver's seat. All put there at different times at least a year apart. Once police arrived on the island, they found more vehicles, with more victims inside."

"That's horrible." Patterson shuddered. Not only were the girls left to die a lonely and lingering death, but they also had to share their unusual tomb with the corpses of previous victims. "You think that's what happened to Julie?"

"I don't know," Quinn admitted. "We've tentatively dated one of the unknown victims to around the same time your sister was in town, so it's certainly a possibility."

"Oh." Patterson didn't know what to say. She felt numb. The thought of Julie being left like that was almost too much to bear. She felt her throat constricting. Her eyes moistening. For the first time she had a solid lead, but it came at a high price. "I want to see the killer's dumping ground. I want to see where my sister might have died."

"I can't do that," Quinn said, shaking her head. "You're not part of the investigation."

"But I'm still an FBI agent."

"Doesn't matter. You're taking personal time." Quinn looked uncomfortable. "I told you this, even though I probably shouldn't have, because you deserve answers."

"So where does that leave me?" Patterson forced herself to remain calm.

"With a better understanding of what might have happened than you had before."

"But I can't be a part of the investigation."

"No." Quinn shook her head. "But like I said, I want to give you answers, as much as I can."

"And how do you propose to do that?"

"By having you come back in so the lab can do a DNA swab."

"To see if there's a match with any of the victims," Patterson said.

"Precisely." Quinn picked up her pint and looked at Patterson over the rim of the glass. "What do you say?"

Patterson didn't hesitate with her answer. "I say the sooner, the better."

TWENTY-SEVEN

Patterson stayed behind in the bar after Quinn left. She ordered a second beer and sat looking moodily down into the pale amber liquid, her mind filled with thoughts of Julie, and the possibility that she had died at the hands of a sadistic killer who left his victims alone and afraid, trapped far from help.

She wondered if it had been worth taking a sabbatical from the FBI and following her sister's fading trail across the country, only to end up contemplating a resolution that was almost worse than not knowing.

But she'd come this far, and like they said, you couldn't put the genie back in the bottle. If she abandoned the quest now, she would forever wonder if Julie had died on that remote island surrounded by a deep, dark Oklahoma reservoir.

The problem was, she was locked out of the investigation. She had an FBI badge, but it was practically useless considering she was far from her own office and on leave. Not only that, but Julie was linked to the bodies on the island only by circumstance. It was far from a foregone conclusion that her sister was one of the unknown killer's victims.

There was only one solution Patterson could think of. She reached into her pocket and withdrew her phone and unlocked the screen, then hesitated, her finger poised over Grant's number. It had just turned 9 PM. Oklahoma City was on Central Time. That meant it was 10 o'clock on the East Coast. He would still be up, no doubt watching a John Wayne Western or some black and white war movie from his streaming collection of classic flicks. He rarely watched contemporary movies, claiming they were all about criminals and serial killers and people doing horrific things to each other, which he said he saw enough of in his day job. Patterson had pointed out more than once that war movies hardly involved people being civil to one another, but he said that was different. They focused on heroes and heroics, not blood and guts. A viewpoint Patterson felt was nothing more than splitting hairs.

She put the phone down, overcome by a rare bout of indecision. She wasn't worried about disturbing his evening. He would be pleased to hear from her. At least until he heard why she was calling. And that was the real reason for Patterson's hesitation. If he refused the request she was about to make, Patterson would remain on the outside looking in. A frustrated and uninformed observer to an investigation that could provide the answers she needed. She paused a moment longer, then scooped up the phone and dialed, deciding that a faint heart would get her nowhere.

When Grant answered, she heard The Duke's familiar drawl in the background and smiled. Her hunch had been right. A moment later the sound stopped as Grant hit pause.

He said, "Patterson. I was thinking about you."

"No, you weren't," Patterson replied with a laugh. "You were watching a bunch of long dead actors playing dress up as cowboys."

"You should watch one of these movies with me some day, you might actually learn to appreciate it."

"Not going to happen."

"Your loss," he said. "Are you calling because you miss me, or did you find something out regarding Julie?"

"I miss you. Always. You know that." Patterson took a sip of her beer, more to delay telling Grant why she'd called than anything else. "But this does concern Julie. I have a request and I hope you'll hear me out before answering."

Grant sighed. "If this is about using the FBI to get information about your sister's whereabouts, you know I can't authorize that. It's not an active investigation, and you're sidelined."

"Just listen a minute before you say no, please?"

"I don't need to listen. I know what you're going to ask."

"You do?" Patterson replied, surprised.

"Yes. I do. Agent Quinn informed me she was meeting with you this evening and also told me the reason."

"Why would she do that?" Patterson was taken aback. Quinn had mentioned none of this to her.

"Because I asked her to keep me in the loop when we spoke this morning, before you arrived to check in with her. I also sent over the file on your sister's case."

"I know that much. She told me she'd read the file." Patterson couldn't help feeling like Grant was keeping tabs.

"I can't put you on the Bracken Island Killer case, Patterson."

"But—" she started to protest.

"I don't want to hear it. The SAC took you off active duty and put you behind a desk until you undergo a psych eval. You promptly removed yourself from the equation by taking your accrued leave. Right now, you're only one rung above a civilian."

"That's not fair."

"Life's not fair, Patterson."

"Don't trot out that tired bull crap to me."

"Then don't tell me it's not fair that I won't reinstate you to go chasing ghosts."

"Is that what you think I'm doing?" Patterson resisted the urge to tell him where to go and then end the call. Maybe she would have if it were thirty years earlier, and she was using a landline. But it was kind of hard to slam the receiver down when you were on a cell phone. "Do you believe I'm wasting my time looking for Julie?"

"I never said that."

"Sure sounded like it."

"Patterson, come on. Be reasonable. If I reinstate you and contact the Oklahoma City office requesting you join the investigation, it'll be my ass on the line when the SAC finds out. And you know damned well Madeline Kahn will find out. She knows everything that goes on."

"So go speak to her tomorrow morning and explain the situation. Tell her how important it is to me."

"Yeah. Not going to happen in a million years. You were sitting right next to me in that meeting when she warned us both not to press our luck. Both our careers are on the line here. She didn't give you a formal reprimand, but if you push it, that might change. Worse, we could piss her off even more and end up transferred to Alaska. Which I might remind you, is much colder than New York."

"Fine. I hear you, loud and clear." Patterson swallowed her disappointment. "I've taken up enough of your time. Why don't you go back to your movie."

"Are you sure?" Grant asked. "What are *you* going to do?"

Patterson looked down at her half-empty glass. "I'm going to drink some more beer."

TWENTY-EIGHT

Feeling frustrated, Patterson returned to the hotel. When she entered the lobby, the manager looked up, as if he were expecting her to press him for the registration card again, but Patterson ignored his gaze and headed straight upstairs to her room. She undressed and climbed into bed, the fruitless conversation with Grant heavy upon her mind.

After their conversation at the bar, she'd spent some time thinking about his predicament and realized she was asking a lot. It wasn't fair to put her search for Julie between their relationship and professional lives. Dating a coworker was not easy, let alone your direct supervisor, but she had always been able to accept the boundaries of their situation before and would have to do so now.

She closed her eyes and lay in the darkness, listening to the sounds of cars passing by on the road below, and the occasional snatch of conversation or bang of car doors from other guests and residents in the surrounding buildings returning home. It took her a while to fall asleep, and when she did, Julie was waiting, trapped inside a rusting old automobile, chained by her wrists, and crying out for help Patterson could not bring.

The next morning, she awoke bleary-eyed and still

exhausted. She had a headache too, no doubt brought on by the two pints of beer the night before. Patterson hardly ever drank these days, and when she did, it left her groggy once the alcohol had worked through her system. She should have kept it to just one drink and made a mental pact with herself to do that from now on. At least until she solved the mystery of her sister's disappearance.

As she brushed her teeth and washed her face, Patterson played the previous evening's conversation with Grant over in her mind. She still felt irked by his attitude, even though she knew deep down that he was right.

Then, as if sensing that he was on her mind, he called while she was getting dressed. She picked up the phone, expecting a continuation of the previous evening's conversation. Instead, he surprised her by saying the exact opposite when she answered.

"I've gotten you access to the investigation."

"Wow. You have?" Patterson was momentarily speechless. "How?"

"I've sent a request to the Oklahoma City office asking them to brief you on their progress with the Bracken Island Killer and keep you informed of any new developments."

"I thought you didn't want me anywhere near the case?"

Grant replied, "I said you couldn't officially join the investigation. And you still can't. However, your sister's disappearance remains unsolved and is therefore an inactive, cold case. If there's a chance she died at the hands of this perpetrator, it's worth looking into. The FBI didn't become involved back when she first disappeared, but that doesn't mean we can't explore the possibility that she's a Bracken Island victim now. With that in mind, your insight could be valuable. At least that's how I'm spinning it."

"Does that mean I'll be able to read the case file?" Patterson asked hopefully.

"You'll have access to the same information as an investigating agent. The only caveat is that you cannot act upon that information in any official capacity as a member of the FBI. It's the best I could do without overstepping the boundaries of my authority."

"Does Madeline Kahn know?"

"No. Which is why we have to tread lightly. While I haven't technically gone against her decision to remove you from duty for the foreseeable future, it's a gray area. I'd rather not find out what her opinion is on the matter if you catch my drift."

"In other words, I should be careful."

"I would appreciate that," Grant replied. "When are you giving a DNA sample?"

"This morning. As soon as I've had breakfast." Patterson felt a flutter of dread at that thought. She wondered how she would cope if they confirmed Julie as one of the murdered girls. "Can't say I'm looking forward to it. Maybe it's better not to know."

"I disagree," Grant replied. "If it turns out Julie is a victim of the Bracken Island Killer, it will be beyond awful, but at least you'll have an answer. You can move on with your life without wondering anymore."

"I guess." Patterson wasn't convinced. "Even though telling dad won't be easy. It sounds crazy, but I think he still clings to a hope she'll just breeze through his front door one fine day and say she was off exploring the world for the past sixteen years. I think that's why he stayed in the house all these years. Even after the divorce he scrabbled together enough money to pay mom her half and keep the place."

"Speaking of your mom. How do you think she'll take it?"

"She decided Julie was dead years ago so the news won't dash her hopes, but I'm sure it'll still be hard, finally knowing the truth."

"I don't envy your position," Grant said. "Let's hope Julie isn't one of his victims."

"Keeping my fingers crossed. I want to find my sister, but not like that."

"Understood." There was a moment's silence on the other

end of the line. Then she heard Grant's muffled voice, as if he were talking to someone who'd stepped into his office. When he came back on again, he sounded distracted. "Hey, Patterson, I have to get back to work. I'll check in again later, make sure you got everything you need."

"Sure thing," Patterson replied. "Go. I have to finish getting dressed and take care of that DNA swab, anyway."

"Great. Love you lots," he said in a hushed voice. "Take care."

"Love you too, sweetie." Patterson hung up and dropped the phone on the bed. She buttoned her blouse and put on her shoulder holster containing the Glock service weapon. She was about to pick up her coat and slip it on over the gun when the phone buzzed.

A text message.

It was from Mary Quinn, confirming that Grant had requested she have access to the investigation.

Patterson replied saying she was on her way then slipped the phone into her pocket and scooped up her car keys. After checking her hair in the mirror near the door, she stepped into the corridor and made her way down to the hotel parking lot. Moments later, she was driving toward the FBI building, and a possible answer to the riddle of her sister's disappearance.

TWENTY-NINE

Quinn was waiting when Patterson arrived at the FBI office. She led her through the building and up the elevator to the third-floor lab, where a technician in a white coat was working. He told Patterson to sit on a stool next to an aluminum bench from which he picked up a buccal swab kit.

"Name and date of birth," he asked, waiting for Patterson to reply before writing the information in permanent marker on the side of a clear tube with a blue screw cap. He also wrote the current date and time, along with his initials. Turning back to her, he smiled. "Open your mouth as wide as possible please and keep your tongue down."

Patterson complied, tilting her head back slightly to allow him better access.

The technician pulled on a pair of latex gloves. He removed a swab from its sterile packaging and held it between his fore-finger and thumb. "This is pretty noninvasive. It won't hurt. Just keep still for me, please."

Patterson nodded. She'd seen this done before and was aware of the procedure.

"Excellent." The technician inserted the swab's tip into

Patterson's mouth and rubbed it back and forth against her inner cheek, watching a wall clock and timing off thirty seconds before withdrawing the swab.

"All done," he said, dropping the swab and his newly collected sample of Patterson's cells into the collection tube before screwing the top tightly closed. "You can relax now."

"Thank you," Patterson said, slipping down off the stool.

The technician said, "It'll take several days to work up a DNA profile to compare with the victims found on the island."

"I understand." Patterson waited while Quinn thanked the technician, then followed her back out of the lab and down to the ground floor.

When they reached Quinn's office, she stepped inside, telling Patterson to wait, and then returned a moment later with a manila folder thick with papers, which she held out. "This is everything we have on the Bracken Island killer. Statements from the woman who discovered the bodies, photographs, psychological profile of the perpetrator."

Patterson took the folder. "This will be a big help, thank you."

"You're welcome." Quinn stepped back into the corridor and started toward the front of the building. "If you'd like to follow me, we're not done yet."

"Where are we going," Patterson asked, hurrying to catch up with the FBI agent.

"Bracken Island. The New York office made a request that we bring you up to speed on the investigation, so you should probably view the crime scene. That is what you wanted, right?"

"Yes, it is," Patterson replied quickly, keeping pace as they crossed the lobby and exited the building.

Quinn led Patterson to a black Ford SUV parked at the curb. Patterson's own car sat a couple of spaces away in an official use only zone that would have gotten most other vehicles towed. But not hers, thanks to the blue federal plates attached to the front and rear.

Quinn pulled out into traffic, and they headed north out of the city following interstate 35. After they had been driving for a while, Patterson glanced over at her companion.

"I really appreciate you doing this," she said. "I know you must be busy and probably think I'm nothing but a nuisance."

"Not at all," Quinn replied, keeping her eyes on the road. "I get exactly where you're coming from. If it were my sister missing, I'd kick down every door in the country looking for her."

"You have a sister?"

"Two, actually. One older, the other younger. Their names are Carly and Denise."

"Are they in law enforcement too?"

"Heavens, no. Carly is up in Seattle and works as a banker. Denise lives in Maryland. She's just had a baby boy."

"Congratulations," Patterson said. "How does it feel to be an aunt?"

"Bit weird. I never thought of Denise as the mothering type. She was always so adamant she didn't want kids."

"People change their minds." Patterson wondered what Julie would be doing now if she hadn't vanished. Would she be married with children of her own, making Patterson an aunt? It made her angry to think that someone, possibly the Bracken Island Killer, had taken that option away from her sister. "Have you seen your nephew, yet?"

"Not yet. I'm hoping to go home at Christmas. I was on duty through the holidays the last two years, so the agency owes me."

"I'll keep my fingers crossed for you," Patterson replied. "How far is it to the lake?"

"Not too long," Quinn replied, taking an offramp and leading them onto a county road. "We're about eight miles away right now."

Patterson fell silent and watched the scenery roll by. They were out of the city proper now. At first the road was lined with big houses sitting on third and half acre plots, but soon these gave way to rolling wheat fields. After a few more miles the fields ended, and they were driving through a thickly wooded area filled with red cedar trees.

Quinn turned shortly after they'd reached the trees, and soon Patterson noticed more housing. Large swaths had been cut from the forested landscape and replaced with sprawling subdivisions called Oak Landing and Cedar Hills. She found this ironic considering the developers had removed every trace of greenery to build houses.

A few minutes later, the road ended at a set of open gates leading into a marina sitting next to a wide expanse of shimmering water. She parked in a bay near the marina office and glanced sideways toward Patterson.

"You ready for a boat ride?"

"Sure." Patterson opened her door and exited the vehicle, then followed Quinn toward the office and waited outside while her companion arranged their transportation.

The marina played host to a variety of leisure craft from small boats to larger pontoons and bowriders. There were even a few cabin cruisers with names like Lady of the Lake, Lazy Susan, and Weekend Dreamer. She found it fascinating that so many people had the money to own these indulgent toys. The mooring fees alone must run hundreds per month for the biggest vessels.

When Quinn came out, she tapped Patterson on the shoulder. "Come along. Our chariot awaits."

Patterson followed her to the end of the nearest pier, where a small skiff with a single outboard motor sat bobbing in the water. Ten minutes later, they were skimming across the glassy lake toward Bracken Island.

THIRTY

Bracken Island was a dark mass sitting low in the silvery waters of Lake Calhoun. Patterson sat in the skiff's bow and watched as the crouching spit of wooded land drew closer.

"This is a perfect dumping ground," she commented, as they approached a narrow wooden dock posted with signs warning that the island was a federal wildlife habitat and unauthorized boats should not approach. "Remote and off limits to the public."

"Which is probably what appealed to the killer. Less chance of discovery." Quinn steered the boat parallel with the dock and cut the engine before hopping out and securing it with a mooring rope. "There are a couple of overgrown trails through the interior of the island, but the cars are scattered over a square mile of land. It took the Oklahoma City PD homicide unit a week to find them all."

"Which means the killer must have had intimate knowledge of the terrain." Patterson let Quinn help her out of the boat and followed her along the dock. Her eyes roamed to the sliver of beach ringing the island. A thin ribbon of gray sand that acted as a buffer zone between water and land. "Maybe the killer keeps a boat at the marina."

"We looked into that but didn't come up with any obvious suspects. No one with a criminal history that would point to this kind of crime. Doesn't rule out the possibility though."

"What about houses backing up to the lake?"

"Again, it's possible our killer has private lake access, but we're looking for a needle in a haystack. There are more than seven hundred parcels of land that abut the shoreline. Also, the killer doesn't need to have lake front property. There are at least three public boat ramps. All he'd have to do is drive to one of those with a small skiff like we used to come here, and he could be on the water within minutes. Plus, even though the boat ramps officially close at sunset, there's actually nothing to stop someone using them under the cover of darkness. They aren't gated, and there are no cameras."

"Meaning it could be anyone within a hundred-mile radius who has access to a boat."

"And therein lies the problem," Quinn said as they stepped off the dock onto the island. She nodded toward the trees towering in front of them, between which a narrow and over-grown path meandered into the gloomy understory. A chain had been strung at the trailhead with a no trespassing sign attached. "It's tough going in there. Stay close."

Patterson nodded, and together they set off, leaving the warm and comforting sunlight behind.

―――――

Quinn wasn't wrong. The trail narrowed not long after they left the shore behind and gave way to thick vegetation that looked indistinguishable from the surrounding woodland. But Quinn appeared to know where she was going, pushing through the tangle of brush with a confidence that suggested she'd followed this route before.

Above them, in the canopy of trees, the song of at least a dozen varieties of birds reached Patterson's ears. To her left a

squirrel raced up a tree, chattering angrily at the human interlopers passing through its domain.

Less than a minute later, Quinn pulled up short and raised a
hand in the air. She glanced back toward Patterson. "We'll need
to take a minor detour."

"Why?" Patterson looked around but saw nothing of note.

"Snake. Big one. It's on the trail ahead of us." Quinn took a
step sideways, moving with slow deliberate footfalls. "Looks like
a copperhead."

"Poisonous?"

"Yeah. Not the most venomous. But getting bitten out on this
island so far from help would still not be good. We should be
okay as long as we don't annoy it. They're not known to be
overly aggressive if left alone."

"I hate snakes," Patterson said, walking in Quinn's footsteps
as she followed her off the trail.

They pushed through the underbrush, skirting the area.
Patterson scanned the ground, wary of stepping on some other
dangerous reptile. When they arrived at the island, she hadn't
even thought about poisonous snakes, but now it was all that
filled her mind.

Rejoining the path, Quinn forged ahead, moving faster than
Patterson thought was appropriate given their near miss. But
soon the trees parted and opened into a small clearing.

And there, sitting in the middle with weeds growing up
through its frame, was a rusting old car with sweeping arched
front wings and chromed bumpers and hubcaps, the once shiny
metal now dull and pitted. Further away, near the edge of the
clearing, a second vehicle stood with its nose poking out of the
bushes. This one looked newer, although still old. She guessed
the first car was from the 1950s. The second, with its more
angular lines, hailed from at least a decade later. Tangled in the
brush to her right were the remains of a dilapidated cattle fence,
complete with a gate that now rested askew off its hinges while

greenery weaved through the slats, tugging it inexorably toward the ground.

Patterson moved further into the clearing and came to a stop. Her gaze swept across the surreal scene. The cars forever trapped in a creeping prison of mother nature's making, their wheels buried deep in the soft earth, oxidized frames shedding what little weathered paint still clung to them. A shudder ran down Patterson's spine. The reason they were here weighed heavy upon her.

Quinn remained silent for a moment, as if giving Patterson time to absorb the clearing's energy, then she turned, a somber expression upon her face, and said, "Welcome to the Bracken Island Killer's charnel house."

THIRTY-ONE

P atterson stepped further into the clearing, thoughts of Julie on her mind. She looked up at the treetops—the arching canopy of branches circling a small patch of cloudy sky-and wondered if this was the last thing her sister had seen. It was a sobering thought, and one that filled Patterson with horror. She could only imagine what terror the victims must have felt, trapped alone in this desolate place with no chance of rescue. But dwelling on such maudlin thoughts would not help her find Julie or move them closer to catching the sadistic creep that had done this.

She took a long breath and pushed her emotions aside, forcing herself to view the scene with an investigator's eye. And what she found surprised her.

"This doesn't look like a crime scene," Patterson said, turning to Quinn with raised eyebrows. "In fact, it doesn't look like anyone's been here for a long time."

"That's deliberate." Quinn replied. "After Homicide removed the bodies, they went to great pains to make it look like the dumping ground hadn't been discovered—"

"Because they believe the killer is still active and will return here," Patterson said, finishing Quinn's sentence for her.

"Exactly. We believe he took another victim not long after dumping his previous one. We're working on the assumption she's still alive."

"You developed a profile of the killer, I assume?"

"First thing we did. He's an older male. At least in his forties, given the length of time he's been operating. Probably white because his victims are all Caucasian. He takes a new victim every twelve to eighteen months on average and probably keeps them for a time before they end up on the island."

"Putting them in the cars is the last phase of his cycle," Patterson surmised. "He's probably driven by some kind of sadistic need, almost certainly sexual in nature. He likes to feel powerful, relishes their fear, and the knowledge that their lives are in his hands."

"That's the conclusion we came up with," Quinn agreed. "He probably tires of them once they become too compliant."

"So he came up with a way to extend the thrill a little longer," Patterson said. "He brings them here, to a remote place he knows they won't be found and leaves them to die. It serves a dual purpose. He avoids the messy act of killing the victims himself, and he gets to feel powerful one more time, knowing he could save them if he chose to do so."

"He goes one step further than that. He leaves the keys to their shackles on the hood of the car, out of reach."

"The means to their salvation right there, a few feet away, if only they could reach it." Patterson grimaced.

"Which they never will."

"And he'll do the same to his next victim."

"Which is why we need him to believe nobody has discovered this dumping ground," Quinn said. "Unless we catch a break and find him first, the only way to save that poor girl is to let him bring her here."

"Because he'll chain her in one of these cars to die a slow death." Patterson felt a surge of revulsion. The Bracken Island Killer was an animal.

"And when he does, we'll catch him in the act and save her."

Patterson looked around, skeptical. Even though there was no evidence the police had ever been here, the killer would know that something wasn't right as soon as he stepped foot into the clearing. "You must've removed the bodies already," she said. "The game will be up when the perpetrator gets close to one of those vehicles."

"It's true, we've removed the victims. We couldn't leave them here. Apart from needing to get them autopsied, it just wouldn't be right. But the killer won't know they're gone."

"How?" Patterson asked, bewildered.

"Go look in the car." Quinn pointed to the nearest vehicle, the one sitting in the clearing. "See for yourself."

Patterson approached, careful not to disturb anything, and leaned forward to peer through the grimy side passenger window. The car's interior was dark, but she could make out the seats, fabric long since rotted away to reveal moldy filling material and bare springs. The headliner was sagging and had torn in a couple of places, the fabric hanging low. She also saw a shape sitting in the front seat, one arm handcuffed to the steering wheel.

She recoiled and turned to Quinn. "There's still a corpse in this car."

"Not exactly." Quinn looked pleased with herself. "The killer has been using old vehicles all over the island to dispose of his victims, but the cars will only hold so many occupants, so he moves on every once in a while, to a fresh automobile. This is the only car used by the killer that didn't contain four bodies, so we made the logical assumption that he would bring the next victim here. To that end, we visited the Oklahoma University College of Medicine. They were kind enough to provide us with a female anatomical skeleton. It's practically indistinguishable from the real thing but made of a hard plastic. We went to a wig shop and matched the hair on the real corpse and the forensic lab guys worked on the skeleton to give it the appearance of advanced decay. Don't ask me how they did it. I don't know, and I'm not sure I want to. Finally, we used the clothes from the real victim to dress the body before we staged it in the car. It might not hold up to a close examination, but we're confident our killer won't pay enough attention to notice."

"He won't be expecting the body to be fake."

"His attention will also be focused on his latest captive."

"This is all very clever," Patterson said. "But you still won't know when he brings a victim here. How are you going to catch him in the act?"

"Trail cams." Quinn nodded toward the trees. "We have twelve of them positioned around the clearing and also on the path leading here. They're camouflaged. Hidden so well you can't see them. There are more trail cams focused on the dock where we accessed the island. It's the most logical place for our killer to come ashore, although we can't be positive he'll take advantage of the dock, of course. There are other, less convenient landing sites around the island."

"How are you monitoring them?" Patterson asked.

"We used wireless models that send photos in real time back to a laptop monitored by Oklahoma City PD homicide squad. We don't have the staff to monitor the cameras twenty-four hours a day, but we don't need to. In all likelihood the perpetrator uses the cover of darkness. We check the laptop several times each evening, and then again in the morning. So far, we've caught a lot of birds and other wildlife, but no homicidal maniacs."

"We're being filmed right now, then." Patterson glanced around the clearing but couldn't see the trail cams.

"The cameras don't record continuously. They take snapshots when they sense movement. But yes, we must have triggered the cameras when we came ashore. It's not a big deal though. I already informed OCPD of our visit today. I will also let them know as soon as we leave the island."

"Let's hope our killer doesn't wait too long to come back

here," Patterson said. The thought that another victim was out there at that very moment, a terrified young woman suffering at the hands of a sadistic sociopath who'd gone undetected for the best part of two decades, made her feel sick. She didn't want to wait for him to grow tired of his victim and decide to discard her. She wanted to capture the bastard right now, before he could inflict one more ounce of misery. But beyond that, Patterson wanted to look him in the eyes and ask him one simple question, even if it meant she wouldn't like his answer. Had he killed her sister?

THIRTY-TWO

Patterson returned to the hotel that afternoon under a dark cloud of depression. Seeing the island and abandoned cars for herself had pressed home the horror of the situation. She had attended many crime scenes during her time as an FBI agent, but none—except possibly the farm raid in upstate New York that had set this entire trip in motion—had ever affected her this deeply. It was one thing to work the scene of a stranger's death, but quite another to straddle the line between investigator and victim. She didn't enjoy having a foot in each world even as she realized it would make her a better, more compassionate agent going forward.

As she walked through the hotel lobby—the folder containing everything the Oklahoma City Police Department and local FBI had gathered on the Bracken Island Killer tucked under her arm—she'd made one more attempt to pry information from the manager. As expected, she had gotten nowhere. If he knew anything about the hotel room break-ins sixteen years before, as Patterson suspected he did, the manager was keeping quiet. She wasn't in the mood to argue with him and instead turned and climbed the stairs toward her room, feeling his gaze upon her back as she did so.

She let herself into the hotel room, then went to the bed and sat propped up with her back against the wall, the folder open on her bent knees. She rifled through the thick wad of papers, reading autopsy reports, and examining photos of the dumping ground taken while the bodies were still in the cars. The images were gruesome, and she paused to gather herself together a couple of times.

The psychological profile worked up by the Bureau's behavioral analysts was in there too. She read it twice, poring over the sections that talked about the perpetrator's probable race and age, marital status, need for control, extreme sociopathic tendencies, and his uniquely hands-off way of committing murder. It was a well-crafted analysis, but with no actual suspects to focus upon, it was next to useless. No better than a roadmap when you didn't have a destination.

Then she came upon the transcript of an interview with the Wildlife Service employee who discovered the bodies. A woman named Margaret Collier who was visiting the island to check on the whooping crane, a species of endangered bird. The interview had occurred on site the day of the discovery, and it was obvious even through the written words on the page that the employee was shaken up, possibly near hysterical. She recounted her arrival on the island and going in search of the bird's nesting area. She hadn't gotten far when she heard sounds in the woods that she thought sounded very much like one of the whooping cranes she was there to observe. It appeared to be in distress. The employee had never ventured away from the narrow beach areas surrounding the island, which were the preferred habitat of the whooping crane, but she ventured inland, nonetheless.

She never found the endangered bird.

But she did discover a mostly decomposed corpse trapped in a rusting old car.

The report was thorough, but brief. The interviewing officer concerned himself only with her account of stumbling upon the crime scene. He asked no questions about previous visits to the island, or how often Fish and Wildlife went there. Patterson felt the interview lacked depth, especially since they had nothing to go on outside of this one solitary witness. An additional page behind the interview mentioned talking briefly to the only other Fish and Wildlife Service employee in Oklahoma City—Holly Cartwright, the original steward of the whooping crane project, now retired for almost ten years. OKCPD had gleaned no new information from this brief interview, conducted more to rule her out as a suspect, than because the homicide unit thought she possessed any valuable information.

Patterson was unimpressed by their lack of thoroughness and had questions of her own the interview transcripts did not answer. In her experience people often possessed more information than they realized, and a question not asked, or badly phrased inquiry, might be a missed opportunity for a new avenue of investigation.

She turned back to the first leaf of the interview transcript with Margaret Collier. The woman's address and telephone number were written at the top of the page. She picked up her cell phone and was about to dial before hesitating. Was this overstepping the line? Grant had warned her not to involve herself actively in the Bracken Island Killer case. But was that actually what she was doing if it overlapped her inquiries into Julie's disappearance? It was a gray area, for sure, and open to interpretation.

The easy option would be to wait for the DNA comparison to come back from the lab. Then she would know one way or the other whether Julie was actually a victim of the Bracken Island Killer. Yet that might take weeks. Unlike television, where an investigator could get near instantaneous DNA results whenever they wanted, real-life labs moved slowly. There was always a backlog of material waiting to be analyzed, all of which was important to one investigation or another. Matching Patterson's DNA to an already dead victim would be low on the agenda despite the lab technician's optimistic assessment that they would have results in a few days. Sitting on her hands until she knew one way or the other would waste valuable time. Making up her mind, Patterson tapped the number into her phone and hit connect.

Margaret Collier answered on the third ring.

There was traffic noise in the background. It sounded like she was driving.

"Hi, Margaret," Patterson dived right in. "My name is Patterson Blake. I'm calling about the incident on Bracken Island. I hope I'm not catching you at a bad time?"

"Oh, no. Not at all. I'm on my way back from a meeting with the National Park Service. We discovered the remains of a Native American settlement at a local wildlife conservation area and we're working with them to preserve it. They have a lot of experience with this kind of thing. It's fascinating stuff, actually." Margaret paused. "But you didn't call to discuss archaeology. You mentioned Bracken Island."

"Yes. I've been reading the police report, and it says you're the person who discovered the bodies."

"Only the first one. And thank goodness for that." Margaret paused again, and this time Patterson got the idea that she was composing herself. "It was horrible. I try not to think about it, but to tell the truth, I've been having nightmares ever since."

"I'm sorry about that," Patterson said, and she meant it. "The last thing I want to do is stir up memories unnecessarily."

"You can't stir up a memory not yet forgotten," Margaret said matter-of-factly. "I don't think you told me what your interest in this is. Are you a reporter?"

"No. I'm not with the press. As I'm sure the police already advised you, they're doing their best to keep this out of the papers."

"They said as much. Yes. Something about not wanting to alert whoever did this so they can catch him in the act. Told me not to discuss the matter with anyone but law enforcement. They think he's still out there taking young women. Isn't it dreadful?"

"Horrific. Which is why I want to see if they missed some detail, no matter how small, when they interviewed you the first time."

"Are you with the police, then?"

"Not local. I'm federal," Patterson said, sidestepping the question to the best of her ability.

"I see. In that case, how can I refuse. Anything I can do to get that monster off the streets…"

"Wonderful. I'd like to meet with you in person if you don't mind. As soon as possible."

"How about this afternoon? I'm on my way home right now, so you can meet me there."

"You work from home?" Patterson asked, surprised.

"Yes. FWS doesn't maintain a location in the city." She replied, using the acronym for the U.S. Fish and Wildlife Service. "Officially, I report to the Wildlife Management Office down in Tishomingo, but I only go there a few times a month. It's a two-hour drive each way and my duties mostly keep me out and about on the lakes around Oklahoma City."

"This afternoon will be fine," Patterson said. "If you text me your address, I can probably be there in an hour, assuming that's not too early."

"Not at all. Come on by."

"Thanks."

"I'll send you my address once we hang up," Margaret said. "See you in an hour."

Patterson said goodbye and watched her phone until Margaret's text message came through. Then she hurried from the room for the second time that day in the direction of the lobby.

THIRTY-THREE

Margaret Collier lived in a brick cottage nestled along a tree-lined street near the outskirts of the city, in a home surrounded by lush landscaping, including rosebushes, sumac shrubs, and flowerbeds full of catmint, primrose, and hyssop.

Patterson made her way up the path and knocked twice, then turned to admire her surroundings, which were clearly the work of an avid gardener. She was still lost in the meticulously planted grounds when Margaret answered the door.

"Patterson Blake, I assume?"

"Yes." Patterson turned back toward the open door. "You have quite the green finger."

"Thank you. Although I can't take credit for all of it. A lot of the plantings were here when I bought the place. I'm just their latest caretaker."

"It's still gorgeous," Patterson said. "I wish I was surrounded by such beauty."

"It just takes a little dedication, that's all." Margaret replied. Then she hesitated, a look of concern flickering across her face. "You know, when we spoke on the phone, I didn't ask which specific agency you're actually with. I probably should have."

"I'm federal, like I said." Patterson hoped the vague reply

would suffice, but she suspected it wouldn't. Her hunch was proved correct when Margaret spoke again.

"Do you have some identification I could see?"

Patterson froze, caught in a moment of indecision. She had promised Grant that she wouldn't abuse her status as an FBI agent while investigating her sister's disappearance. She'd also promised to stay out of the Bracken Island investigation. Talking to the woman who discovered the killer's dumping ground might overstep the line on both counts, even though she'd convinced herself that it was a gray area. One that had now turned decidedly murkier. But what choice did she have? If she didn't comply with this woman's request, she wouldn't get past the doorstep. Reluctantly, she reached into her pocket and withdrew her credentials, then held them out.

"You're a special agent with the FBI?" Margaret said with a note of surprise in her voice. "You don't look the type."

"What type would that be?" Patterson asked, closing the wallet and slipping the credentials back into her pocket.

"I don't know." Margaret shrugged. "I always thought of FBI agents as big burly men who like to kick in doors. You'll have to excuse me. I guess I'm a bit outdated."

"Don't worry about it. It's not the first time someone's done a double take when I tell them what my job is."

"That's kind of you to say, but I shouldn't have jumped to conclusions. After all, anything a man can do, a woman can do better, at least as far as I'm concerned." Margaret stepped back and held the door open for Patterson to enter. "Come on in."

"Thank you." Patterson stepped across the threshold and followed Margaret to a living room decorated in warm shades of yellow and ochre. A fireplace with a thick wood mantle dominated one wall, above which hung a painting of birds flying across the open water. The room felt fresh and cozy.

Margaret motioned for Patterson to sit on the couch, then took a seat across the coffee table on a smaller loveseat. She placed her hands in her lap and looked at Patterson. "Ready when you are."

Patterson took her cell phone and opened the voice recorder app. "You mind if I record our conversation?" She asked. "It's easier than making notes."

"Not at all." Margaret smiled and edged closer to the coffee table and the phone. "Now, my dear, what is it you'd like to know?"

"Well, for a start, I'd like to hear how you discovered the body, and why you were on the island."

"Oh, that's easy. I go to the island about once a month, especially in the summer, to check on an endangered species of bird that nests along the shoreline."

"The whooping crane."

"That's right. The island is a designated wildlife sanctuary. It's off-limits to the public, but not to me."

"Because you work for the U.S. Fish and Wildlife Service."

"Yes. I'm a wildlife biologist. I don't just work with the whooping cranes. I oversee several monitoring programs in the area, and I also liaise with environmental scientists and biologists from other agencies and non-profits trying to preserve endangered habitats."

"And archaeologists too, apparently," Patterson said, remembering what Margaret had told her on the phone.

"Yes, sometimes. Some of our habitat areas contain archaeological sites, and we also work to preserve those. It's a fascinating job, actually. Every day is different. Much like being an FBI agent, I would imagine."

"It has its moments," Patterson replied. "And a lot of paperwork too."

"Don't talk to me about paperwork." Margaret shook her head. "We might be at opposite ends of the spectrum, but we both work for federal agencies—in my case the Department of the Interior—and one thing the government loves is paperwork."

"That's true," Patterson said. They were getting off topic. Patterson decided to reel her back in. "So tell me about that day. Try not to leave anything out."

"I've already gone over this with the police. I spent two hours with a homicide detective. He made a lot of notes. Surely you've seen them."

"I'd like to hear it from the source."

"Very well. It's pretty straightforward. I went out to the island to check on the birds. There's a dock maintained by the Fish and Wildlife. That's where I tied my boat up. I went ashore and was walking along the beach looking for signs of nesting, although it's really just more of a strip of gritty dirt between the water and the trees. I hadn't gone far when I heard a bird that sounded like it was in distress."

"A whooping crane?" Patterson asked.

"That's what I believed it to be. Yes. There are several primitive trails leading into the center of the island. They're mostly used by wildlife coming out to the shore to drink water. I followed one of those inland. We try not to disturb the interior of the island because human presence upsets the ecology, but I couldn't leave an injured animal there."

"Did you find the bird?"

"No." Margaret shook her head. "I found something much worse. The trail was overgrown. It was hard going in places, but after a while I came to a small clearing. And there was a car in the middle of it. A really old car. I'd heard stories about stuff being left on the island when the Corps of Engineers created the lake back in the seventies. It was all farmland around here before that and the rumor was that one of the farmers collected automobiles. I guess he wasn't a good collector because the cars were still there. At least some of them, anyway."

"What did you do then?" Patterson asked.

"I did what anyone would do. Let my curiosity get the better of me and took a peek inside." Margaret's demeanor had changed now. Sorrow creased her face. "There was this poor girl in there. Dead."

"How did you know was a girl?"

"I don't know. It just looked like a girl. The body had long hair, for a start. Scared the living daylights out of me. I think I screamed. Then I turned and hightailed it all the way back to the beach as fast as my legs would carry me. My cell still had reception—there's a tower on the shore near the marina—so I called the police. They told me to stay where I was until they got there. I really didn't want to do that. I'd just found a dead body after all."

"But you did."

"Sort of. I went and got back in the boat and took it about a quarter mile off the island. That's where I waited for the police. I returned to the dock after they arrived." Margaret's face was ashen as she relived the horror. "It sounds silly, but I was afraid that whoever killed that young woman might still be on the island."

"It doesn't sound silly at all." Patterson said in her most soothing voice. "I would have done the same."

"That's kind of you to say, even though I don't believe it. You're trained for this kind of thing. Plus, you have a gun."

"Doesn't make it any easier," Patterson replied. "Other than the girl in the car, did you notice anything else unusual that day?"

"Not that I recall. But I wasn't looking, either. My mind was on whooping cranes not crime scenes."

"Point taken. But you probably would've noticed footprints or other signs of an intruder being on the island, wouldn't you?"

"I suppose. Footprints would only be on the sandy areas near the shore, and they wouldn't last long. In case you hadn't noticed, it's been raining a lot around here recently. Water levels have been higher the past few months. Also, the lake might not be tidal, but it does still have some wave action at the shore." Margaret wrung her hands together. "I'm sorry, Agent Patterson, but I really didn't notice anything other than the body. If someone was coming on to the island, I didn't see any trace of it."

"That's okay. I just wanted to make sure nothing had been overlooked." Patterson was disappointed. She'd hoped to discern some previously overlooked detail from the Fish and Wildlife employee. Something that would give her a direction in which to head. "I won't take up too much more of your time, but I have one more question."

"What's that?" Margaret asked, some of the color returning to her face.

"Other than yourself, is there anyone else who has official access to the island?"

"Theoretically anyone who works for my organization, but in practice it's just me. Like I said on the phone, the nearest office is two hours away down in Tishomingo. I'm the only Fish and Wildlife employee in this area."

"I see." Patterson nodded.

"Well, except for Holly."

"That would be your predecessor, Holly Cartwright?"

"Yes. I took over her duties when she retired about ten years ago, but she'd been working with the cranes over on the island for at least twenty years before that. If anyone knows Bracken Island, it's her."

"That's very interesting," Patterson said. It was already in the back of her mind to talk with Holly Cartwright. But hearing that she visited the island regularly for at least two decades prior to her retirement made that conversation even more important. The Bracken Island Killer had been operating for at least half that time, using the small hump of land in the middle of Lake Calhoun as his dumping ground. It was a long shot given the years that had passed, but if anyone would remember something strange on that island, it would be her.

Patterson knew where she had to go next.

THIRTY-FOUR

The interview Oklahoma City Homicide Unit conducted with Holly Cartwright had been brief and uninformative. If there was any actual investigating going on, Patterson could not see it.

She was sitting in her car outside Margaret Collier's house. The folder Quinn had provided was open across the steering wheel, with the page detailing Cartwright's dialogue with OCPD topmost on the pile of papers.

As she hoped, the detective had written Holly's address and phone number atop the transcript, just as they had on Collier's paperwork. But Patterson had no intention of calling ahead this time. There was no point. Holly was retired, which meant she would probably be home, and Patterson didn't want to set the woman's mind churning ahead of time in case she subconsciously constructed a false narrative or second-guessed her own memory. A lot of time had passed, and Patterson knew that a person's first recollections, before they had a chance to mentally deconstruct them and put them back together in what they felt was a more logical way, were often the most accurate. Even then, researchers had proven that memory was fickle. People would forget actual events or relay details of scenarios that had never occurred. Eyewitness testimony was more unreliable than most people assumed. But it was still a valid investigative tool, because there were few viable alternatives.

Patterson entered the address into her cell phone's GPS software and placed the phone on the car's central console before pulling away from the curb. Thirty-five minutes later, and halfway across town, she pulled up at her destination.

Holly Cartwright's residence was nothing like that of the woman who had taken over her job. Where Margaret Collier's house could have graced the cover of Better Homes and Gardens, Cartwright's abode was better suited to a spread in Unkempt Slums Monthly. The former boasted neatly laid flowerbeds, trimmed bushes, and carpets of manicured grass. A bare dirt lot choked with weeds and rambling undergrowth surrounded this home. It might once have been presentable but had since become wild and tangled with only the barest hint remaining of its former appearance.

Patterson sat in her car for a moment and observed the scene, allowing her first impressions of the property to percolate before exiting the vehicle and navigating the cracked concrete path leading to Holly Cartwright's front door.

The retired biologist was indeed home, answering the door only moments after Patterson rang the bell.

This time Patterson had her FBI credentials ready and flashed them right away. Deciding she'd already crossed the Rubicon at her previous port of call and using her ID once more would make little difference at this point. The result was an instant invitation inside the house. A moment later, she found herself in a living room as different from Margaret Collier's spic and span abode as was the home's exterior. It wasn't that the room was actually untidy, Patterson thought, but more the outdated style of the furnishings, and drab walls that didn't look like anyone had painted them in at least two decades.

"I have to say, I'm rather surprised to get a visit from the

FBI," Holly said, motioning for Patterson to take a seat. "Whatever could you think I've done?"

"You haven't done anything wrong, Mrs. Cartwright," Patterson reassured her. "I just want to have a chat, that's all. Nothing to worry about."

"Well, in that case, we should do so over a cup of tea, don't you think?" Holly turned toward the living room door, then glanced back over her shoulder. "I don't have any iced tea, I'm afraid. Just a breakfast blend, which I prefer hot with a slice of lemon. It's so much more refined."

"Hot tea will do just fine," Patterson replied with a smile. "Lemon too."

"Very well. I'll be right back," Holly said as she left the room. "Please make yourself comfortable."

Patterson watched the old woman go, then studied her surroundings. The room contained two wingback chairs, and a sofa covered with a floral pattern slip that had come away in one corner to reveal the sofa's original tan upholstery. A mid-century modern coffee table that had seen better days occupied the center of the room. Piles of magazines covered the table. They were mostly supermarket tabloids promising to dish out the dirt on whatever celebrity they thought would sell the most copies. A pair of frames containing photographs sat on the fireplace mantle. Patterson stood and approached these. The first was of a much younger Holly with her arms around a man that Patterson assumed was her husband. There were no manly touches to the living room and no sign of a male presence in the house, which meant he was probably long deceased. The second photo also contained a younger Holly. This time she was standing flanked by a woman about Holly's age on one side, and a boy whom Patterson guessed was in his mid-teens on her other. The difference in body language within the group was striking, with Holly and the woman grinning broadly, and the boy staring dully toward the camera with narrowed eyes. She wondered if he was

Holly's son, but then a voice spoke from her rear, breaking her train of thought.

"Here's the tea," Holly said, entering the room and placing two china cups sitting atop dainty saucers down on the coffee table. "I already had the tea bags steeping when you came, so it's rather strong, I'm afraid."

"I don't mind strong tea," Patterson said, turning back toward the old woman and retaking her seat. "Is that your husband," she asked, nodding toward the first of the two pictures.

"Yes. Larry. He died young. Not long after that photo was taken, actually."

"I'm sorry to hear that."

"Please, don't be. He's been gone a long time. I'm used to it. I have to say, though, not having him around still gets lonely. Especially since I retired."

"Do you have any other family?" Patterson asked, eyeing the second photo.

"I have an aunt in Dallas. She lives in a nursing home now because she's in her nineties, so I haven't seen her in a long time. I don't like to travel." Holly picked up her cup by the handle and took a sip of tea before returning it to the saucer. "I also have a sister out west. Salt Lake City. She has a son named Scott."

"Is that him in the photograph," Patterson asked, still looking at the second frame.

"Yes. I used to visit my sister regularly, but I haven't seen her in a couple of decades. We don't see eye to eye. I couldn't even tell you where she's living right now, to be honest, or even if she's still alive."

"That's a shame," Patterson replied.

"It's life. Now why don't we get down to business. I'm sure you didn't come here to talk about my family issues."

"No. I didn't."

"Then what did bring you to my door?" Holly picked up the

teacup again and took another sip, then studied her guest over the rim. "Is it that dreadful business on Bracken Island?"

Patterson nodded. "I want to make sure nothing was overlooked during the original interview."

"I see." Holly looked thoughtful. "I'll happily tell you the same thing I told the homicide detective last month, but I can't imagine you will discover any new information. To tell the truth, I couldn't be of much help. I haven't even stepped foot on the island for many years."

"Do you remember noticing if anyone else was coming ashore there?" Patterson asked.

"If anyone else was coming on to the island, they weren't making it obvious. At least so far as I can remember. That's really all I have to say. My job took me to the island on a monthly basis for the better part of two decades, but I was only there for a few hours each time. I really can't be of any help to you. I told that detective the same thing."

"Yes. I read the interview report."

"Then you must surely have been aware that driving out here would be a waste of time," Holly said. "I'm just an old woman fading into retirement with no knowledge of any crimes that were committed on that island."

"I was hoping there might be something you deemed too small to mention during the last interview," Patterson said. "People sometimes dismiss information as irrelevant, when it isn't."

"I didn't do that. I relayed what I knew, which was nothing." Holly paused and observed Patterson for a moment, then her brow furrowed. "If you don't mind me asking, why are you really here?"

"I already told you."

"I wasn't born yesterday, Agent Blake. The FBI surely has better use for its agents than wasting time on follow-up interviews with people who clearly have no relevant information. Do you think the Oklahoma City Police Department are not doing their job correctly?"

"It's not that," Patterson said.

"Then what is it?"

"Look, I'll be honest with you," Patterson said. She picked up her cup and drank the tea, then replaced it on the saucer. "I'm not exactly here in an official capacity."

"Oh?" Holly's brows raised. "Go on."

"It's true that the FBI are working with the Homicide Squad on this case, but I'm not officially part of that investigation."

"Really?" Holly's demeanor became guarded. "But you are a genuine FBI agent?"

"Yes, I am." Patterson didn't want to go into detail about her true reason for visiting Holly Cartwright, but she had no choice. If the woman followed up with the Bureau, it would get back to Grant, and probably Madeline Kahn. "I'm on what you might call a sabbatical. My sister went missing on a road trip sixteen years ago and I've taken time off to look for her. She was last seen alive in Oklahoma City. I'm trying to determine if she's a Bracken Island Killer victim."

"My goodness. That's awful. You poor thing. Are you having any luck finding out what happened to her?"

"Not so far. As much as I hate to admit it, this killer is the only avenue of investigation I have right now. I'll just keep digging until I get an answer."

"I certainly hope you find what you're looking for," Holly said. She glanced at Patterson's empty cup, then toward the living room door. "If you don't have any more questions, I'll show you out. I'm not trying to be rude, but I like to take a nap around this time of day. The joys of old age."

"I don't have any further questions at this time." Patterson reached into her jacket pocket and removed a business card. "My cell number is on this card. If you think of anything, I hope you'll call me."

"I will. I'll do my best to think back and if I remember

anything new, I'll get in touch." Holly stood and led Patterson from the living room to the front door. "Will you be in town for a while?"

"At least until I find out if my sister died on that island," Patterson replied.

"I see." Holly nodded thoughtfully. "Where are you staying while you're in town? Somewhere nice, I hope."

"Not so much. A dive called The Welcome Inn. It's the same place my sister stayed, so I thought it would be a good starting point."

"I'm not sure I know of it. But then again, that isn't surprising. I live here already so I don't have any need for hotels." Holly opened the front door and waited for Patterson to step outside. "Good luck, Special Agent Blake."

"Thank you. I think I'll need it," Patterson replied, then turned and started down the path toward her car.

The afternoon had turned gloomy now, Patterson noted. Gone was the bright sunshine, replaced by scudding gray clouds that raced across the sky on a stiff eastward breeze. Then, as she reached her car and unlocked the driver side door, the rain started to fall.

THIRTY-FIVE

It was getting late in the afternoon when Patterson arrived back at the hotel. She parked and hurried to the entrance with her head bent low against a persistent drizzle of rain. She still hadn't picked up an umbrella and made a note to get one at the first available opportunity.

She stepped into the lobby and approached the registration desk. She had failed to get the information she wanted from the hotel's manager on her last two attempts, but now she decided to bring out the big guns.

"Did you find that registration card yet?" She asked, leaning on the counter and looking at him through the hatch.

"Not yet," he responded, eyes glued to the computer monitor. "Still busy. I'll get to it when I get to it."

"And what about the theft in my sister's room?"

"Look, lady, I told you this twice already. I don't know anything about any room thefts, and certainly not from that long ago."

"And I said I'd give you some time to think on it and see if your memory got any better." Despite the manager's insistence that he knew nothing, his own body language gave him away. It convinced Patterson he was lying.

"Well, it didn't. I don't know what you want me to tell you."

"The truth would be nice," Patterson replied. She slipped a hand into her pocket and removed the slim black wallet containing her FBI credentials. For the third time that day, she was about to step over the line Grant had drawn in the sand.

When she placed the open wallet on the counter in front of him, the manager's eyes grew wide. "You're a cop?"

"I'm a special agent with the Federal Bureau of Investigation." Patterson felt a rush of satisfaction as the manager recoiled.

"Shit. You never said anything when you checked in."

"Why should I?"

"I don't know." The manager was stumbling over his words. "Aren't you supposed to announce that you're the law? Isn't it, what's the word…Entrapment…if you don't?"

"That's not a thing. I'm under no obligation to tell you I'm a law enforcement officer, even if you might commit a crime in my presence. You've been watching too much TV. And even if it were a thing, it doesn't apply to renting a hotel room." Patterson smiled despite herself. She had the manager on his heels. She decided to press her advantage. "You should think about the repercussions of lying to an FBI agent, though."

"Look, if I don't remember, it's not lying." The manager's complexion had turned pale. "Right?"

"That's true. But I think it's only fair to warn you I'm trained to spot deception." Patterson could sense the manager's resolve crumbling like so many stacked playing cards. "You know, we've chatted a few times now, and I don't even know your name yet."

"Hank." The manager's reluctance to provide this information was clear from the tone of his voice. "Hank Lasky."

"Good to meet you, Hank," Patterson said in the friendliest tone she could muster. "How about you give it some thought and see if that memory of yours has gotten any clearer."

"I'll do my best."

"That's all I ask." Patterson put her ID away before continuing. "Now why don't we try this again. Do you, or do you not, remember a series of room thefts at this hotel around the time my sister stayed here, sixteen years ago?"

"Yeah. I remember now. Went on for about five years. Guests reporting items missing from their rooms. It was mostly money, small electronics like iPods, cell phones. That kind of thing. Some of the guests, mostly women, reported clothes going missing too."

"My sister and her friend had clothes stolen. The thief took their underwear."

"The underwear thing was weird. He was definitely a freak."

"He? Are you telling me you know who the thief was?"

The manager hesitated, realizing he'd let his tongue slip. "Yeah. We caught the little perv back in 2008. Guy named Justin Ferrera. He'd been working here for about ten years as a part-time desk clerk. The rest of the time he handled maintenance."

"How did you catch him?" Patterson asked.

"There was a young woman staying here. Pretty thing, if I recall. I guess he didn't want to wait until she went out to get ahold of her panties. She woke up in the middle of the night and found him standing over her bed. Created a hell of a ruckus, I'll tell you. He ran when she screamed, but not before the woman got a good look at him. That was enough for us. We fired him on the spot."

"What about the police?" Patterson asked. Had Justin Ferrera broken into her sister's room while she was sleeping? Did he do more than that? "I assume you had him charged."

"Yeah. Right. Like we wanted to advertise that one of our employees was a creep. Like I said, we fired him. Problem solved."

"What about the girl whose room he broke into? Didn't she call the police?"

"She wanted to. Kept screaming about how violated she felt. Said she thought he was going to rape her. Took us a while to talk some sense into her. In the end a free room and a thousand bucks cash did the trick."

"You paid her off to keep quiet." Patterson was aghast.

"No. We compensated her for the problems she'd encountered while staying here. You can't prove we did otherwise."

"That's true. I can't." Patterson didn't bother to mention that it was irrelevant since the statute of limitations would have long expired on any crimes committed during that timeframe by either the maintenance man or the hotel's management. Except murder. There was no ticking clock on that offense. If Justin Ferrera was involved in her sister's disappearance, he could still face charges. "Do you know if Justin Ferrera still lives in Oklahoma City?"

Hank the manager shrugged. "How on earth would I know that? It's not like we were best buds. I thought the kid was creepy even before we caught him stealing panties. He had that look about him, you know?"

"What kind of look?" Patterson's mind drifted to the Bracken Island Killer, and the young women he'd chained in cars to die a lingering death. Could the hotel's ex maintenance man have anything to do with that? She might just be able to provide local investigators with their first person of interest. "Can you elaborate?"

"Unsettling. Like he was thinking stuff in his head when he talked to you." Hank shuddered visibly. "He wasn't a pleasant person to be around. Had a vibe about him."

"What about a phone number or address? You must have had those on record when he was working here."

"That much I can do." Hank turned to the computer and pecked at the keyboard. Seconds later, a desktop laser printer came to life and spit out a single sheet. Hank handed it to her. "His employment record. I can't vouch for how accurate it is after so many years, but that's the last contact details we had on file before we booted his ass."

"You can find this in ten seconds flat, but you can't locate my sister's registration card?" Patterson asked, glancing down at the sheet of paper.

"We put all the employee records onto the computer not long after we got it. Made it easier for payroll. Couldn't see the point in entering the old registration cards though. You're the first person who ever asked us about them."

Patterson nodded. "I trust you'll make a renewed effort to locate my sister's card now we've leveled with each other."

"I'll do my best," the manager grumbled. He glanced up at Patterson and met her gaze. "A word of advice..."

"Yes?"

"You might want to be careful about flashing those credentials while you're staying here. Some of my guests are—shall we say—averse to being in the company of law enforcement, if you catch my drift."

"I catch your drift," Patterson replied. "Does that include you?"

"I guess that depends on the circumstances."

"In that case, you'd better find me that registration card." Patterson returned the manager's gaze for a moment, then she stepped away toward the stairs and spoke over her shoulder without looking back. "We'll talk again real soon, Hank."

THIRTY-SIX

P atterson called the number on the sheet of paper the manager had printed out as soon as she reached her room. She thought it was a long shot that he would still be using the same number after so many years, and she was proved right. The person who answered had never heard of Justin Ferrera, and curtly hung up after informing her she had a wrong number.

But Patterson wasn't giving up. She had an address too, and assuming it wasn't a rental, Ferrera or one of his relatives might still live there. Patterson sat on the bed and opened her laptop, then typed the address into Google, which returned several pages of results. It heartened her to see that none of these were real estate websites, which meant the property—a one story block house according to Google Earth-probably hadn't changed hands in a long time. More good news.

What the search results did return though, were several websites run by companies hoping to sell background checks to whomever would pay their monthly fee. Some of the information was free, provided as click bait.

Patterson browsed to the first such website and got a hit on Justin Ferrera's name along with a list of potential family members. There were three phone numbers, too. The first she already had and knew was incorrect. She jotted down the second and third ones.

When she dialed the second one, all she got was a bleating tone interspersed with a message telling her the number was out of service.

The third number connected.

It rang four times.

On the fifth ring, a harried sounding female voice answered. "If this is another goddamned debt collector, I've already told you people, you'll get your money when I get some money."

"I'm not a debt collector," Patterson said quickly. "I'm looking for a man named Justin Ferrera. Do you know of him?"

"I know him well enough. He's my worthless brother."

"Can I speak to him?"

"If you can find him, you can."

"He doesn't live there with you, then?" Patterson asked. "I got your address and phone number from one of his previous employers."

"Must be a really old employer then. He hasn't used this address in over a decade." The woman hesitated. "Who is this, anyway? Are you a cop or something?"

"I'm working with the local police, yes." Patterson wondered why the woman jumped to an immediate conclusion, upon receiving a call about her brother, that it was from the police. "Has Justin been in trouble before?"

"He's been in trouble his whole life. Alcohol. Drugs. You name it. What's he gone and done now?"

Patterson said, "He hasn't done anything as far as I'm aware. I need to talk with him regarding an incident that occurred many years ago at a hotel where he was working as a maintenance man. The Welcome Inn."

"I remember that place. Friggin' rathole. Technically, he wasn't living with me. He was just using my address to receive his mail. Like I said, he's had a lot of drug problems. Been homeless on and off for a couple of decades. The hotel were paying him part-time to work the front desk and letting him stay there in a basement room if he made up his hours doing maintenance work."

"He was living at the hotel?" Hank hadn't mentioned that little detail.

"Sure was. At least until he went and got himself fired. Then he came and lived with me for a while, at least until I couldn't take it no more. I had young kids, and he was bringing drugs in the house. In the end my husband kicked him out."

"I take it you don't keep in touch with him, then?"

"What do you think?"

"And you don't have a current address?"

"Well, we kicked him out of our house and told him not to come back, so we aren't exactly exchanging Christmas cards."

"That would be a no, then?"

"That would be a most definite no. If I were you, I'd try the homeless shelters first. Even if he ain't in one of them, someone there might know where he hangs out."

"I'll do that. I'm sorry to have disturbed you."

"No biggie. I'd rather be talking to you than some scumbag debt collector. Even when you tell 'em you're broke, they don't believe you. Think we're dodging our bills for the fun of it. Like we enjoy not being able to make ends meet."

"It's a tough world, for sure," Patterson sympathized. "I can call you back when we find your brother, if you'd like. Put your mind at rest that he's okay."

"Don't bother. I washed my hands of him years ago. Last thing I want to do is get back on that merry-go-round."

"Understood," Patterson replied before saying goodbye and hanging up.

She'd struck out tracking down Justin Ferrera with the meager resources at her disposal. But the Oklahoma City Field Office would have no such limitations. Her next call was going to be Agent Quinn, anyway. Even though there was no proof Ferrera was the Bracken Island Killer, his crimes at the hotel all those years ago, including his obsession with stealing women's underwear, suggested he might possess sociopathic tendencies. She dialed Quinn's number and wasted no time passing on what she'd learned. The special agent was interested and said she'd pass it along to the OCPD homicide unit to follow up on. Then she said something that caught Patterson off guard.

"What are you doing for the rest of the evening?" Quinn asked.

"Nothing much. I'll probably go grab some bad takeout food and bring it back to the hotel room."

"That's absolutely not going to happen," Quinn replied. "You're coming to our house for dinner, instead."

"It's really sweet of you to invite me, but I couldn't do that. It's such an imposition."

"Nonsense. You're FBI. There's no way I'm letting a fellow agent eat a hamburger and fries along with the cockroaches in a cruddy hotel room when you could be enjoying turkey lasagna with us. Leah always makes too much anyway so you'll be saving me from four days of leftovers."

"And Leah would be?"

"She would be my enormously talented wife, who cooks better Italian food than most restaurants."

"With an endorsement like that, how can I refuse?"

"You can't."

"I feel like I should bring something. Can I pick up dessert?" Patterson asked.

"You don't need to bring a thing. We already have dessert. Tiramisu. But if you're feeling super guilty, a bottle of Pinot wouldn't go unappreciated."

Patterson said, "I think I can handle that. What's the address and what time you want me there?"

"I'll text you the address," Quinn said. "It's almost six right now. Shall we say half past seven? That should give you enough time."

"Perfect. I'll see you then," Patterson said before hanging up.

She went to the mirror and gave herself a quick once-over. Her hair was a mess and the clothes she was wearing were unacceptable for a dinner with people she hardly knew. She went to her travel bag and found a fresh pair of jeans and a white top. She had worn most of her other clothes already and would need to find a laundromat soon. Unless she wanted to start recycling underwear, which wasn't happening.

But that could wait until tomorrow. She had an hour and a half to make herself presentable and drive over to Quinn's. Feeling more upbeat than she had in a while, Patterson grabbed a couple of clean towels from a stand near the hotel room door and headed down the corridor to take a shower.

THIRTY-SEVEN

Patterson didn't linger in the shower. She washed as quickly as possible and then stepped out of the cubicle onto a towel she'd laid on the floor to protect her bare feet from the disturbingly dirty tiles beneath.

She dried herself and dressed in the clean clothes brought from her room, then dumped the used towels into a laundry hamper before stepping into the corridor.

She was almost back to her room when the door next to hers opened, and a man in a pair of dark jeans and a blue shirt stepped out. Neatly groomed and clean-shaven, he looked to be in his late thirties or early forties.

He turned and locked his hotel room door, then pocketed the key. When he noticed her approaching, he smiled and nodded a greeting.

"Evening, neighbor," he said in a baritone voice that carried the barest hint of a Midwestern accent. "What do you think of the accommodations?"

"I've stayed in better," Patterson replied as she reached her own door.

"Me too. I only checked in today. It wouldn't be my first choice. Hopefully, I won't need to stay here too long."

"Are you in town on business?" Patterson asked as she unlocked her own room door.

"Personal business," the man replied. "I'm not sure how long it will take."

"Well, good luck." Patterson stepped into her room.

"You too." The man smiled again. Then he started down the corridor toward the stairs.

Patterson watched him for a moment, until he turned onto the stairs, then closed her door and added the dirty clothes she'd been wearing before her shower to the laundry pile. She brushed her hair and donned the best pair of flat shoes she'd brought with her, because she didn't have any heels. Whenever she wasn't carrying it, Patterson kept her Glock service weapon out of sight in the nightstand drawer, since there was no room safe. Now she transferred it to a red Coach purse. She couldn't leave the gun in the room unattended but didn't want to bother wearing a holster.

With the purse over her shoulder, Patterson exited the room and made her way downstairs.

When she walked through the lobby, she noticed that the double doors leading to the lounge bar were open. An aroma of cigarette smoke and stale beer wafted out. Glancing inside, Patterson noticed the man she'd spoken to in the corridor sitting at the bar, a pint in his hand. He lifted the drink in her direction and nodded. Patterson nodded back, then continued to the parking lot and her car.

Mary Quinn's home was in the city's Shepherd Historic District. On the way, Patterson stopped at a liquor store and picked up a bottle of Pinot Grigio.

The house was a two-story Tudor revival with bricks on the lower level and half timbers above. Patterson parked in the driveway to the side of the house behind Quinn's SUV and walked up a brick path laid out in a herringbone pattern to the front door.

Quinn was there to greet her. She accepted the bottle of wine with an approving nod. "Come on in," she said, waiting for Patterson to enter, and then closing the door behind them.

"You have a lovely home," Patterson said, her gaze roaming across the neat entrance hall and comfortable living room off to her left.

"Thank you." Quinn led Patterson toward the back of the house and into the kitchen. "I can't take credit for the decor, though. That's all Leah."

"She has a good eye," Patterson replied, noting the modern bright kitchen with gleaming quartz countertops and shaker style cabinetry that reached almost to the ceiling.

"I wouldn't go that far." An unfamiliar voice spoke from Patterson's rear. "I mostly just copy what I see in magazines."

She turned to see a slender woman of about the same age as Quinn, with short, dark hair and dusty gray eyes. "You must be Leah."

"And you must be Patterson Blake." Leah smiled and removed the corkscrew from a drawer in the kitchen island. "I think you might be the first coworker that M's ever brought home."

"You'll have to excuse Leah," Quinn said. "She calls me M even though I'd prefer not to be referred to by nothing but an initial. After eight years together, it's an affectation I'm going to have to live with forever, it appears."

"I think it's adorable," Patterson said with a smile.

"See! I'm not the only one who thinks it's cute." Leah was opening the bottle of wine. She pulled the cork out with a pop, then glanced toward Patterson. "Nice choice on the vino, by the way."

"Thanks." Patterson waited for Leah to pour three glasses. She set her purse down on the center island and took one. The air was redolent with the scent of cooking. "It will be refreshing to have a home-cooked meal for a change. I've eaten nothing but fast food since leaving New York."

"That's right," Leah said. "You live back east. What brings you all the way to Oklahoma City?"

"Didn't Mary tell you?"

"We try not to talk about her work. We decided a long time ago to keep our home life separate from M's job. The evils of the outside world have no place here."

"Then I'm not sure I should burden you with the details of my stay in Oklahoma City."

"We can make an exception. If only to satisfy my curiosity."

"Very well, then. I'm not actually here on official FBI business. I'm looking for my sister. She went missing sixteen years ago. The last place anyone saw her was here."

"How awful," Leah said. "I can't imagine losing someone like that. Have you gotten any closer to finding her?"

"No." Patterson shook her head. "But I had a minor breakthrough today. A person who could be involved in her disappearance."

"Speaking of which," Quinn chimed in, "I passed the information you gave me on to Homicide. They're going to look at Justin Ferrera, see if he fits the bill for the Bracken Island Killer. I'll keep you informed."

"I'd appreciate that." Patterson said. Her eyes wandered to a picture in a silver frame hanging on the wall near the door. A portrait of Leah, Quinn, and two boys of about twelve years of age. She wondered to which of the pair the boys belonged, considering they'd only been together for eight years.

Leah provided the answer, reading Patterson's mind. "Those are my kids. Aiden and Michael. They're from my previous relationship. My ex is the biological mother. That's where they are right now. We have joint custody."

"They're a handsome pair," Patterson said. "They look so much alike."

"That's because they're twins. We weren't expecting that. There's no history of twins in my ex's family. Must have been the donor. It came as quite a shock."

"I bet." Patterson sipped her wine and soaked in the relaxing atmosphere of Quinn's home. It was a departure from the rundown hotel she was currently staying in.

"All right then," Leah said, turning toward the oven and checking on the lasagna. "I think we're about done. Who's ready to eat?"

THIRTY-EIGHT

With a full belly, Patterson departed Quinn's house at ten o'clock and drove back to the hotel. When she entered the lobby, the bar was still open despite there being few patrons left within. One lonesome figure, sitting on the same stool as when she left, was the man occupying the bedroom next to hers.

Previously intent upon heading upstairs to bed, Patterson changed her mind and veered left into the bar instead. She ordered a drink—the only import they had on tap—and turned to her temporary neighbor.

"There are better places than this to while away an evening, you know," she said half-jokingly.

The man looked up from his beer. "I'm sure there are. But being new in town I don't know any of them." He glanced around the smoky room. "Besides, this place has a certain ambience."

"That's one way to describe it." Patterson tasted her beer. It had a sour, vinegary tang. She winced and wondered how long it had been since the bar cleaned its draft system. If they relied upon the same person who mopped the shower room floor, that would be never. "A word of advice. If you're still in town tomorrow night, and you want somewhere to go, try Bricktown.

I haven't been here long myself, but there's a great brewpub, and the food's not half bad either."

"Thanks. I'll remember that." The stranger tipped his glass. "I'm John. What's your name?"

"Patterson."

"That's an unusual moniker, especially for a girl."

"You are not the first person to point that out." Patterson looked down at her beer, decided against it.

"I suppose not." John paused a moment before he spoke again. "What brings you to town?"

"Just some unfinished family business," Patterson said, guarded.

"Are you going to be here long?"

"Not sure, yet. How about you?"

"Oh, I don't know. I guess we'll see." John glanced at his watch, then back to Patterson. "I don't mean to be rude, but I'm beat so I think I'll go back upstairs and hit the sack."

Patterson nodded. "I understand. I saw you were still in here and just thought I'd come in and say hi, that's all."

"And I'm thrilled that you did," John said. He finished the last of his drink and asked the bartender for the bill. He paid in cash and stood up. "I guess I'll see you around, Patterson."

"We are right next door to each other, so probably."

"That's true." John lifted his hand in a parting gesture, and then he was striding away toward the lobby and the stairs beyond.

Patterson leaned on the bar and contemplated whether she could be bothered to finish her beer.

The bartender observed her with narrowed eyes while he casually wiped a glass with a stained cloth before putting it on a shelf. He was young, probably no older than his mid-twenties, with slicked back hair and a greasy goatee. A dragon tattoo weaved its way from his wrist up one arm before disappearing under the sleeve of his faded black T-shirt. Hank the hotel manager had told her the owner's son ran the bar. This was obviously not him. The hotel owner had apparently retired to Florida several years earlier, so his son must be older than the man currently standing behind the bar.

Deciding the skunky beer wasn't worth her time, she reached into her pocket, found a five-dollar bill, and placed it on the bar next to the mostly full pint glass. Then she stood and followed in the footsteps of John—the man who wasn't sure how long he would be in town—up the stairs and was soon asleep in her bed.

THIRTY-NINE

Patterson's phone rang at 7 AM and woke her.

She reached out to the nightstand, groggy, and scooped it up, answering without looking to see who it was.

Mary Quinn's voice filled her ear. "We've got a hit."

"A hit on what?" Patterson sat upright, confused and still half asleep.

"Bracken Island. The trail cams." There was excitement in Quinn's voice. "Homicide was checking the photos that came in overnight and caught two figures coming ashore. A male and a female."

"Is it our guy?" Patterson was already out of bed and pulling on her clothes. "You think he's dumping his next victim?"

"No idea," Quinn replied. "I only just got the notification. I'm heading down to the precinct to look at the images. You want to come with?"

"Try to stop me." Patterson had her phone on speaker now. She laid it on the bed while she strapped on her shoulder holster and secured the Glock. She concealed it with a light jacket, then picked the phone back up. "Tell me when and where."

"I can swing by and pick you up. I'm already in the car and heading your way. Should be there in fifteen minutes."

"Great," Patterson replied. "I'll meet you outside the lobby."

"Roger that," Quinn replied, then hung up.

Patterson grabbed her toiletries bag and headed down the hall. Ten minutes later, she was on her way down the hall again, this time to meet Quinn.

———

The Oklahoma City Police Department's investigative Bureau, tasked with handling homicide investigations, was located in the downtown police headquarters. It was a newly constructed brick and glass building that sat in the center of the city and was a far cry from the older police precincts in New York.

She followed Special Agent Quinn through an expansive lobby with a soaring ceiling that rose three floors through the middle of the building. They passed through a security door next to the information desk and rode the elevator to a second-floor operations room where a cluster of three plainclothes officers were observing a large wall-mounted screen upon which was a blurry picture of a woodland trail at night. The fuzzy outlines of two figures stood in contrast to the darker backdrop of foliage. A fourth man sat at a desk below the monitor, working on a laptop computer.

"Agent Quinn." The tallest of the officers, a stocky gentleman in his late fifties wearing gray suit pants, a white shirt with the sleeves rolled up to his elbows, and a shoulder holster that contained a Glock similar to Patterson's, turned toward them as they entered the room. "We'll backtrack the images so that you can see the sequence from the beginning."

"Thanks." Quinn moved further into the room.

"Who's this?" The detective's eyes shifted from Quinn to Patterson. "You get yourself a partner?"

"Not quite." Quinn shook her head. "This is Special Agent Patterson Blake from the New York Field Office. She's in town temporarily and providing her expertise."

"Lucky her," the detective said. He extended a hand toward Patterson. "Frank Ballard."

"A pleasure to meet you." Patterson shook the proffered hand.

The detective jerked a thumb toward the man to his right. "This here is Eddie Kittrell with the Oklahoma State Bureau of Investigation. They've been helping us process the killer's dumping ground on Bracken Island. They also set up surveillance for us."

"The trail cams."

"Correct."

Kittrell turned toward her and nodded a perfunctory greeting, then turned his attention back to the screen.

Ballard indicated the man standing to his left. "This is Carlos Gimenez. My partner."

"Hello," Patterson said as the man glanced toward her.

"Now the introductions are over, let's get back to business." Ballard tapped the seated technician on the shoulder and told him to start the sequence of photos over. "We've been checking the trail cam footage several times a day for over a month. Until now we've captured a lot of wildlife, mostly blurred shots of birds flying into the camera's field of vision. There aren't many large mammals on the island. No deer, bears, or bobcats. There are smaller animals like black-tailed jackrabbits and Eastern wood rats, but the cameras won't pick those up. What we have picked up are feral pigs. A small population has survived and even thrived on the island. There's ample food for them and hardly any natural predators there. They've wandered in front of the trail cams several times."

"You'll have to excuse Frank," Gimenez said. "He fancies himself something of a naturalist."

"Just providing background," Ballard said. He pointed to the image frozen on the screen. A black and white night vision shot of the dock Patterson and Quinn had moored at the day before. There was another boat tied up there now. A small cabin cruiser tied with the bow facing them. "This was the first image showing our interlopers." He motioned for the technician to move on. Another image of the dock popped up, this time showing two people walking toward shore. A man with a hoodie pulled over his head, disguising his features, and a young woman wearing a halter top and shorts. "There are three more images that captured one or both of them. One more on the dock, a single picture near the beginning of the trail, and a final photograph that appears to show the male returning to the boat. Either the girl wasn't with him at that point, or she wasn't in frame and boarded the boat in between photos. There's an eight second delay before the camera can take another shot."

Gimenez added, "It's a limitation of the equipment we're using."

"None of the cameras around the car tripped?" Quinn asked.

"No. We don't know where they went once on the island." Ballard sounded frustrated. "If he took her to an abandoned vehicle, he used one we're unaware of."

"Shit. If that's our killer, how are we going to find the victim?" Quinn grimaced. "I was sure he'd use all the available space in one vehicle before moving on to another. That's been his pattern so far."

"Maybe he changed it." Gimenez rubbed his chin.

"Why would he?" Quinn shook her head. "That doesn't make sense."

"What about facial recognition?" Patterson asked. "We've used it with some success back in New York."

Ballard said, "We're working on it. But as I'm sure you know, it's not exactly reliable. Also, thanks to the hoodie, none of the photos captured enough of the male's features to run through the databases. We might have more luck with the woman, but I wouldn't hold your breath considering the quality of the images. There may be too much motion blur."

"So where does that leave us?" Quinn asked.

"With this." Ballard tapped the technician's shoulder and instructed him to bring up the last photo.

An image showing the boat flashed up on the screen. It had departed the dock and was motoring away from them as it returned to the far shore.

Patterson squinted at the image. "There's a name written on the back of the boat, but I can't quite read it."

"How about now?" Ballard asked as the screen changed to another image. An enlargement of the boat's transom. "We blew it up and enhanced the image to make the lettering clearer."

"Salty Miss," Quinn said. "The boat's name is Salty Miss."

"That makes things easier," Patterson commented. "All we need to do is find out who owns the Salty Miss, and we'll have our culprit."

"I have someone working on that already." Ballard glanced at his watch. "I expect we'll be receiving our answer any time now."

As if on cue, Ballard's phone rang. He answered and conversed briefly with the person on the other end before hanging up.

His gaze wandered from the picture of the boat's stern to the pair of FBI agents. "Looks like we have a winner. Kevin Robert Grayson. Home address is in Nichols Hills."

"Wow." Quinn raised an eyebrow. "Looks like we're off to see how the other half lives."

Ballard added, "And there's no time like the present." He picked up a jacket that had been hanging over the back of an empty chair next to the technician, then slipped it on. "Let's go see what Mister Grayson has to say for himself. Who's with me?"

"What about the island?" Patterson asked. "Shouldn't someone check on that?"

"Already have a team on the way," Ballard replied. "If there's a victim over there, we'll find her."

"Good." An image of the derelict car popped into Patterson's head. Was there a terrified girl chained inside it at that very moment?

Ballard left the room, followed by Kittrell and Gimenez.

Patterson glanced at Quinn, hoping she wouldn't object to an out-of-town FBI agent, technically off-duty, riding along. In answer, Quinn merely turned and followed the men with nothing but a casual, "Come on, then."

FORTY

I t didn't take long for Patterson to realize what was so special about Nichols Hills. Million-dollar plus homes with stately façades were spread out around the scenic Grand Boulevard Park, a lush green corridor which ran through the middle of the district. The area abounded with upscale salons, restaurants, and bars. It was even home to an exclusive country club where businessmen could hold informal meetings on the front nine before retreating to the clubhouse to enjoy a chef prepared meal and a glass of fine wine. It was about as far from her own working-class neighborhood in New York as one could get.

Kevin Robert Grayson did not live in one of the biggest houses Patterson had seen on their drive through the trendy suburb, but it was far from the smallest. As they pulled through the property's open gates and onto a semi-circular brick driveway that curved around a large three-tier stone fountain, she craned her neck to marvel up at the imposing residence sitting amid lush green lawns and manicured hedgerows. It was large, at least six thousand square feet, with vines creeping up its red brick walls, and a glass conservatory on one end.

Patterson was riding with Quinn, following another unmarked vehicle driven by Ballard. He pulled up next to a red

Porsche 911 Turbo S that was sitting with its nose pointing toward the first bay of a large three-car garage. Quinn brought her own vehicle to a stop behind Ballard's, and the two women climbed out. They joined Ballard, Gimenez, and the Oklahoma State Bureau of Investigation agent, Kittrell, and mounted a set of stone steps leading to the front door.

When they knocked, a tall woman in her late forties with cascading black hair and a hawkish face answered. She observed them with some surprise before asking what their business might be.

"We're looking for Kevin Robert Grayson," Ballard said. "Is he here?"

"And who might you be?" the woman replied, her eyes narrowing.

Ballard removed his credentials and showed them to her. "My partner and I are from the Oklahoma City Police Department. The remainder of my companions are with the OSBI, and the FBI."

"FBI?" The woman's demeanor changed from one of haughty indifference to shock. "Whatever business could the FBI have with us?"

"I'm sorry," Ballard said. "But I don't believe you introduced yourself. You would be…?"

"I'm Laura Grayson. Kevin's wife. Would you please tell me what this is about?"

"I'm sorry, Mrs. Grayson. That's something I need to discuss with your husband. Is he at home?"

"Is this to do with Transpacific Oil and Freight?"

"I have no idea what that is," Ballard said. "If you would just answer my question, I'd appreciate it."

"So you're not here about the shares my husband sold?"

"No, we're not here about your husband's stock market dealings." Ballard shook his head.

"Well, thank goodness for that. I told him not to do anything rash when he heard they were intending to file Chapter 11. Told him to be careful. They send you to jail for insider trading. But he always knows better."

"I wouldn't be too relieved, Mrs. Grayson. I'm actually a homicide detective."

"Oh." Laura Grayson looked like someone had pulled the rug out from under her. A momentary flash of indecision washed across her face before being replaced by a hardened expression. "Whatever you think my husband has done, he didn't. Unless you have a warrant, I don't think it would be wise for me to let you inside the house."

"Mrs. Grayson, we just want to talk to your husband. We're not here to arrest him." Ballard folded his arms. "Not yet anyway."

"If you want to talk to my husband, you'll need to go through our lawyer."

Quinn stepped forward, possibly hoping a softer female voice would defuse the situation. "This will be so much easier if you just let us talk to him, Mrs. Grayson. Your husband may have information that can help us with our inquiries. We have no intention of charging him with any crime at this time, I assure you."

"Be that as it may, I still think it would be best if we—"

"Laura, honey, it's okay." A man's voice spoke from within the house. "If these people want to ask me some questions, just let them do it."

Laura Grayson glanced back over her shoulder toward a gray-haired man in his early fifties wearing a pair of khaki shorts and a white polo shirt. "I really don't think that's a good idea. They're from the police, something to do with a homicide, apparently."

"Actually, I said I'm a homicide detective," Ballard corrected her. "I did not say we were here about a murder, only that we wish to speak with your husband."

"And are you here about a murder?" Kevin Grayson nudged

his wife gently aside and stood in the doorway, facing the group with arms folded.

"That's something I'd prefer not to discuss on your doorstep, if you don't mind," Ballard replied.

"In that case, why don't you come in." Grayson moved aside to allow them entry. "We can talk in my study."

Ballard made no move to enter. "I was thinking a better venue would be an interview room at police headquarters."

"So you are looking to implicate me in something," Grayson said, his face unreadable. "I can't imagine what."

"If you come with us, you'll know soon enough." Ballard was giving nothing away.

"Is that an order, or a request?"

"At this point, your cooperation is purely voluntary. We just want to talk to you. Ask some questions. What happens after that depends upon your answers."

"And if I refuse?"

"Then we'll need to secure your cooperation with an arrest warrant, but I'd prefer not to waste the time."

"I see. It's unlikely you'll be successful getting a judge to sign off on a warrant given that I've done nothing wrong, and certainly nothing that would draw the attention of homicide detectives."

"That remains to be seen."

"That it does. While I'm tempted to refuse your kind offer of a trip downtown and see which judge in this city would actually sign a warrant against me, I have a feeling you won't give up regardless." Grayson turned to retreat back into the house. "Give me a minute to get my keys."

Ballard reached out and placed a hand on Grayson's arm, stopping him before he could reenter the house. "Actually, sir, we'd prefer that you ride with us."

"Very well." Grayson shrugged. "Perhaps it would be better if my lawyer is involved, after all."

Laura Grayson had remained quiet throughout the exchange, but now she spoke up. "I'll call him right away."

"Follow us to the police station once you've done that," Grayson said to his wife. "I can't imagine these fine people will offer me a ride home once they're done, and I'd rather not have to take a taxi." Then he turned back to Ballard with a resigned look upon his face. "Alright. Let's get this over with."

FORTY-ONE

Patterson and Special Agent Quinn stood in the observation room and watched the detectives seat Kevin Michael Grayson in the interview room beyond. A one-way transparent mirror separated the two spaces. There was also a computer monitor sitting on the desk which showed a live feed from the interrogation room's recording equipment. The same system relayed sound through wall-mounted speakers.

His lawyer, who was already waiting when they arrived back at police headquarters, accompanied Grayson. Dressed in a sharp charcoal gray Armani suit and wearing a wristwatch that probably cost more than a year of Patterson's salary, Nelson Ottermeyer looked exactly like a high-priced corporate legal eagle, well-versed in wrangling his clients out of uncomfortable situations simply by invoking their contacts and status. He took a seat next to Grayson with a look of smug assurance on his face, clearly expecting to walk back out of the interrogation room within minutes.

Detective Ballard ignored the lawyer's display of arrogant bravado and took a seat on the opposite side of the table. Detective Gimenez followed suit.

Patterson wondered what had happened to the Oklahoma

State Bureau of Investigation agent, but then he opened the observation room door and strode through, taking up position next to them with his arms folded.

Ballard had already begun speaking, reiterating for the benefit of the recording that Grayson was merely helping with their inquiries, was free to leave at any time, and was not currently under arrest. He then got right to it.

"Mr. Grayson, are you the registered owner of a boat named the Salty Miss?" Ballard asked.

Grayson glanced toward his lawyer, who merely nodded. Having received the go-ahead to answer, he kept his response curt and to the point. "Yes."

"And where do you keep the Salty Miss docked?"

"The Twelve Acres Marina."

"Where is that Marina located?"

"The south shore of Lake Calhoun."

"How long have you owned the Salty Miss?"

"At least ten years."

"And you've always kept it on Lake Calhoun?"

"Yes."

"Did you own a boat before that?"

"Well, I..." Grayson paused. He looked down and rubbed his chin absently with one hand. "No. Not as such."

"You sound unsure." This was Gimenez. "Would you mind elaborating?"

Grayson's lawyer leaned in and whispered in his ear. The man nodded, as if agreeing with the lawyer's unheard statement, and then turned his attention back to the detectives. "My business partner and I had a boat jointly before the Salty Miss. It wasn't actually owned by us. It was a corporate asset. We used it to entertain clients."

"But you had access to that boat whenever you wanted?" Ballard asked.

"Yes. Mostly." Grayson nodded.

"Did you ever take either boat out at night?"

"Sometimes. Not very often." Grayson looked perplexed by this line of questioning. "Why?"

Ballard ignored the question and pressed ahead with one of his own. "When was the last time you took the Salty Miss out at night, Mr. Grayson?"

"I don't know. Maybe a few months ago. We mostly use it on the weekends. To be honest, I took it out more when my son was younger. Tried to get him interested in boating, and he was pretty good too. Could almost handle her better than me. Not lately though. He's nineteen now and has a girlfriend, so he's lost the interest. Probably for the best, though. My business has exploded over the last few years. It's crazy. I barely have time to do anything. I should probably sell the damned boat. It costs a fortune to maintain."

"What is your business, Mr. Grayson?"

"I'm a corporate accountant. Mostly forensic accounting. Companies that think they're being embezzled, mismanaged trust funds, that kind of thing."

"Judging by your house, and the car parked outside, you're doing pretty well. Why not just hire more staff?"

"It's not that simple. I have a business partner, like I said, but it takes a certain skill set to be a good forensic accountant. It's not unlike your line of work, actually. You can't just hire any old person fresh out of college with a degree in accounting. There's an investigative aspect to it too. It's difficult finding employees that understand not just the intricacies of bookkeeping but are also proficient in following a trail of deception. People who steal money try to hide their malfeasance, and some of them are extremely good at it."

Ballard replied, "You're well versed in the art of deception, then."

The lawyer reacted to this question. He held a hand up to stop his client from responding, then leaned forward toward Ballard and Gimenez. "Just because Mr. Grayson investigates accounting anomalies does not mean that he has ever used that information to commit any crime, or that he knows how to."

"I'm not saying he used his knowledge to commit a crime," Ballard responded.

"But you alluded to it with your line of questioning," the lawyer replied. "And the fact that you're interviewing my client at all indicates you suspect him of some wrongdoing."

"We're merely trying to establish the facts of the situation," Ballard replied in an even tone.

"Then why don't you just cut to the chase so that we can settle this matter and get out of here." The lawyer's tone was polite but forceful. "My client has already told you he's a busy man. He came here voluntarily, even though it meant stepping away from his business. But if you continue to dance around the issue, you'll force me to advise him to leave and not communicate further until such time as you have a warrant."

"Very well." There was a folder on the desk in front of Ballard. He opened it and removed a printout of the enlarged photo section showing the Salty Miss moving away from the dock. After removing a second print of the original, he slid them both across the desk in front of Grayson. "Can you tell me where you were between the hours of 9 PM and 10 PM yesterday evening?"

Grayson looked down at the photos, perplexed. "What is this?"

"I was hoping you could tell me." Ballard said. "A hidden camera took these last night on Bracken Island."

Grayson shook his head. "That's impossible. I haven't even visited the boat in weeks, let alone taken her out."

"So you're saying you didn't take this boat out last night and visit Bracken Island?"

"No. Why would I do that?"

"That's an excellent question."

"I can't have taken the boat out last night. I wasn't even in town. I've been away on a business trip for the past four days, only came back this morning. My wife went with me. If you don't believe me, check with the airport. We were on a flight back from Seattle at ten o'clock last night. The flight landed here at eleven fifteen. Didn't get home until almost one in the morning."

"How do you explain this, then?" Ballard removed a third photo showing the hoodie wearing man and the girl accompanying him. He slipped this across the table to show Grayson.

"Well, that's not me, obviously. Do I look like the kind of man who wears a hoodie?"

"Perhaps you can tell me who it is then?" Ballard asked. "Did you lend the boat to someone?"

"Hell, no. I paid almost three hundred grand for that boat. You think I'd lend it out to just anyone?"

"You're sure you don't recognize either of these people?"

"Not that I…" Grayson stopped mid-sentence. He picked up the photo and stared at it. Then he turned to his lawyer, leaned close, and whispered in his ear.

The lawyer listened, nodded, then looked at Ballard. "My client would like to know if you intend to charge either of the people in this photo with a crime."

"Not at the moment," Ballard replied, shaking his head. "We're just making inquiries. Technically, the people in this photograph were trespassing on restricted federal land, but I have no interest in that. The crimes I'm investigating are much more serious. If Mister Grayson knows either of them, he should tell us now. If he doesn't, we may charge him with obstruction of justice later on."

Grayson gave the lawyer a concerned glance.

The lawyer nodded silently.

Grayson cleared his throat. "I know who both these people are."

"Would you care to elaborate?" Ballard leaned forward.

Gimenez did the same.

There was a moment of expectant silence before Grayson

spoke again. "This is my son. The young woman with him is Nicole Crawford, his girlfriend."

In the observation room, Patterson and Quinn exchanged glances.

Eddie Kittrell turned away from the window with a disappointed grunt. "If that guy's telling the truth, we don't have our killer. It was just a couple of horny rich kids looking for somewhere to screw around and stealing daddy's boat to do it."

"On an overgrown island in the middle of the night?" Patterson asked. "Hardly seems very comfortable."

Eddie shrugged. "That's teenagers. I once took a girl to a graveyard thinking she'd be all into it."

"And was she?" Patterson wondered if she'd led a sheltered life.

"Not so much. I didn't get another date with that girl."

Quinn snorted. "I can't imagine why."

"I was young and stupid."

"You said it, not me," Quinn shot back.

"Speaking of young and stupid," Patterson interjected, "someone should probably confirm if this Grayson guy is telling the truth."

"That should be easy enough." Kittrell jerked a thumb toward the door. "Kid's right outside in the waiting area. Grayson's wife brought him with her. Guess she didn't trust him alone at home. Now we know why."

"Someone should probably get him into an interrogation room, make sure his story matches Grayson's," Quinn said.

"Looks like Detective Ballard is way ahead of you." Patterson was looking through the one-way mirror. Ballard had suspended the interview and stood up. So had the lawyer. They made their way toward the door. As they reached it, Ballard glanced over his shoulder toward the observation room, his expression unreadable. Then he stepped into the corridor and was gone, with the lawyer right behind.

A minute later, Eddie Kittrell's phone buzzed as a text

message came through. He took it out, read the message, then turned to Quinn and Patterson. "They have the kid across the hall in interrogation room two. Our presence is requested."

"Great," Patterson said, stepping past Kittrell toward the door. "Let's get this over with so we can go back to hunting our killer."

FORTY-TWO

Three hours later Patterson was in Quinn's car, returning to the hotel. Grayson's son had owned up to taking the boat out without permission. It took him all of a minute to crumble once he was sitting opposite a pair of hardened homicide detectives. As Agent Kittrell suspected, the teenagers had gone to the island to fool around, unaware they were encroaching upon the domain of a serial killer, or that they were tripping the cameras laid to catch him.

Just to be on the safe side, they dispatched a uniformed officer to the home of Nicole Crawford, the girlfriend. She arrived at police headquarters, looking shocked and embarrassed, accompanied by her parents. Ballard put her in the now empty interrogation room that the senior Grayson had recently occupied. Just like her boyfriend, she wasted no time in owning up to their shenanigans.

"I would hate to be in the girlfriend's shoes right now," Patterson said as she thought back upon the day's events. "She might not see daylight again until her thirtieth birthday."

"She stole a boat and snuck off to an island for sex with her boyfriend," Quinn replied. "She's hardly innocent."

Patterson looked sideways toward Quinn. "And you did nothing like that when you were younger?"

"I think I'll plead the fifth on that one." A faint smile creased Quinn's face. "It's a shame, though. I really thought we'd struck gold with Grayson. He was the right age, had the kind of job that might appeal to a sociopath given how easy it would be to fade into the background, and maintained an air of outward respectability."

"Except the profile worked up by the Behavioral Analysis Unit suggested he would be a loner. Probably unmarried and incapable of forming normal bonds." Patterson had wanted it to be Grayson. It was so neat. But in hindsight, he just didn't fit. "Grayson is the opposite. Successful, married, and sure of himself. Plus, where would he have kept the girls? I doubt he was walking them past his wife and locking them in his study."

"Doesn't mean he didn't have another property somewhere. Like you said, he's rich enough."

"It's irrelevant." Patterson stared out the window and watched the urban landscape roll by. "It wasn't him. Ballard should charge those kids with wasting police time."

"Good luck with that one." Quinn chuckled. "You saw the family lawyer. He'd get the charges dropped before they even crossed the DA's desk."

"Yeah. Still irks me." Patterson lapsed into silence.

Quinn said, "Hey, we still have the lead you uncovered. Justin Ferrera."

Patterson noted. "The panty thief."

"I sent his details over to homicide. Ballard and Gimenez have their people on it."

"How's that going?"

"They haven't tracked him down yet. It's a big city, and it sounds like he sleeps rough most of the time. Might not even be holding down a regular job anymore. Makes him difficult to locate."

"Assuming he's still in the area."

"Right. Assuming that. Chances are he is, though. He was born and raised hereabouts, has family here. And I'll say this, he fits the bill for the Bracken Island Killer much better than Grayson."

"Except that he's homeless according to his sister." Patterson wanted to believe Ferrera was the killer. It was neat. Easy. But in her experience, the dominoes rarely fell in such a predictable manner. "Don't forget our killer's MO. He keeps his victims alive, probably for months at a time. He needs somewhere to take them. To hold them."

"Hey, don't write him off just because he has no fixed abode. Most of these homeless people live in makeshift camps, although I admit it's unlikely that he would keep his victims there. But he probably knows about abandoned buildings around town. It's amazing how many forgotten spaces there are if you look for them."

"We don't actually know that he's homeless. His sister hasn't seen him in years. Who knows what he's doing now."

"Exactly." They were approaching the hotel. Quinn pulled into the side parking lot and came to a halt. After shifting into neutral, she turned to look at Patterson. "PD will find him, and when they do, we'll have our answer."

"I know." Patterson nodded. "It's been sixteen years since my sister disappeared. I can wait a few more days."

. "I won't pretend I know what it's been like for you," Quinn replied. "But I will say that we wouldn't have this lead if it wasn't for your tenacity. If Ferrera looks good for this, you might get the answers you're seeking, and take a dangerous killer off the streets."

"I know," Patterson agreed. She unclipped her seatbelt and opened the car door. "I meant to say this earlier, but thanks for dinner last night. It was a welcome change from hamburgers, and your wife is lovely. Such a great host."

"Well, thank you. I'll tell her that." Quinn smiled. "Leah is awesome. I consider myself incredibly lucky to have found her."

"You should." Patterson slid out of the vehicle and stood up, then leaned through the open door. "Call me as soon as you know anything, okay?"

"I promise," Quinn replied.

Patterson said goodbye and closed the car door, and watched as Quinn turned around and drove away. Then she walked around to the front of the building and made her way inside and up to her room.

FORTY-THREE

After Quinn dropped her off at the hotel, Patterson spent the next two hours in her room browsing the internet and looking through the online archives of *The Oklahoman*, the city's most widely read daily newspaper, searching for news articles dated back to the summer of 2006 that might contain a clue about her sister. She wasn't sure exactly what she was hoping to find, figuring that she'd know it when she saw it, but unfortunately nothing leaped off the screen.

She would just have to wait and see if Ballard and Gimenez found Justin Ferrera, and what the hotel's old maintenance man had to say for himself.

Even if he wasn't the Bracken Island Killer, Patterson still wanted to look into the face of the man who'd set this entire chain of events in motion by breaking into her sister's room all those years ago. She wanted to know why he picked Julie and Stacy's room over all the others he could have targeted. Was it because they were two attractive young women traveling alone? Hank, the hotel's surly manager, had already informed her that Ferrera worked occasional shifts on the front desk. Had he checked her sister and Stacy in? If so, he would've seen them leave to get food, thus providing ample time to sneak into their room and go through their stuff at his leisure. It made sense, but she would not know for sure until he was in police custody.

With no option but to wait, Patterson decided to call her father. She hadn't spoken to him since leaving Long Island and wanted to check that he was okay all on his own. She glanced at her watch. It was almost six in the evening, and an hour later on the East Coast, so he should have left work by now if he was on the day shift.

When she dialed his number, he answered almost immediately. "Hey, Peanut, this is a pleasant surprise."

"Hi, dad. How are you doing?"

"Not so bad. Can't grumble. Well, I could, but no one cares enough to listen. You?"

"I'm good," Patterson replied. "And you know that's not true, there are people that care to listen. Me for a start."

"I know you do, Peanut." He cleared his throat before continuing. "Wish you were here, though. I'll miss our dinner date next week."

"I'm sure you can get by without me for a few weeks. When I get back, we'll go wherever you want."

"Deal." Her father hesitated. "Have you found out anything about Julie?"

"Not as much as I'd like," Patterson replied. She told him about visiting Stacy in Chicago, and how Grant had gotten her a car to drive down to Oklahoma City. She told him about The Welcome Inn, and that she'd discovered the identity of the thief who broke into Julie's room, but hadn't been able to track him down. What she didn't mention were her living arrangements. If her father knew she was staying in the same place Julie had all those years ago, he would probably worry. She also didn't mention the corpses found on Bracken Island or that there was still an active serial killer on the loose. She could see no point in upsetting him unnecessarily. If her sister turned out to be one of the Bracken Island Killer's victims, that would be another matter, but right now there was no proof either way. It was also an active investigation, and as such she could not officially discuss it with anyone, even her own father. Those were the rules, and as an FBI agent she had to follow them.

"Gee, it doesn't sound like you're getting very far," her father replied after listening to everything Patterson had to say. "You can always come home, Peanut."

"I know you want me to," Patterson admitted. "But I have to do this. I'm aware of the odds. Even if I never find out what happened to Julie, at least I'll know I've tried."

"Well, that's true." Her father made a tutting sound as if he wanted to say more but was holding back. "You're a grown woman and I can't stop you. I just don't want you wallowing in the past. It isn't healthy."

"I'm fine, dad." Patterson was getting hungry. Quinn had gone through a McDonald's drive-through on the way to police headquarters that morning and she'd picked up a much-needed coffee and a breakfast sandwich. Since then, she had relied solely on cans of soda, chocolate bars, and bags of chips bought from the vending machine in the police canteen. Now her stomach rumbled in protest at its shoddy treatment. "But it was good to hear your voice."

"Yours too." Her father sounded almost wistful.

"I'll call again soon and keep you up-to-date, okay?" Patterson replied. She knew her father had been lonely ever since the divorce, and now he didn't even have the midweek dinner appointments with Patterson to look forward to. She made a mental pledge to spend more time with him when she returned to New York.

"Make sure that you do."

"I promise," Patterson replied before saying goodbye and hanging up. Now that she was on her own again, the hotel room felt too quiet. She turned on the TV to mask the silence and changed out of the professional attire she'd worn that day, opting instead for a pair of jeans and a navy blue V-neck T-shirt with the FBI motto written upon it in white block lettering. Three words stacked one above the other. Fidelity. Bravery. Integrity. She pulled on a pair of sneakers.

Last, Patterson slipped her Glock into an inside the waistband holster that she'd put on when she was changing. Previous to this, she'd been wearing her shoulder holster under a light jacket, but the strong side hip carry allowed her to conceal the service weapon while not needing a coat. After arranging her T-shirt, which she wore loose, to further disguise the gun, Patterson made her way downstairs.

As she passed through the lobby, Hank looked up. "Hey, I just want you to know. I dragged some of those boxes out from under the stairs today. Started looking through them. I haven't found your sister's registration card yet, but I'll find it."

"I appreciate you letting me know," Patterson said. Apparently, the revelation that she was an FBI agent had jolted the previously desultory hotel manager into action. It had also changed his demeanor toward her. Where before he'd been prickly and unhelpful, he was now grudgingly polite. She suspected it was because he had skeletons he would rather not have law enforcement drag out of his closet. Either that, or he was just an upstanding citizen with a respect for authority. Patterson thought she knew which of the two it was.

"You heading out for the evening?" He asked.

"For a couple of hours." Patterson nodded. "I ate at a fantastic little brewpub over in the Bricktown district a few nights ago. Figured I'd give it another try."

"Canalside Beerworks?"

Patterson answered, "That's the place."

"I've eaten there a few times myself. Food's good. Beer too. But man, do they overcharge just 'cause it all has fancy names. Give me a Bud anytime. Am I right?"

"I guess we'll have to disagree on that one." Patterson was at the main entrance now.

"Yeah, well, have fun."

"I will," Patterson replied, stepping out onto the sidewalk.

She turned right and headed toward the parking lot, keys in hand. Her car was parked in the third space back. A battered pickup truck with a white tonneau cover enclosing the bed, outdated political campaign stickers slapped on the rusting tailgate, and a finish more primer than paint, occupied the drivers-side bay. The parking space nearest the passenger side was empty save for a discarded beer can resting against the concrete curb stop.

Patterson crossed to the car, unlocking it as she went. She walked between her Toyota and the battered truck, was about to open the driver's side door, when she noticed the front wheel.

It was resting on the rim; tire deflated.

She mumbled a curse under her breath, ignoring the hunger pangs that filled her stomach. It would take at least a half hour to change the wheel, and that was assuming the spare was any good and there was a jack in the trunk. She glared at the wheel for a moment longer, wondering if Hank's new attitude extended to changing car tires, but then decided that it wouldn't. Besides, she could do it herself. She didn't need any man to come to her rescue.

Her mind made up Patterson started to turn back toward the rear of the car to open the trunk. At least until a lightning-quick arm snaked around her shoulders, and a powerful gloved hand pressed a five-inch blade tight against her exposed throat.

FORTY-FOUR

T ry to scream and I'll cut your throat." The man's voice was
gravelly. Barely more than a hoarse whisper.

For a split-second Patterson froze as her brain processed the
situation, but then her instincts and FBI training took over.

She quickly lifted her arms, keeping them in front of her
body to shield the movement from her assailant. Then, letting go
of her car keys, she gripped his wrist and forearm with her
hands and tugged downward to the left and away from her
neck. This was important. Her attacker was holding the knife in
his right hand. If she dragged his arm down the other way, she
would do the job for him and slit her own throat.

The sudden and unexpected motion twisted her attacker's
upper body, pulling him momentarily off balance. In the same
fluid movement, Patterson lifted her right shoulder, lowered her
head, and pivoted sideways, keeping her opponent's forearm
close to her collarbone to prevent giving him enough range of
motion to turn the knife back upon her.

Keeping her grip tight, Patterson slipped out from beneath
her assailant's knife arm and turned to face him, noting that he
wore a bandanna around his face, concealing his features.

Momentum was now on her side. She hadn't loosened her

grip on the man's wrist or released shoulder pressure on his forearm, which meant he was now standing partly bent with the knife pointing inward toward his own gut. It would've been easy for Patterson to drive his arm forward, using the weight of her body, and slide the knife into the soft flesh beneath his ribs. But she was an FBI agent, and that wasn't something she was willing to do. She already had the tactical advantage and knew she could disarm him effectively without such drastic measures thanks to her excellent law enforcement training at Quantico.

Which is precisely what she did next.

Finally releasing her shoulder pressure, Patterson stepped back and twisted her assailant's wrist, bending it forcefully downward at the same time. This had the effect of keeping the knife pointed inward and far away from her own body.

The man let out a surprised grunt of pain, even as he tried to turn his hand and stab her.

But her assailant's grip on the knife was weak now thanks to the pressure she was applying to his wrist. Patterson was able to shift one hand down and onto the knife's handle, then strip it away from him in a rapid movement. At the same time, she kicked upward with her right leg, toward his down-turned face. Her foot caught him under the chin, snapping his head backwards, and the man squealed in pain.

Patterson quickly released her grip on his wrist and scurried backwards, out of range, with her attacker's blade still in her hand.

Now she got her first look at him. The man was about the same height as herself, of medium build, with dark hair. The bandanna still obscured his features, although it had twisted higher upon his face. His knife hand was now empty, because Patterson had already disarmed him, but in the other he held a pair of handcuffs, no doubt meant to restrain her.

Patterson experienced a moment of horror. This was no simple mugging. It was an attempted abduction. Images of Julie flashed through her mind, and she briefly teetered on the edge of losing focus. But then her training came to the rescue again. She discarded the lethal hunting knife, tossing it far behind her, out of reach, and went for the Glock concealed in the waistband of her jeans.

But her attacker wasn't waiting around to be arrested. He retreated backwards, keeping his gaze upon her, even as she brought the gun up and leveled it at him.

"Armed FBI agent," Patterson barked, identifying both the fact that she had a gun and her standing as a law enforcement officer, just in case it wasn't already obvious to him. "Stay where you are and keep your hands where I can see them."

But he didn't stay. He hesitated a moment, clearly wondering if she would shoot, then he turned and bolted toward the street.

"Stop!" Patterson lowered the gun and sprinted after him. She reached the road in time to see her attacker duck to the right into an alley between two buildings a block distant.

Patterson gave chase but pulled up short of actually running headlong into the alley. That would be a rookie mistake and open her up to all sorts of bad scenarios. It was improbable, but he might be waiting for her to round the corner, ready to launch another physical attack.

A more likely danger was walking into a bullet.

He could be standing in the alley with a weapon pointed back at the entrance, waiting for her.

Running blindly into the unknown was a good way to end up dead.

Instead, she stood with her back flattened against the wall and peeked around the corner.

The alley, a cut through to another road, was empty. There was also nowhere for an assailant to hide. The building she now sheltered against was a pawnshop, while a convenience store occupied the corner opposite. Behind this, fronting the next road over, she could see the back of a squat one-story building that might once have been a residential home with a hair salon sign affixed to the side.

Patterson stepped into the alley, gun at the ready, and proceeded down it, her gaze sweeping from left to right in anticipation of the unexpected.

But there was no sign of her attacker.

He wasn't in sight when she reached the next road and didn't appear to be hiding anywhere close by. Not that he needed to. There were gaps between most of the buildings on the street, and her attacker could have picked any of them to make his escape.

Annoyed that the man who attacked her had escaped, Patterson swore under her breath. She paused a second to catch her breath, leaning against a lamp post next to the salon. When she saw a car drive by, its occupant staring in surprise at her openly visible gun before quickly speeding up, she slipped the Glock back into its holster and turned in the hotel's direction.

Back at the parking lot, she scooped up her car keys, dropped in the scuffle. Patterson kneeled by the deflated tire and examined it, noting a two-inch slit on the sidewall that matched the knife blade still laying nearby. As she suspected, the flat tire was no accident. Her assailant had laid a trap by disabling the car and then waited for her to walk into it.

Patterson straightened up and took out her cell phone.

Her first call was to Mary Quinn.

FORTY-FIVE

FBI Special Agent Mary Quinn arrived twenty minutes after Patterson's call. Ballard and Gimenez also arrived, along with a pair of uniformed officers who wasted no time in cordoning off the parking lot.

Patterson, who had been leaning on her car during the interim to guard the crime scene, now pushed off and met Quinn. "You got here quick, and you brought back up."

"I dropped everything when I got your call," Quinn replied. She shot Patterson a concerned look. "Are you okay?"

"A little shaken up, but no physical damage." Patterson was relieved to no longer be alone. Despite having a gun and knowing she could take care of herself, waiting in the parking lot by herself was still nerve-wracking after having a knife pushed against her throat.

"That's good to hear." Quinn glanced around, taking in the scene.

Ballard said, "You want to tell us what happened?"

"Sure." Patterson filled them in, starting when she approached the car and discovered the flat tire. She took her time, making sure not to miss anything out. When she got to the chase, she grimaced in frustration. "I can't believe he got away. I shouldn't have given him the chance to run."

"Sounds like you did everything you could, from where I'm standing." Quinn reached out a comforting hand and placed it on Patterson's arm. "It was a scary situation, and you handled it like a pro."

Ballard glanced down at the flat tire and then back to Patterson. "This was no opportunist crime. Your attacker planned this. Targeted you specifically."

"That's what I'm thinking," Patterson agreed. "And I believe I know why."

Quinn said, "You've been asking around about your sister and rattled someone's feathers."

"Can you come up with another reason someone would attack me out of the blue like this?"

"Not off the top of my head." Quinn stepped past Patterson and looked down at the knife. "This guy meant business. Did you get a good look at him?"

"He was wearing a bandanna. Disguised his features. All I know is that he was of medium build, had dark hair, and appeared to be around fifty."

"Are you thinking what I'm thinking?" Ballard asked, looking around the group.

Quinn nodded. "That it might be the Bracken Island Killer. We know he's still active, and while we can't yet prove if Patterson's sister was a victim, there's a distinct possibility."

"Bracken Island Killer or not, it means I've gotten too close and spooked someone, and the obvious suspect is Justin Fererra." Patterson didn't like that thought, but she also realized it was progress. If she was now a target of the man abducting and leaving women on Bracken Island, an answer to her sister's disappearance might be close at hand.

"It also means that our serial killer case, and your investigation into Julie's disappearance, have now officially intersected."

Quinn's gaze roamed around the parking lot and the road beyond. "Question is, what was he planning to do with you?"

"He could have stabbed me before I even realized anyone was there if he just wanted me dead. The guy was stealthy. I never heard him coming."

"Yet he took the time to put the knife against your throat and tell you not to scream," Quinn pointed out.

"And you said he was carrying handcuffs," Ballard added.

Gimenez voiced what they were all thinking. "He wanted to abduct you."

"Which means he must've had transportation parked close by. He couldn't exactly take you away on foot." Quinn was still inspecting their surroundings. Her gaze finally settled upon the beat-up truck parked next to Patterson's car. "This is the only vehicle that fits the bill. There's nothing else parked close enough."

Patterson followed Quinn's gaze. It made sense. The truck was parked in the bay next to her driver's door, while the few other cars in the parking lot were toward the back or on the opposite side. There was also the road, but her attacker would not want to risk that. It would leave him exposed and in view of any passing cars or guests exiting the hotel. Quinn had picked her up that morning, meaning she hadn't moved her car all day. Ample time for someone to park the truck, then wait on the assumption that she would eventually go somewhere. "Once he had me under control, he could just bundle me in the passenger side of the truck."

Ballard was pulling on a pair of blue latex gloves. He circled the truck, examining it. When he reached out and tried the driver's side door handle, it opened. "Vehicle's unlocked."

"How many people do you know who park up and don't bother locking their truck before leaving it?" Quinn asked.

Gimenez replied, "Off the top of my head, none. Not in this area of town." He followed his partner's lead and went to the passenger side, pulling on his own set of gloves. When he tried the handle, that door opened too. Finding nothing, he went to the back of the truck, lifted the tonneau cover enclosing the bed, and dropped the tailgate. His eyes widened. "This is definitely the attacker's getaway vehicle."

Patterson and Quinn joined the detective at the tailgate, looking over his shoulder, followed by Ballard, who slammed the driver's side door and joined them.

There, hidden inside the truck's bed, were a roll of gray duct tape, zip ties, and a bandanna like the one Patterson's attacker wore. There was also a length of chain looped through the truck's tie-downs, and a sturdy padlock.

"Sweet Jesus," Quinn breathed, shocked. "This guy meant business."

"It's like a ready-made abduction kit," Ballard said. "Once he had you in the bed of that truck, he would've zip tied your legs, taped your mouth, and blindfolded you."

"And those chains would've held you in place. An added insurance policy to make sure you didn't somehow get the cover open while he was driving."

Patterson's blood ran cold. "I don't think there's any doubt who this guy was. I can't imagine what would have happened if he'd succeeded in taking me." But even as she spoke the words, Patterson knew one thing. Her father would have lost both his daughters sixteen years apart, possibly abducted by the same man, and in the same location. It didn't bear thinking about. She shuddered and pushed the awful thought out of her mind.

"You think this truck belongs to our killer?" Gimenez asked hopefully.

"It would not surprise me," Quinn replied. "He made no attempt to flee in this vehicle, possibly because his plan had failed, and he knew it was compromised."

"Not to mention the fact that he'd never outrun a police cruiser in this if they caught up with him. The thing's a clunker. Must be twenty years old."

"Which would've made it a breeze to steal," Patterson said.

"Much easier than a modern vehicle with electronic ignition. I bet it doesn't even have an immobilizer. Check the steering column and you'll probably see it's been jumped."

Ballard returned to the cab and stuck his head inside, careful not to disturb anything. "Yup. Cover's off the steering column. He bypassed the ignition."

"You're one lucky woman," Gimenez said, turning to Patterson. "This guy meant business."

"Not lucky." Patterson shook her head. "Well trained."

Quinn nodded. "The Academy has one of the toughest regimens you'll ever find. Twenty weeks of intensive training including advanced self-defense tactics. We're literally built for this stuff."

"Good thing our killer didn't know that," Ballard replied. "Otherwise, he might just have opted to cut your throat instead and leave you to bleed out."

"Thanks for that brutally honest assessment of the situation," Patterson replied.

"Hey, it was a compliment." Ballard rejoined them at the back of the truck. "You're clearly badass."

"Thanks, but I don't feel like a badass right now," Patterson admitted. "I'm feeling a little shaky, to be honest."

"That's natural," Gimenez said. "You're coming down from the adrenaline rush."

"Which is why we need to get you out of here." Quinn glanced toward Ballard. "Can your guys wrap up the crime scene?"

"It would be my pleasure." Ballard nodded. "I'll call forensics down here and get this parking lot and the truck examined inch by inch, although I don't expect we'll find much." He glanced toward the discarded knife. "I bet we won't get much off that either. Perp was wearing gloves."

"You'll get my prints," Patterson told him. "My hand was all over the knife when I disarmed him."

"Right you are," Ballard said. He glanced back toward the

road. "I don't suppose that hotel has any external CCTV cameras."

"What do you think?" Patterson replied. "It doesn't even have private bathrooms. Everyone has to share."

"I thought as much." Ballard looked disappointed. He looked at Quinn. "You guys should get out of here. Get Agent Patterson a strong cup of tea with lots of sugar. That will calm her nerves. If we find anything at all, no matter how small, I'll call you right away."

"It's not like I have far to go," Patterson said. "My hotel room is literally a hundred feet away."

"Oh, hell no." Quinn was having none of it. "You're done staying in that hotel. We're going straight to your room to pack up your belongings, and then you're coming home with me."

"I can't do that," Patterson objected. "It's too much of an imposition. Besides, you haven't even asked Leah."

"Leah will be fine with it. I promise. In fact, if I go home without you tonight, she'll just send me back here."

"If you're sure." Patterson hated to impose upon someone she'd only known for a few days, but at the same time, she really didn't want to spend another night at The Welcome Inn.

"I'm sure." Quinn steered her toward the police cordon.

Hank was there, standing on the other side along with some of the hotel's guests, including the man staying in the neighboring room to hers.

They ducked under the yellow crime scene tape, ignoring the curious stares of the onlookers, and headed back into the hotel.

Fifteen minutes later, Patterson was in the passenger seat of Quinn's SUV, riding across town to the FBI agent's home, with her meager belongings stashed in the back.

FORTY-SIX

When they arrived at Quinn's house, Leah was already waiting anxiously at the door. Quinn had already called ahead and told her that Patterson would be staying with them and telling her shocked wife the basics of what happened.

Leah rushed out to meet the car as it pulled up to the curb and tugged on the handle, opening the passenger side before Patterson could even unclip her seatbelt.

"Oh my gosh, I can't believe what happened." There was genuine concern in Leah's voice. "Are you okay?"

"I'm okay. Just a bit shaken up," Patterson admitted, climbing out of the car.

"Thank goodness for that." Leah waited for Quinn to join them before heading back inside the house. "I've got a pot of tea brewing, unless you'd prefer something stronger."

"A mug of tea will be just fine," Patterson said as they reached the kitchen. She placed her travel bag on the floor and took a seat at the kitchen's center island. "I really appreciate you taking me in like this."

"It's absolutely no trouble." Leah went about preparing three mugs of hot tea and then passed one to Patterson. "You must be absolutely starving, too."

"That's an understatement." In all the excitement, Patterson had forgotten about food. But now, with her adrenaline rush wearing off, the hunger pangs were creeping back in full force. "I haven't eaten anything since lunchtime, and even then, it was just a bag of chips and some chocolate at police headquarters."

"I'm sure we can fix that," Leah replied. "We have plenty of deli meat. I can make us all sandwiches, or if you prefer, I can take a pizza out of the freezer and make a Caesar salad to go along with it."

"A sandwich sounds heavenly." Patterson picked up her mug of tea. It was sweet, strong, and hit the spot.

"We have turkey and ham. There's also provolone or Swiss cheese."

"Ham and Swiss if you don't mind."

"I'll take the same," said Quinn.

"On it. Three ham and Swiss sandwiches coming right up."

"And after that, I'll show you where the spare bedroom is, so that you can settle in," Quinn said.

"Thanks."

"I can't believe someone tried to abduct you," Leah said, as she went about preparing the sandwiches. "It must've been terrifying."

"To be honest, I didn't really have time to be scared," Patterson admitted. "It all happened so fast. One minute I was walking to my car, the next there was a knife at my throat. My training kicked in and I just reacted. Luckily, he wasn't expecting it."

Leah said, "What I don't get is how the guy intended to actually take you. I mean, you weren't just going to climb into his vehicle willingly. Did he have chloroform or something?"

"Nothing so exotic." Quinn shook her head. "Despite how TV and the movies portray it, chloroform doesn't actually work like that. If you gave someone a dose big enough to instantly render them unconscious, you'd probably kill them instead. At the very least you might cause brain damage. Plus, to keep a person knocked out, you'd need to keep administering it. The same with an injected drug. Anesthetics and sedatives have to be closely monitored and carefully administered. Besides, it isn't actually that easy to get ahold of drugs like that unless you're a medical professional. You can't just walk into Walmart and buy them."

"Which is why he had handcuffs," Patterson said. "No doubt he wanted me to put my hands behind my back so he could cuff me before taking the knife away from my throat. Then he was going to put me in the bed of his truck and finish the job. Zip ties for my ankles. A gag and blindfold. Then chains to keep me from moving around while he took me to wherever he holds his victims."

"Holy crap." Leah had gone pale. "That's horrifying. I can't believe there are actually people like that wandering around out there passing as respectable human beings. I guess ignorance really is bliss."

"Which is why I like to keep my work life separate from my personal life," Quinn said. "I see enough evil during the day. I don't need to bring it home too."

"I think we'll make an exception in this instance," Leah said. She had finished making the sandwiches now and cut them in half on the chopping board before transferring them to three plates. She went to the pantry and took out a couple bags of potato chips—one barbecue flavor, and the other sour cream and onion—which she opened and placed on the island. Then she passed a sandwich to Quinn, one to Patterson, and kept the third for herself. She looked at the two women. "Well, what are you waiting for? Dig in."

———

When the meal was over, Quinn led Patterson through the house and upstairs to a bedroom at the end of the landing. She opened the door and let Patterson enter before stepping in, herself.

The comfortably appointed room had a queen bed against one wall. A dresser stood on the side wall, opposite a window hung with room darkening curtains. A comfortable plush chair sat in the corner with a small reading desk next to it, upon which stood a lamp.

"Here it is," Quinn said. "It's hardly the Ritz, but miles ahead of that hotel room at The Welcome Inn."

"It's lovely," Patterson said. "I'm sure it will be very comfortable."

Quinn hovered near the doorway. "Leah already changed the sheets. There are fresh towels in the top drawer of the dresser if you want to take a shower. Bathroom is the second door on the left."

"You really didn't need to do all this." Patterson wasn't accustomed to such attention. "I really would've been fine back at the hotel."

"Nonsense." Quinn folded her arms. "There was no way I was leaving you in that place after what happened. Frankly, I can't believe you wanted to stay there."

"It was where my sister stayed," Patterson said. "I wouldn't have chosen it otherwise. Besides, it wouldn't have mattered which hotel I was staying in. That guy clearly targeted me, and we both know why."

"I'm just happy you're not staying in that dump anymore."

"I appreciate that, but I don't want to outstay my welcome. I'll look for another hotel in the morning."

"Not happening. You'll stay here until you're done in Oklahoma City," Quinn replied resolutely. "And I don't want to hear anymore arguments about it, okay?"

Patterson nodded. "Okay."

"Good. I'll leave you to get settled in, then." She turned to leave, softly closing the door.

Alone now, Patterson put her travel bag on the bed and unpacked the essentials. Her stomach was full and for that she was grateful, but the attack earlier in the evening had left her with an uncomfortable feeling sitting in her gut. Had she come face to face with her sister's killer? The only way to know that would be to catch him. And that was exactly what Patterson intended to do.

FORTY-SEVEN

Patterson slept better than she had in a week. Quinn's bed was comfortable, and twice the size of the narrow twin bed at the hotel. She woke at seven-thirty the next morning feeling refreshed.

When she went downstairs, Quinn and Leah were already in the kitchen preparing breakfast. Blueberry pancakes with maple syrup and sweet breakfast sausage. The aroma was heavenly and made Patterson salivate at the thought of yet more home-cooked food.

It was Quinn's day off, but she was up early, anyway. Having gotten into the habit of waking early the rest of the week, she said, it was now part of her routine even when she wasn't going to work.

"There's fresh coffee, if you'd like some," Leah said with a smile.

"I never say no to coffee." Patterson approached the kitchen island and poured herself a mug, then turned to the other two women. "Is there anything I can do to help?"

"Not at the moment. We've got it all covered." Leah was busy piling pancakes onto a plate and making yet more. Patterson wondered what it would be like to be with a partner who loved cooking. Grant's culinary skills stopped at pop tarts. The one time he'd tried to cook her a fancy meal, two years ago on Valentine's Day, it had ended in disaster. This was anything but. They demolished the stack of pancakes in no time at all and then sat chatting around the island while drinking coffee.

"What made you join the FBI?" Leah asked, looking at Patterson. "It still seems to be a predominantly male occupation, at least from what M has told me."

"It depends on what you're doing in the FBI. On the support side, women outnumber the men by twenty percent. That's not the same for special agents where the men outnumber the women five to one. It's a sad fact, but better than it used to be."

"Exactly. I can't imagine wanting to be in an environment like that. And yes, I know M does it, but even she says the sexism gets to her."

"It's a boys' club, alright," Patterson agreed. "But I love my job, and I don't want to do anything else."

"You still haven't told me why you joined the Bureau in the first place," Leah pointed out. "I assume it has something to do with your sister?"

"That was part of it," Patterson admitted. "I saw how badly the LAPD botched the investigation into her disappearance back when I was growing up, and it stuck with me. I felt like the world needed better police officers. For the longest while, they brushed my dad off as though he were just an over-protective parent who didn't know when to step back. Nothing much was done, even when they started to take it more seriously. They asked around a bit. Asked local PD in Chicago to interview her best friend. Entered her information into ViCAP, but it all went nowhere."

"ViCAP?" Leah looked confused. "What's that?"

Quinn answered. "It's the Violent Criminal Apprehension Program run by the FBI. It collects and analyzes information on all sorts of crimes, from murder, to assaults and missing persons. We can use DNA to link unidentified human remains back to living family members, and even make connections between violent criminals and missing persons."

"Of course, it doesn't work if there's nothing in the system," Patterson said. "As in my sister's case. It was like she fell off the face of the earth."

Leah said, "I know I said this the other night at dinner, but I'm truly sorry."

"Thank you," Patterson replied. "We might be one step further to get an answer on Julie's case after what happened last night. If the person who attacked me really is who we think he is, then he may hold the answers I'm looking for."

"Assuming we can find him," Quinn chimed in. "I've already spoken to Ballard this morning and got an update. Pickup was stolen, as we suspected. Owner didn't even know it was gone yet. They have a construction business and it's a work vehicle, but they were out of town yesterday visiting a friend."

"Which gives them a perfect alibi," Patterson noted.

"It does. Truck was clean, too. Forensics went over it inside and out. No fingerprints, and nothing that can identify the thief."

"Damn." Patterson was hoping against hope that her attacker had slipped up.

"Same with the knife. They pulled a set of your prints from it, but nothing else. It doesn't look old so we're trying to track down if it was purchased locally. But honestly, I wouldn't hold your breath. It's a popular brand of hunting knife that can be found in all sorts of retail establishments, like feed stores, sporting goods stores, and even Walmart. It's a long shot, for sure."

"That's a shame," Patterson said. "What about Justin Fererra?"

"We're looking into that angle. We also ran a background check on Hank Lasky, the manager of the hotel, just to be sure. He's definitely in the right age range."

"Except I passed him on my way out last night. Spoke to him, too. There's no way he could've gone out of the hotel, changed his clothes, and attacked me in that short period. Plus, he has the wrong body build. It's not feasible."

"Doesn't mean he didn't have an accomplice."

"True, but I don't think it's him. Besides, he told me about Justin Ferrera."

"Only after you flashed your badge at him."

"True. So what did your background check show?"

"Not much. Couple of outstanding parking tickets. A drunk and disorderly ten years ago in the bar attached to the hotel when he was off duty one night. Typical bar brawl. Responding officers only issued him a warning. Besides, the earliest identified Bracken Island victim was around the year 2000. He wasn't even in Oklahoma City. He was working in Houston at the time. Spent almost a year down there. Rules him out as the Bracken Island Killer, at least."

"So that brings us back to Justin Ferrera."

"Who Ballard and Gimenez are working to find as we speak."

"How long do you think it will take them to find him?" Patterson asked.

Quinn shrugged. "Your guess is as good as mine."

"In that case, I'm going to head back to my room and do some research. There are some leads I want to follow up with on the internet." Patterson stood up and thanked Leah for the fantastic breakfast, then went back up to her room.

She returned to The Oklahoman's online archives and spent the next two hours browsing them, still searching for any old articles that might have relevance to her sister's disappearance. But she drew a blank. Then, just as Patterson was giving up hope, there was a knock on her bedroom door and Quinn appeared.

"Hey," she said. "I just got off the phone with Detective Ballard. They found him."

"Ferrera?"

"Yes."

"Really?" Patterson swung her legs off the bed and jumped up. "Where is he now?"

"They're bringing him in. I'm heading over to police head-quarters. Want to tag along?"

"Hell, yes." Patterson didn't need to be asked twice. She buckled her shoulder holster, threw on a jacket, and headed to the door. "What are we waiting for? Let's go."

FORTY-EIGHT

Justin Ferrera sat in the same interview room that Kevin Robert Grayson had occupied a mere twenty-four hours earlier.

When Patterson and Quinn arrived, Detective Ballard was standing outside the interview room door, deep in conversation with Gimenez, no doubt discussing their strategy for interrogating the suspect.

He looked toward them as the two female FBI agents approached.

"How are you feeling this morning?" He asked Patterson.

"Not too bad," Patterson replied. "Even better now you have Ferrera."

Quinn glanced toward the closed interview room door. "What's his deal, is he still homeless?"

"No." Gimenez shook his head. "That's what made him so easy to find."

Ballard picked up where his partner left off. "We ran his name through the DPS. They had an updated address from last year. Turns out he was still there."

"DPS?" Patterson asked, confused.

Quinn was the one who answered. "Oklahoma Department

of Public Safety. They're responsible for issuing driver's licenses."

"Ah. Got it. His sister thought he might be homeless."

"Maybe at one time. Not anymore. He was living in a studio apartment above a garage on the east side of town. Not anywhere I'd want to make a home, but hey, I guess it's better than living on the streets."

"You ready to go do this thing?" Gimenez asked his partner.

"Yeah. I think he's sat in there long enough." Ballard looked at Quinn and Patterson. "We wanted to wait until you guys got here before we started."

Gimenez added, "And we thought some time sitting alone in the interrogation suite might soften him up. People get nervous when they're dragged downtown."

Quinn glanced around. "Is Agent Kittrell joining us this morning?"

Ballard shook his head. "No. He's busy working another case. We'll keep him informed, though."

"We'll watch from the observation room, same as yesterday," said Quinn.

"Sounds like a plan," Ballard replied, nodding. He led them to the observation room and opened the door, then followed them in with Gimenez on his heel.

All four investigators looked through the one-way glass at the suspect.

Justin Ferrera was clearly uncomfortable. He rubbed his chin and jiggled one leg up and down, probably without realizing he was doing it. More than once he glanced toward the interview room door, then up to the camera mounted in the corner. He was wearing a dirty pair of jeans and a white T-shirt stained with what looked like different colors of paint.

"He claimed he was getting ready to leave for work when we knocked on his door," Gimenez said. "He does house painting. Said he works for a guy that has a renovation business. Probably a day labor type of arrangement, cash in hand."

"Hey, everyone has to make a buck," Quinn replied.

"Not knocking it. Just filling you in." Gimenez folded his arms. "He look like the guy that attacked you?"

Patterson studied the man on the other side of the mirrored glass. He appeared to be about the right build and age. She hadn't seen her attacker's face, so she couldn't give a definitive answer one way or the other, but there was one distinct difference that jumped out at her. "He has a shaved head. The man that attacked me had hair."

Ballard answered her. "Means nothing. Your assailant had a good twelve hours between the attack in the parking lot, and this morning when we arrived at Ferrera's place. Even though he wore a bandanna, you might still recognize his haircut. Simplest solution would just be to shave his head."

"Or it could just be coincidence," Quinn said. "Lots of guys shave their heads. Doesn't make them murderers."

"We have no proof that he is a murderer," Ballard pointed out.

"But we know he broke into my sister's room sixteen years ago." That alone made him a prime suspect in Patterson's eyes. She desperately wanted to accompany Ballard and Ramirez into the interview room but knew she would not be allowed. She would have to content herself with watching through the glass, just as she had done the previous day. "We also know he was stealing women's underwear, and that he entered the room of a female guest at The Welcome Inn while she was sleeping."

"According to the manager of the hotel," Ballard said.

"Yes."

"And they reported none of this to the police at the time." Ballard glanced toward Patterson. "I'm sure you know that a defense attorney would pick that testimony apart in a second. They would ask why nobody reported the crimes and try to frame them as hearsay."

"They were reported. At least in my sister's case."

Quinn said, "I bet some of the other people who had stuff going missing filed police reports, too."

"Maybe they did," Ramirez countered. "Problem is, Ferrera wasn't implicated in those crimes. The hotel apparently paid off the one person who could have fingered him to avoid the negative publicity. They never filed a complaint."

Quinn nodded. "The girl who caught Ferrera standing at the end of her bed, looking at her."

"Precisely. We only have the hotel manager's word that Ferrera was the culprit. Even then, he hasn't made an official statement."

"Shouldn't we get him to do that?" Patterson asked.

"We already tried. I went around there first thing this morning to talk to him while the uniform was bringing in Ferrera. He was less than helpful. Told me he didn't want to get involved."

"That sounds about right," Patterson said. "He stonewalled me until I pushed my credentials in his face. Even then, I think he only told me anything because it took him by surprise."

"Plus, you're FBI," Ballard pointed out. "That carries a lot of weight. Probably didn't want the feds poking into his past. Especially when one of them was staying at his hotel."

"That's the way I see it," Patterson replied. "Maybe you should use that tack to get a statement out of him."

"It crossed my mind. I've met his type before. I'm sure he's been involved in some sort of shady dealings we don't know about even if he isn't right now."

Gimenez jerked his head toward the door. "In the meantime, we have Ferrera to busy ourselves with."

"Let's get to it then," Ballard said. He looked at Patterson. "If this is the guy that attacked you, we'll do our best to get him to admit it."

"I know," Patterson replied.

Ballard met her gaze momentarily, then looked at Gimenez. "All right then. Let's go see what he has to say for himself."

FORTY-NINE

Justin Ferrera was about as cooperative as Patterson expected him to be. He sat opposite the two detectives, Ballard and Gimenez, with a suspicious scowl on his face and his arms defiantly folded across his chest.

"I don't know what you guys think I done, but whatever it was, I didn't do it," he protested within seconds of the two detectives sitting down before they could even say anything to him.

"If that's true," Ballard said, "then you have nothing to worry about and you'll be out of here in no time."

"How about I just walk out of here right now," Ferrera responded in a growling voice. "I was supposed to work today. I have rent to pay."

Ballard replied in an even voice. "We won't keep you long if you answer our questions, Mister Ferrera."

"Assuming you're as innocent as you claim," Gimenez added.

"You better get on with it, then. I'll answer your questions."

"Pleased to hear that." Ballard leaned forward, getting down to business. "You used to work at The Welcome Inn, is that correct, Mister Ferrera?"

"Yeah. I worked there for a while." If Ferrera was rattled by Ballard's opening salvo, he didn't show it. "Place was a dump. Not fit for rats."

"That's a harsh assessment considering your own living arrangements," Ballard replied. "You rent above a garage if I'm not mistaken. The officers that brought you in weren't very complementary about the place. They seem to think you could use a maid."

"So what?" Ferrera shrugged. "Where do you live? The White House?"

Ballard ignored the barb. "Your employment at the hotel included front desk duties, as well as performing maintenance. Is that correct?"

"Sounds right. It's been a long time."

"And you also received free accommodation in the basement as part payment for the aforementioned duties?"

Ferrera nodded. "I needed somewhere to crash, and they wanted someone on site twenty-four hours. You wouldn't believe how often the lowlifes renting rooms at that place blocked their toilets. It was a win-win."

"So you had a passkey that granted access to all the guest rooms?"

"I was the maintenance man. What do you think?"

"Just answer the question with a yes or a no, if you wouldn't mind."

"Yes. I had a key that got me into the rooms. Kinda hard to do my job without it."

"And did you ever take anything from the rooms?" Ballard asked.

"Sure. All the time." Ferrera leaned back in the chair with a smirk on his face. "Broken TVs. Parts from the air conditioning units. Couple of dead rats."

"Did you take anything you weren't supposed to?"

"I don't remember."

"Yet you remember the rats?"

"You try picking up a rodent that's been rotting underneath a nightstand for a week and see if you forget it."

"Fair enough." Ballard paused for a moment before continuing. "Did you ever enter a guest's room while the occupants were sleeping?"

"That would be wrong," was Ferrera's only answer.

"I'm glad we agree on that," Ballard said. "But that is not an answer to my question."

"Don't remember."

"You don't remember entering a room while an occupant was sleeping?"

"That's what I said."

"And you don't remember stealing any items from the guest rooms during your employment?"

"It was a long time ago."

"Were you consuming alcohol or taking any drugs during your time at The Welcome Inn?"

"Probably."

"Drugs, alcohol, or both?"

Ferrera shrugged.

"Is it true that after you lost your job at the hotel, you went to stay with your sister, who subsequently asked you to leave because of a drug problem?"

"Like she's never done anything," Ferrera snorted.

Gimenez spoke now. "Is that a yes?"

"Don't remember."

"Your memory's not very good, is it Mister Ferrera?" Ballard observed.

"Like I said before, it was a long time ago. I've lived a lot of places since."

"Tell us how you lost your job at the hotel."

"What does that have to do with anything?"

"Just tell us what we want to know."

"All right. I didn't see eye to eye with the management. We had a disagreement, and I left. That's not a crime."

"Did you quit, or were you fired?"

"It was mutual."

Ballard nodded. "I should probably advise you we've spoken to the hotel manager, Hank Lasky. He worked there at the same time as you. Still does. He was your direct supervisor. According to his version of events, it wasn't mutual."

"So why bother asking, if you already know."

"I want to hear from you."

"I've given my answer."

"And I'll ask you one more time, did you ever enter a guest room while an occupant was sleeping?"

Ferrera remained silent.

"Was that why you got fired?"

Still, he didn't speak.

"What about the panties and bras?" Ballard asked, referencing the underwear that Julie and Stacy had reported stolen when they filed their police report back in 2006. Hank Lasky had also confirmed there were underwear thefts when Patterson spoke to him. "Did you take those?"

"Underwear?" Ferrera's lips curled up at the edges. "What kind of freak do you think I am?"

"You tell me."

"Look, even if I took all that stuff, and I'm not saying that I did, it's irrelevant."

"How do you figure?" Ballard asked.

"Because you ain't got nothing on me. All these thefts at The Welcome Inn don't mean squat. You're talking about stuff that happened over ten years ago. I haven't even worked there for longer than that. No one questioned me at the time. Never even saw a cop."

"Doesn't make it right."

"Who cares? We got something called a statute of limitations in this country. You can't do shit to me even if you have video of me stealing the stuff, and a hundred witnesses who claim they saw me do it. It's been too long."

Ballard nodded slowly. "You think you're pretty clever don't you, Mr. Ferrera?"

"What I think, is that this is a waste of my time. And since you haven't charged me with anything, maybe I'll just get up and leave."

"Try it," Gimenez grumbled menacingly. He leaned forward, spearing Ferrera with a deadly glare. "Just because we can't prosecute you for thefts everyone in this room knows you committed back then, doesn't mean you're off the hook."

"Yeah. It kinda does." The smirk on Ferrera's face was growing bigger.

"You're forgetting one thing, smartass."

"What's that?"

Now it was Gimenez's turn to smile. "There is no statute of limitations on murder."

FIFTY

The reaction on Justin Ferrera's face when Gimenez mentioned murder was instant. It was like he'd been slapped.

In the observation room, Patterson and Quinn exchanged glances.

"Whoa." Ferrera held his hands up. "I don't know anything about no murders. I might have done some stupid things in my life, but I ain't killed nobody."

"Does the name Julie Blake mean anything to you?" Ballard asked.

"Should it?" Ferrera's demeanor changed from one of cool arrogance to fear.

"She stayed at The Welcome Inn with a friend when you were working there back in 2006. Someone broke into her room and stole cash and other valuables. The thief also took underwear. Despite your protestations of innocence and refusal to answer our questions, we have it on good authority that your particular proclivities involved underwear stealing."

"Even if I did go into that room and took stuff, and I'm not saying that I did, what does that have to do with murder?"

"I think you know very well what it has to do with murder," Ballard replied. "Do you remember Julie Blake, or not?"

"A lot of people stayed at The Welcome Inn when I was working there. You expect me to remember one person I might not even have met sixteen years later?"

"Under normal circumstances, no," Ballard replied. "But these aren't normal circumstances, are they, Mister Ferrera?"

"You tell me."

"Fine. I will. Julie Blake checked into The Welcome Inn during the time you were working there. Someone broke into her room and stole the items we've already discussed. We strongly suspect that someone was you. At some point afterward, we don't know how long, Julie Blake disappeared." Ballard sat back and observed Justin Ferrera for a moment. "Do you see where I'm going with this?"

"When you say disappeared, you mean missing, like someone took her?" Ferrera said. "Right?"

"Now you're getting it. And guess who our prime suspect is."

"Look. I never abducted no one." Ferrera's eyes were wide. "Besides, just because she went missing doesn't prove she was murdered. I mean, you need a body to know that."

"We do have a body," Gimenez said. "We have lots of bodies belonging to over a dozen girls that were abducted, abused, and killed over the past twenty years. All by the same person. Now we don't know yet if one of those murdered women is Julie Blake, but rest assured we will find out."

Ballard picked up where his partner left off. "At this moment, given what we know about your past, we're thinking you might have had something to do with those murders. Especially since you had the means and opportunity to abduct one of the potential victims."

"How long have you lived in Oklahoma City, Mister Ferrera?" Gimenez asked.

"This is bullshit." Ferrera shook his head. "You've got nothing. You 're fishing, that's all."

"You want to take a gamble on that?" Ballard asked, calling Ferrera's bluff.

"If you had any proof that I'd murdered even one person, you'd have read me my rights and slapped a pair of handcuffs on me by now. Like I said, you've got nothing."

"You're absolutely right," Ballard admitted. "We would have. But that doesn't make you innocent."

"Doesn't make me guilty either."

"No, it doesn't," Gimenez said. "I have one more question, though."

"What?"

"Where were you last night between 8 and 10 PM?"

"What does that have to do with anything?"

"Just answer the question," Ballard said.

"Fine. I was at home in my apartment."

"Can anyone vouch for that?"

"Maybe, maybe not. My landlady lives in the main house. I guess it's possible she saw me when I went out on the stairs for a smoke."

"You were there the entire time?" Asked Ballard.

"Yeah. I was." Ferrera scratched his chin. "Actually, now that I think about it, I did step out briefly."

"When?"

"Probably a little before ten. Went to the liquor store two blocks from my place, picked up a bottle of Wild Turkey."

"Did you go anywhere else?"

"No. Just the liquor store. Mike, the owner, he'll vouch for me."

"We'll check up on that," Ballard said.

Gimenez added, "and talk to your landlady too."

"You do whatever you have to," Ferrera said, the arrogance creeping back into his voice. "I think I'd like to go now."

"Not until we have some answers from you," Gimenez replied.

"Then charge me with something if you want to keep me here." Ferrera was defiant. He waited a moment for the detectives to respond, then grinned. "That's what I thought."

In the observation room, Patterson stiffened. She was standing less than ten feet from the man who robbed her sister, and possibly murdered her, and now he was going to get up and walk out without admitting to a damned thing. Worse, they couldn't stop him. There was nothing to link Justin Ferrera to the murdered women found on Bracken Island.

Everyone realized he was responsible for the thefts at The Welcome Inn, but that didn't automatically make him a serial killer. If one of the victims turned out to be her sister, Julie, then there would be a link directly back to Ferrera, but even then, it would be almost impossible to prove he was the murderer without DNA or other corroborating evidence.

Hell, she couldn't even say for sure that he was the man who attacked her the previous evening. If only there was some way to say for sure, like an identifying tattoo, or a visible birthmark. But she had nothing. The only fact she knew for sure was the color of her attacker's hair, and that didn't help because Ferrera had shaved his head. Short of waiting a month or two for his hair to grow out, she couldn't make a comparison.

"It's okay," Quinn said next to her, no doubt sensing Patterson's frustration. "If it's him, we'll prove it."

"And what if we can't?" Patterson asked. "He just gets away with murder?"

"Let's cross that bridge when we come to it."

Patterson didn't reply. She was watching Ferrera stand up and walk toward the door with the detectives at his rear. He was walking out, and there was nothing they could do to stop him. It filled her with anger. Murderer or not, her sister would probably still be alive if it weren't for the actions of this man.

She turned toward the door.

"What are you doing?" Quinn took a step toward her.

"Getting answers." Patterson was at the door now. She pulled it open.

"Wait. You can't go out there and confront him."

"Why not?"

"Because you're an FBI agent. That's why. You can't harass people without proof just because you think they're guilty, even if they are," Quinn replied. "We're held to a higher standard."

"I'm not doing this as an FBI agent," Patterson shot back. "I'm doing it for my sister."

FIFTY-ONE

Justin Ferrera was on the front steps of police headquarters when Patterson caught up to him. When she shouted to catch his attention, Ferrera stopped and turned, surprised.

"You talking to me?" he asked, clearly suspicious of her motives.

"Julie Blake," Patterson shouted at him while still fifteen feet away, across the plaza in front of the building. "I don't care what you said in there, I know you recognize that name."

Ferrera rolled his eyes. "I already said all I have to say. You people are crazy. Leave me alone."

"You broke into that room at The Welcome Inn, and you know it." Patterson was closing on Ferrera now. "Why don't you just admit it and do us all a favor."

"You never heard of the Fifth Amendment?" Ferrera shook his head and turned to leave. "This is harassment."

"Hey! I'm not done with you yet." Patterson raced to catch up.

"Yeah? Well, I'm done with you." Ferrera was still descending the steps, moving quicker now. "All of you."

"Don't walk away from me." Patterson closed the gap with

Ferrera and reached out, gripping him by the shoulder. "You're going to answer my questions, one way or the other."

Ferrera spun around. "Like hell I am. Who are you anyway? You weren't in the interview room. You a cop, or something?"

"It doesn't matter who I am." Patterson could feel her face growing hot with anger. "Just tell me what I want to know."

"Course it matters who you are." Ferrera's voice was calm but firm. "Because if you're a cop, I can file a complaint against you. This ain't legal."

"Like you care about the law," Patterson spat back. "You've been breaking it your entire life."

"And how would you know that?"

"I know you stole from my sister and her friend. And lots of other people at that hotel. That's why you got fired." Patterson knew she was on dangerous ground. If Grant found out about this impromptu interrogation, let alone Madeline Kahn, she could find herself drummed out of the Bureau and looking for a new job. But in the moment, she didn't care. "I also know you're a pervert. Stealing women's underwear. Creeping into their rooms while they sleep so you can watch them. What else were you planning to do?"

"Wouldn't you like to know?" The sneer that had been a fixture of Ferrera's face during the police interview was back.

"Were you satisfied with just watching them sleep, or did you take it further?" Patterson was barreling down a dark tunnel with no good destination. But the thought of her sister falling victim to this man drove her on, regardless. "Tell me."

"Look, if I didn't tell those two cops in there, I sure as shit ain't telling you."

"Julie Blake." Patterson repeated the name, as if this would somehow compel Ferrera to relent. "What did you do with her?"

Ferrera smiled. "What do you think I did with her?"

"Don't play games with me," Patterson replied, her voice trembling. "I need to know."

"Go fuck yourself." Ferrera shook his head and turned away.

"Hey. I'm not done with you yet." Patterson took a step forward, but then a restraining hand fell on her shoulder.

"That's enough."

She glanced backward to find Quinn standing there. "He knows what happened to my sister."

"He might, or he might not. Either way, this isn't how to go about dealing with it."

Ferrera glanced back. "You should listen to her."

"Don't you dare tell me what to do," Patterson replied, anger flashing in her eyes.

Ferrera held his hands up. "Whatever." He continued on a few steps more, and then paused. "What did you say your sister's name was?"

"You know very well." Patterson clenched her jaw. "Julie Blake."

"Oh yeah. That's right. I remember her now. She was a fine piece of ass. Easy to look at."

Patterson shot a look at Quinn. "I told you he knew."

"He's just winding you up," Quinn replied. "Trying to get a rise out of you. Let it go."

"Yeah. I'm just joking around," Ferrera said. "An upstanding citizen. Never took those panties and had fun with them. Never did nothing." Ferrera paused, then cocked his head. "Gotta say, your sister looked real cute when she was sleeping. Didn't even wake up when I pulled the covers down to get a better look."

Patterson saw red. She shrugged Quinn's hand away and started after Ferrera again. Would've reached him if Quinn hadn't stepped in her path.

"Just let him go," Quinn said. "He's not worth it."

"Not to you, maybe." Patterson tried to walk around Quinn without success.

"He's on our radar now," Quinn said. "If he's guilty, we'll hold the bastard accountable. I promise you that."

If the FBI agent's words worried Ferrera, he didn't show it. "I

had some fun with your sister. She was one of the better ones."
He met Patterson's gaze. "Did you know she slept naked?"

"Screw you," Patterson snapped. She tried to push past
Quinn, but the other woman held her back. "Don't do it. You
touch him right now, and we'll never be able to prosecute. Even
the worst public defender in town would have a field day with
it. A federal law enforcement officer attacking a suspect? He'd
walk free. That's assuming the DA was even willing to proceed."

"Dammit." Patterson swiveled and walked away. She knew
Quinn was right, even if she didn't want to admit it. Behind her,
Ferrera chuckled, the sound taunting and merciless. When she
looked back, he was already on the street, moving in the other
direction.

"Just because he said those things, doesn't make it true."
Quinn watched Patterson with a look of concern on her face.
"He's a scumbag, for sure, but chances are he was just looking to
get a rise out of you."

"He remembers my sister," Patterson said. "I could tell.
Maybe he was lying about some of that stuff, or maybe he
wasn't. Either way, he's the one who broke into her room."

"That doesn't mean he's responsible for her disappearance,"
Quinn pointed out. "I'm not saying he's innocent, I'm just saying
you need more proof."

"Then I'll have to find it."

"What you need to do right now is simmer down," Quinn
said. "You got your car keys on you?"

Patterson nodded. "Figured I get uniform to give me a ride
over to the hotel and collect my car."

"No need." Quinn motioned toward the multistory parking
lot next to police headquarters. "Ballard had your car towed here
last night after we left the scene. It's waiting for you on the
bottom level of the garage."

"Thanks."

"Don't thank me, thank Ballard," Quinn said. "But right now,
you need to go back to my place and stay out of this. Let cooler

heads prevail. I'll catch you up on everything when I get home this evening. Okay?"

"Sure." Patterson nodded. "Thanks for keeping me out of trouble just now."

"Don't mention it," Quinn replied. "Now go home."

Patterson glanced beyond Quinn, toward Ferrera, who was almost out of sight. Then she turned and headed toward the parking garage.

Her car waited in a bay near the front. The tire had been replaced, probably by the Oklahoma City PD motor pool. The old tire, no doubt, was sitting in an evidence locker somewhere.

She approached and unlocked the door, but before she could climb in, her phone rang. When she answered, it was Holly Cartwright, the original wildlife biologist—now retired—responsible for the whooping crane program on Bracken Island.

"Is this Patterson Blake?" The woman asked.

"Yes, it is." Patterson leaned against her vehicle. "How can I help you Mrs. Cartwright?"

"You told me to call if I remembered anything," Holly replied. "Anything at all, no matter how small."

"That's right."

"Well, I did remember something. It probably isn't relevant—I hate to even waste your time—but I thought you should know. Can you come by the house?"

Patterson glanced at her watch. "I can be there in twenty minutes. Would you mind if I bring someone with me?" Patterson asked. "The special agent working the case for the FBI."

"I really don't want to get involved officially if I don't need to. Like I said, it's probably nothing. How about you come over and I'll tell you, and if you think it's relevant, I'll make an official statement."

"Fine," Patterson agreed. "I'll be right there."

FIFTY-TWO

Patterson arrived at Holly Cartwright's house fifteen minutes later. She parked outside and hurried up the path toward the front door.

It opened while she was still a few steps away.

Holly Cartwright stood there, waiting for her. "Special Agent Blake, you got here quickly. I really appreciate it."

"It's no problem. I was on my way home, anyway." Patterson entered the house and followed Holly into the living room. "What did you remember?"

"Oh, goodness." Holly shook her head. "That can wait a few minutes. I should make you a cup of tea. It's the least I can do since you rushed all the way over here at a moment's notice."

"There's really no need, Mrs. Cartwright." Patterson shook her head. "You don't have to do that."

"Oh, but I want to." Holly was already moving toward the door. "What kind of host would I be if I left you thirsty while we talk?"

"Well, okay then." Patterson gave in. If Holly Cartwright wanted to drink tea while they talked, then so be it. "Just a small cup, though. With lemon, like before."

"Right you are," Holly replied over her shoulder as she left the room. "One tea with lemon coming up."

Patterson took a seat on the sofa and waited for her host to return. She glanced around the room. It looked just as it had on her last visit, except there were more supermarket magazines on the coffee table now. Holly Cartwright certainly had a soft spot for the tabloid press. Patterson wondered if she believed the sensationalized headlines splashed across the front pages. As a professional investigator, it never ceased to amaze her how gullible people were. If they read it, it must be true. It was no wonder the country was in such a state, with everyone living in their own little echo chamber divided by whichever form of reality they chose to believe. Was she doing the same thing with Justin Ferrera? She hoped not.

"Here we are," Holly said cheerfully, reentering the room with two cups of tea and a plate of chocolate chip cookies on a tray. "I brought something for us to munch on, too."

"Great," Patterson said with a smile. "I haven't had lunch yet."

"Well." Holly looked mortified. "Skipping meals isn't good for you, I hope you know that."

"I'll make it my next priority once I leave here," Patterson promised her.

"You should have a cookie, to keep you going," Holly said.

"I will." Patterson waited for Holly Cartwright to sit in one of the wingback chairs opposite the sofa, then got down to business. "Why don't you tell me what you remembered."

"Like I said on the phone, it's probably nothing," Holly said.

"Why don't you let me be the judge of that."

"Of course." Holly nodded. "Don't forget your tea, my dear."

Patterson picked up her cup and drank, not wanting to offend the woman. The tea was strong with a bitter, lemony taste. It wasn't as good as the last time she was here.

Putting the cup down, she turned her attention back to Holly. "About Bracken Island, what is it you remember?"

"All in good time, my dear." Holly smiled. "Let's enjoy the tea first. You don't have to be all business."

Patterson reached for the half-empty cup again, thought better of it. Something was off. A tingle of apprehension wormed its way up her spine. "I think I've had enough tea, Mrs. Cartwright. I'd really rather we had that chat now if you don't mind."

"Oh, very well." Holly sat back in her chair. "I wasn't entirely truthful when you were here last time. I saw someone on the island. More than once, actually."

"What? Who did you see?" Patterson asked, suddenly aware that her speech felt odd.

She was slurring her words.

She felt weird, like she was drunk.

"That didn't take long," Holly said, sipping her own tea. She picked up a cookie and bit into it. Crumbs fell onto her lap.

"What's happening?" Patterson asked. It was hard to think, and her eyes kept losing focus. She looked down at the tea, too bitter to finish drinking, and understood. "You drugged me."

"Only a little," Holly said in a jovial voice. "I didn't want to use too much. Scott said it might kill you. We couldn't have that. At least, not right away."

"Scott?" Patterson was finding it hard to stay awake now. Her eyelids felt heavy. She struggled against the drug's effects, but could feel herself slipping away, anyway. She tried to stand, fell back to the sofa when her legs gave out. "Who's Scott?"

"My nephew," Holly said. "He's such a good boy. Not like his mother. She was a useless, drug addicted harlot. Probably still is. That's why he came to live with me. I gave my best, tried to raise him right, but you know what they say."

"No. What do they say?" Patterson tried to stand again. She reached for her gun tucked in its holster at her side, but her coordination was gone.

"The apple doesn't fall far from the tree. I think that's how it goes." Holly stepped around the coffee table and reached past Patterson's flailing hand. She pulled the Glock from its holster and set it out of reach on the fireplace mantle. "Still, I think I did my best with him. We came to an understanding."

"That's enough, Auntie," a male voice said from somewhere to Patterson's rear. She tried to look toward him, but her muscles weren't responding.

"I was just making polite conversation with her until you arrived," Holly said, looking past Patterson. "It's the least a good host can do."

"I know." The man came into view. "You did well."

Patterson struggled to make out his features but couldn't because her vision was blurred.

"It won't be long now," the man said, standing over her. He kneeled and took her hand, cradled it in his.

Patterson tried to pull away but couldn't. She wanted to tell him what a mistake he was making, that she was FBI, but all that came out was an incoherent mumble. Then, as the man gently patted her hand, Patterson slipped into darkness.

FIFTY-THREE

Patterson crawled back to consciousness like a diver kicking toward the water's surface. She opened her eyes and groaned. Her head hurt. A dull ache that throbbed behind her forehead. Her back hurt too, probably because of the hard surface she was currently lying on.

Patterson rolled onto her side and saw that it was a rough wood floor. The planks stretched away from her, a seemingly endless expanse of wood from her low angle, head resting on the ground.

Her vision was blurry and unfocused.

She blinked several times, and it got better.

Now she saw the names.

They were scratched into the floor a few feet away. Three of them, one above the other, etched in block capitals yet different enough that Patterson knew they were not written by the same person. Helen, Jessica, and Amy.

A wave of panic gripped Patterson. Where was she?

The last thing she remembered was confronting Justin Fererra outside police headquarters after he walked free. Then Quinn had told her to go home. Except that hadn't happened because Holly Cartwright had called and asked her to come over.

So how had she gotten here, laying on a wood floor?

The answer struck Patterson like a slap in the face.

Holly Cartwright had put something in her tea. A drug. Probably flunitrazepam, more commonly known as Rohypnol, although there were others.

But it wasn't just Holly. There was someone else, too. The memory was vague because the drug had already been kicking in, but he was there.

Holly's nephew. She had called him Scott.

Patterson shifted, ignoring the jolt of pain that flared inside her skull, and raised her head, noting that her jacket was gone. Her shoulder holster had been removed, too. Not that it mattered. Holly Cartwright had relieved her of the Glock while she was passing out. When she was working, Patterson kept a second weapon. A Glock 27 subcompact which she wore in an ankle holster. She hadn't brought that gun with her, opting to leave it locked in the safe inside her bedroom closet at home. But even if she'd brought the backup weapon, Holly or her nephew would have confiscated it, no doubt.

Pulling herself together, Patterson took stock of her situation. She was in a small room with block walls, no bigger than twelve by twelve. It was stiflingly hot and smelled of sweat, urine, and feces. There was a narrow horizontal window set high on the opposite wall. The glass was streaked with dirt, cutting down on the light and rendering the space even more gloomy. The room had only one door, which was reinforced with a sheet of metal and had no interior handle. A single piece of furniture stood against the wall below the window. A cot with a filthy mattress, next to which sat a plastic bucket swarming with flies.

But it was the figure laying on the cot that caught Patterson's attention.

A young woman with tangled long black hair and wearing a dirty sweat stained shift. She was curled, facing away from

Patterson with her bare legs, bruised in places, pulled up toward her waist. The soles of her feet were black.

"Hey," Patterson said, noting how croaky her voice sounded. "You on the bed."

The woman didn't respond.

At first Patterson wondered if she was dead, but then noticed the slow rise and fall of her chest.

She tried again.

"Hey, what's your name?"

This time the girl moved. She rolled over to face Patterson and spoke in a timid, low voice. "Abigail."

"Hi, Abigail. Do you know where we are?" Patterson pushed herself up on one elbow. There was a rattle of metal, and she realized a collar circled her neck, connected to a short length of chain secured to a metal bracket attached to the floor a few feet away. Patterson lifted her hands and ran them around the collar. It was loose, but not enough to remove. There was a hinge on one side and a padlock holding it closed on the other.

Abigail watched her with dull eyes. "We shouldn't talk. He doesn't like me to talk without permission."

"Who doesn't like it, Abigail?" Patterson asked. She licked her lips and swallowed. Her throat was dry, and she had a raging thirst. "Are you talking about the man named Scott?"

"He makes me call him master."

Patterson took that as a yes. "How long have you been here?"

The girl looked at her blankly. "Don't know."

Patterson tried a different tack. "What time of year was it when he took you, Abigail?"

"Summer. I was getting ready to go back to college." She smiled as if remembering a far off, better place. "I'm going to be a schoolteacher."

"What month?" Patterson asked. "August?"

Abigail nodded.

August. Patterson was shocked. It was June now, which meant Holly's nephew had kept Abigail in this stinking, disgusting room for ten months. It was sweltering inside the structure right now, but in the middle of winter, it would be freezing. Patterson looked down at the floor, and the three names scratched there. Abigail was not the first person to endure this.

Then a thought occurred to Patterson. Had Julie been imprisoned in this same room sixteen years ago? She looked around for other names scratched on the floor or walls. Thankfully, she didn't see any. While that didn't mean Julie had not been here, it made Patterson feel a little better. She wanted to find her sister, but not like this.

"He'll be coming soon," Abigail said. "He always comes when it gets dark."

Patterson glanced up toward the narrow slit of window near the ceiling. The daylight was fading; the room growing dim. A bare, unlit bulb hung from the ceiling. There was a switch near the door, too far to reach, thanks to the chain. Another forty-five minutes and it would be dark. Without the light on, it would be pitch black inside the room. That would make it exponentially harder to escape.

Patterson tried to stand, but the chain wasn't long enough. No more than three feet. She only made it to her knees before it pulled tight. Even moving closer to the floor ring provided little leeway.

She leaned forward and tugged, but there was no give. She set her feet and tried again, with the same result. If only she could work the floor ring loose, pull the screws out, she could bust through the door. Maybe. Even if she couldn't, the loose chain would then become a weapon to be used against Scott. She could wait behind the door, wrap it around his throat when he entered, and incapacitate him. If the Glock was still in her possession, she could have just shot a link out of the chain to free herself. Or put a bullet through Scott's chest, for that matter. But it wasn't.

She looked back toward Abigail, who was not shackled. "Hey. Come over here and help me."

Abigail watched her but didn't move.

"If you come and pull with me, we might be able to get this chain free of the floor. Then I can get us both out of here."

Abigail shook her head.

"Don't you want to go home?" Patterson asked. "If you help me, I'll take you home."

"I can't go home." Abigail's voice was a monotone. "If I try, he'll be mad. He hurts me when he's mad."

"I won't let him hurt you," Patterson said, sinking back to the floor because the collar bit into her neck when she was kneeling. "I promise."

"We need to be quiet now." Abigail's eyes shifted to the door. "He's coming."

Patterson followed her fellow captive's gaze. She couldn't hear anyone approaching. But a moment later, the sound of a key grating in a lock on the other side of the door proved Abigail correct. Then it opened to reveal Holly Cartwright's nephew, Scott.

He stood and observed the pair of women with a look that made Patterson's skin crawl.

Patterson scooted back instinctively. Then, from her left, she sensed movement.

It was Abigail.

She heaved herself off the mattress, swung her legs from the bed, and climbed to her feet. Reaching up, she pulled the shift's shoulder straps sideways and let the garment fall to the ground. Then she stepped out of it, arms by her sides, and stood naked in front of her master.

FIFTY-FOUR

S cott stepped into the room and approached Abigail. He cupped her chin with his hand, smiling, then glanced sideways toward Patterson. "Isn't she special? So tame. She'll do anything I ask."

Patterson glared at him. "You're sick."

Scott ignored Patterson's insult. "She wasn't like this when I took her, though. First couple of months, she was always scratching and biting and screaming. That's what makes it so fun. Breaking them. Oh, how they plead and beg. Gives me goosebumps." He moved away from Abigail, closer to Patterson. "What about you, Special Agent Patterson Blake? How long would it take before you lose the will to fight?"

"Take this chain off my neck and I'll show you," Patterson spat back. She looked up at him. "Oh, that's right. I already did last night in the parking lot of The Welcome Inn. That was you, right?"

Scott's cheeks flushed red. His face contorted into a mask of anger. "Bitch."

He raced forward, connecting a vicious kick to Patterson's stomach that lifted her off the ground and sent her toppling sideways, gasping for air. As she rolled back to face him again, he planted a second kick under her rib cage, then a third.

Patterson cried out in pain. Tears welled at the corners of her eyes.

She wheezed and gritted her teeth against the pain. The metal collar had pulled so tight against her neck that she could feel blood running down where it cut into the soft skin under her chin. She flinched, expecting a fourth kick, but Scott was done.

He stood over her, breathless, the fury still etched into his features. "Fucking bitch. Coming around to auntie's house, worrying her like that just when I'd convinced her that everything was going to be okay. Those first cops that came to see her, they didn't have a clue. I promised I'd find somewhere else, that I wouldn't use the island again. I couldn't, anyway. Not after they found my cars. But they hadn't found me, and they wouldn't. Then you showed up asking all those questions. Even asked her about my photo on her mantle. Now she says I have to stay away from her. Says it's not safe for me to be there anymore. And it's all your fault."

"How is any of this my fault?" Patterson gasped between gulping breaths. She looked up through watery eyes, knowing that one wrong word could antagonize him all over again, and she would be on the receiving end. But a deeper part of her wanted to hurt him with her words, the same way he'd hurt so many innocent women. Maybe even her own sister. "You're the freak that likes to murder helpless women."

"I never murdered anyone," Scott screamed. "If they died, it was their own fault."

"How did you come to that sick conclusion?" Patterson pushed herself up on one elbow again. The pain in her stomach was receding, but she was still finding it hard to breathe.

"When I left them, they were alive." Scott glared at Patterson. "I even left the padlock keys there. Put them on the hood of the car. All they had to do was reach them and they'd be free. They chose to die."

"More like you are back here fantasizing about having the power of life or death," Patterson said. "You could have gone back to Bracken Island at any time and set them free, but you didn't."

"I went back, all right. I went there every day to see if they wanted to live. None of them did. They were weak. They just sat in those cars and begged me to set them free. Even at the end, when they could barely lift their heads up, they still begged and cried. It was pathetic."

"Why there?" Patterson wanted to understand the mind of the man who might've killed her sister. "How did you even know about that island or that the cars were even there?"

"It's all because of auntie." Scott's voice had cooled now. His face was still red, but slowly returning to normal. "She's the only one that understands me. My mother was useless. An alcoholic drug addicted harlot. Didn't even know who my father was. Auntie took me away from all that, took me in. She also took me to that island every time she went over there to check on those stupid whooping cranes. I was fourteen when I found the cars. I got bored watching her putting tracking tags on their legs, so I wandered off into the woods. That's when I came across the first car. It was calling from under all the leaves and branches and vines, wanting me to find it. It wanted to be useful again. So that's what I did. I gave it a purpose. And all the other cars too. I gave them passengers that would never leave."

"Why?" Patterson shook her head. "Why do it at all?"

"Janine Bradshaw."

"Who's that?"

"First girl I ever kissed. That was when I was fifteen. Janine was a year older. We'd gone to the movies on our first date, and I told her I'd find somewhere extra special for the next one."

"You took her to the island."

Scott nodded. "I borrowed auntie's boat. She was all into it. So excited. We went across to the island. Her parents didn't even know she was out with me. She lied to them and said she was studying with her friend. I tied the boat up and took her into the woods. She was scared because it was so dark, but I'd brought a flashlight so that I could show her my cars. When she saw them, she thought they were neat too. We got into the back of one. A big old Studebaker. I told her I wanted to play a game, asked her to close her eyes and not open them until I said so. I'd found some chain in auntie's garage and brought it out to the island earlier in the day. She used it to keep the back gate closed before we had the fence repaired. Now it had a better use. I wrapped it around Janine's neck and padlocked it, all the while telling her not to open her eyes yet. You should've seen her face when I put the key on the car's hood. I could hear her begging halfway back to the boat."

"Oh my God," Patterson breathed. "You started at fifteen?"

Scott ignored the comment. "I went back day after day, and each time she was a bit quieter. Then she stopped speaking completely."

"That's because she was dead, Scott." Patterson said in the strongest voice she could muster. "You killed her."

"I know that. I'm not stupid." Scott said. "That's when I had the idea to keep them longer. It was great, putting her in the car, and all. But I should have stayed with her a while first. Got to know her better. That would've made it even more fun. I wanted to spend time with them in the cellar at auntie's house, but she didn't like that idea. That's why she gave me the money to buy this place when I turned eighteen. It was her birthday present."

Patterson recoiled. "You mean that sweet old woman knew what you were all along? She helped you?"

"She raised me the way she thought best," Scott said. "She was a good mother."

"She isn't your mother."

"She's the only mother I've ever known. Better than my real one."

"You realize she'll go to jail," Patterson said, sensing an opening, but she had to tread carefully. Avoid angering him again.

"She'll spend the rest of her life behind bars and die there. And it will be because of you. But I can make sure that doesn't happen."

"I don't want her to go to jail."

"I know you don't, Scott. You love your auntie. I can tell." Patterson wondered if he could hear the fear in her voice. "If you let us go, if you allow me to take Abigail out of here and get her medical help, I'll say that your auntie had nothing to do with it. That she didn't know what was going on."

"You'd do that for me?" There was a flicker of indecision in Scott's voice.

"Yes," Patterson replied. "Because it's only a matter of time now before they catch you. The FBI are involved, and they don't give up. It's not like dealing with the local cops, Scott. They know about you now. Let us go free, and I'll make sure your auntie stays out of prison."

Scott was silent for a long minute. He looked between Patterson, chained to the floor, and Abigail, who was still standing subservient and naked in the same spot as before. Then he shook his head. "You're lying. You just want me to set you free. You're not going to help my auntie. I'm the only one who can help her."

"Scott, that's not true," Patterson said, trying to rescue the situation.

"Shut up!" Scott screamed the words, his face flushing red a second time. Then, just as quickly as the anger erupted, it receded. He turned to Abigail, looked her up and down with a disdainful glance. "Put your nightdress back on and get on the bed. I'll be back for you later."

Then he turned and stomped out slamming the door. Moments later, Patterson heard a key turning. They were locked in again.

FIFTY-FIVE

Abigail pulled the shift up again to cover herself, then retreated to the bed and lay curled facing the wall. Her shoulders moved as if she was crying, but there was no sound.

Outside, crickets chirped, and frogs started their evening chorus as the sun slid lower. Long shadows crept across the floor as the light slowly faded.

Patterson was still in pain from the beating Scott had inflicted upon her, but she knew it was just a prelude to whatever he planned to do next. None of the girls he'd kept in this room had ever lived to talk about it, and Scott hadn't been swayed by Patterson's impassioned pleas to release her and Abigail for the sake of his aunt. He had seen through her ruse, and she might even have made things worse. Scott clearly suffered from an antisocial personality disorder. His violent assault on Patterson, lack of empathy, and the ease with which he flew into a rage and then came out of it again put him squarely into the sociopath category. Both he and his aunt had mentioned the moral failings of Scott's mother. If she were as bad as they made out, this could have been the catalyst for his aberrant behavior. She could have been abusive toward Scott during his formative years and might even have been physically violent. Given the right circumstances, his deviant personality traits would have festered and grown, turning him into a monster. Unlike a psychopath, who was hard-wired from birth, the sociopath was a product of their upbringing and environment. Patterson almost felt sorry for him, going from a mother who laid the seeds of evil, to an aunt who nurtured it, and might even possess her own sociopathic tendencies, albeit better hidden. The behavioral analysts at the Oklahoma City FBI Field Office had been spot on, which didn't surprise her.

It also didn't help, given her current situation.

But there was something that might.

Scott had found a uniquely dissociative way to dispatch his victims once he grew tired of them. Placing a means of escape—the keys to their restraints—close at hand but out of reach allowed him to reason that he wasn't actually a killer. This wasn't for the sake of his conscience. He did not possess that particular mechanism. Rather, it was to allow his crimes to fit within the preconceived narrative he had written for himself. He even said as much. If his victims didn't escape, it meant they wanted to die. That wasn't all of it, Patterson was sure. There were power issues at play too. He liked to break and control women, just as he had with the subservient Abigail.

But it was the keys that got Patterson thinking. She wondered if his habit of placing a means of escape nearby but out of his victim's reach extended to their imprisonment, too.

Were a set of keys to Patterson's shackles in the room at this very moment?

If so, they would not be obvious.

Patterson looked around the room. There were few places to conceal anything, even a small object like a set of padlock keys. It would need to be out of Patterson's reach, too. The most obvious place was the bed—either under the mattress or beneath the pillow that lay on top of it—but Scott would probably not hide keys there. He might believe he'd broken Abigail's will, but he couldn't take a chance on the girl discovering them by accident and giving them to Patterson.

But there was nothing else in the room except the bucket that acted as a makeshift toilet, and that was just too gross to contemplate. Not to mention that he'd have to fish them out when he changed the bucket. He might be a sociopath, but Scott probably didn't like to poke through poop. Patterson discounted that particular hiding place.

Then her eyes drifted upward to the window.

The building was constructed of concrete blocks. The window was set back, which meant there was a narrow ledge underneath it. From her angle on the floor, she could not see if any keys were hidden there. Even if she were standing up, it would be impossible since the window was close to the ceiling. But it was the only place they could be. Assuming Scott had actually left any keys in here with her.

There was only one way to find out. The scared young woman curled up on the filthy mattress.

"Abigail," Patterson said in a soothing voice. "Abigail, honey, can you do something for me?"

There was no response.

"I just want you to stand up and look on the window ledge for me. Can you do that?"

Abigail rolled over to face Patterson. Her grubby face was lined with tears. Proof that she had been silently crying. "He won't like it if I do that."

"Abigail, if you do as I ask, I'll get you out of here," Patterson said. "You must have family. A boyfriend. They'll be worried about you. You want to see your family again, don't you?"

Abigail nodded. "They don't hurt me like he does."

"I know." Patterson felt a lump in her throat and swallowed. "All I want you to do is stand up on the bed and see if there's a key on that windowsill. If there is, you can go home."

"I'm afraid," Abigail replied. "If he finds out, he'll hurt me even worse. One time I missed the bucket when I was peeing. It went on the floor. He beat me so bad it hurt when I lay down."

"I won't let him do that again. I promise. But the only way I can help you is if you look for that key."

"You promise?" Abigail was sitting up now. She glanced nervously at the locked door and then back to Patterson.

"I promise. All you need to do is stand up and look."

Abigail hesitated a moment, and Patterson wondered if she was going to lie back down and turn away toward the wall again, but she didn't. Abigail clambered to her feet, pausing to adjust her balance on the shifting mattress, then turned to the window, which was now level with her eye line.

"There is a key here," she said. "A little one."

Thank God, Patterson thought, relieved. Her hunch had been correct. The one weakness of sociopaths was that when you knew their habits, they were easy to predict. "Take the key down and bring it to me."

Abigail reached up and took the key from the windowsill. She gripped it between her thumb and forefinger, then made her way unsteadily off the bed.

She held the key out.

Patterson took it and reached up to the shackle around her neck. It took her a few seconds to get the key into the padlock because she couldn't see what she was doing, but then it slid in. When she turned the key, the shank popped upward with a click, and she was able to swing the lock barrel sideways and remove it from the metal collar encircling her throat.

Abigail had retreated to the bed and now sat looking at her. "If he knows you took that off, he'll hurt you."

"He already hurt me," Patterson replied. "And if we let him, he'll hurt us a lot more."

"Are you going to take me home now?"

"That's the plan. But first we need to get out of this room." Patterson glanced toward the door. Scott was probably using one or more heavy-duty locks. It was unlikely she could bust through it. Even if she could, the noise would probably alert their captor.

She glanced up above the bed.

The window was the only option.

It was wide enough, at least two feet, but skinny. She estimated the distance from the sill to the top of the window was fourteen inches, maybe less. That might be big enough to wriggle through, but it would be tight. Patterson wasn't overweight, but she wasn't model-thin either, with medium breasts that would probably make squeezing through the gap even more arduous.

But there was only one way to find out, and time was not on her side.

Scott could return at any moment.

With that in mind, Patterson got to her feet and approached the bed. She used the wall to steady herself as she stepped past Abigail and up onto the mattress.

The window was even more filthy now that she could see it up close. The glass was so dirty that she couldn't even see through it in the waning light as day gave way to night. Spiders had built thick cobwebs in all four corners of the window casing. The sill was littered with the carcasses of dead flies that had wandered too close and ended up consumed.

At first, she thought the window was built in and didn't open, but then she noticed a latch sitting at the bottom of the frame in the middle. She lifted it and pushed on the window.

It didn't move.

She wondered if she was doing it wrong but didn't think so. The window was hinged at the top and there were two arms—one on the left side and one on the right—that held the window in place when it was swung vertically out and upward.

It was probably just stuck shut through lack of use. It didn't help that someone had painted around the frame without bothering to crack the window open first. Now it was painted shut.

But that didn't matter. It was their only way out.

Patterson tried again, pushing with all her might. The exertion made her stomach muscles hurt where Scott had repeatedly kicked her, but she ignored the pain and applied more pressure, grunting with the strain.

At first, nothing happened, and she thought her efforts were in vain. But then, with a satisfying crack, the frame broke free of the hardened paint and grime holding it shut and swung outward on stiff hinges.

Patterson felt a rush of relief.

At least, until the window hit an obstruction and stopped less than halfway open. Someone, presumably Scott, had attached security bars to the exterior frame. She could see them through the narrow gap.

They were still trapped.

FIFTY-SIX

Patterson stood looking at the window, and the bars beyond, in disbelief. Even if she could wriggle through the small gap between the window and sill, the bars were too close together.

Still, at least it smelled better in the room. A cool breeze was wafting in, taking the edge off the stench coming from the toilet bucket.

She jumped off the bed and looked around for something, anything, with which to pry the bars loose. The bedframe was metal. Patterson told Abigail to stand up, then dragged the mattress off onto the floor. She examined the frame. There were several pieces that might be long enough to use as a pry bar, but without tools she could not disassemble it to get at them.

Disappointed, Patterson pulled the mattress back onto the frame.

She glanced up at the ceiling. Exposed rafters supported the roof. She could see where they rested on the blocks forming the building's walls. There was nothing removable. Then she noticed a pipe running along the side of the first rafter, above the bed. It was made of metal, probably iron, and went from one end of the building to the other. A second pipe branched off into the middle of the room and ran to the light fixture. Inside would be wiring.

The timber rafter was only a couple of feet from the window. The pipe was secured with hanger straps screwed into the wood. It was impossible to know how sturdy the pipe was, but it gave Patterson an idea.

She jumped back onto the bed and reached up. With her arms fully extended, her fingers brushed the bottom of the rafter but were still several inches short of gripping the pipe.

She bent her legs, careful to maintain balance on the squishy mattress, and jumped upward. As her hands closed around the pipe, she swung her legs forward so that her feet dropped onto the windowsill.

She was now hanging horizontally with her legs bent. The pipe was holding her weight, at least so far. She prayed it would keep doing so, otherwise she would tumble to the ground and probably hurt herself.

There was no time to waste.

Patterson drew one leg back, supporting herself with the other, and aimed at the gap between the partially open window and the frame.

She kicked; the sole of her shoe connecting with the bars on the outside of the window.

The result was a jarring shock that traveled up Patterson's leg and into her back. But the bars remained stubbornly solid. She ignored the pain and drew her leg back again, delivering another hard blow to the base of the bars.

Now there was movement. The metal cage flexed outward before dropping back to its original position. The screws holding it to the wall were pulling from their anchors.

She repeated the action twice more until the fastenings holding the bottom edge of the bars broke free completely with the fourth kick.

With a grunt of relief, Patterson swung her legs down and let go of the pipe, dropping back to the bed. When she looked up, the pipe had bent under her weight. Another minute or two and it would probably have pulled away from the beam completely, sending her crashing to the ground. But it had served its purpose.

She turned her attention back to the window and slipped her hands through the gap. She could now push upward on the bars. After moving them back and forth a couple of times, the screws holding the top gave way, and the bars came off the wall.

She swung the bar cage sideways and let go, letting it fall to the left of the window. She still had to climb out and didn't want them directly below, where she might land on them.

She turned and looked at Abigail, who was standing in the middle of the room, watching with a concerned expression on her face. "Come up on the bed. I'll help you climb through the window first, and then I'll follow."

Abigail shook her head. "I can't."

"Yes, you can." Patterson motioned for Abigail to join her. "It's okay. There's a drop on the other side, but you'll be fine. I promise."

Abigail shook her head again and retreated backwards away from Patterson and the bed. When her back contacted the far wall, she slid down and sat with her knees pulled up to her chest, arms wrapped tightly around them.

It was no use, Patterson realized. The girl was terrified. Scott had treated her so badly, abused her so much, that she wasn't even willing to leave when the opportunity for freedom presented itself.

"I'll take care of Scott, and then I'll come back for you," Patterson said.

The girl didn't respond.

Patterson couldn't wait. If their captor returned now, she would lose her opportunity. "I'm going to climb out now."

When Abigail still didn't react, Patterson turned her attention back to the window. She pushed it all the way open and used the sill to pull herself up, pushing her head through the gap at the same time.

She wriggled forward.

It was tight, but her shoulders went through. Her breasts were another matter. It felt like she was being squeezed through a toothpaste tube. She only managed a few more inches before the back of her bra caught on the metal window casing and she couldn't go any further. No matter how much she tried, it would not go past, and there was no room to maneuver.

Frustrated, Patterson extricated herself and dropped back onto the bed. She undid the buttons of her shirt and took it off, peeling the fabric away from her sweat drenched skin. After removing her bra and discarding it, she put the shirt back on and pulled herself up and through the opening for a second time.

Without the extra bulk of the undergarment, the going was easier. She gritted her teeth and pushed her chest past the frame, biting down against the pain as her breasts scraped against the unyielding window surround.

She wriggled through until she was balancing on her stomach, partly outside the building with her legs providing a counterweight to stop her from tumbling in an uncontrolled fall. Patterson was still a good six feet above the ground, which was covered with a thick carpet of leaves. What lay beneath, she could not tell. The earth might be soft, or there could be jagged rocks, old bricks, or any number of other injurious items hidden under the vegetation.

It was a chance she would have to take.

She reached out with bent arms. If she landed with them straight, there was a risk of breaking her wrists, or worse.

Bracing herself, she swung her legs up and slid free of the window.

Patterson dropped quickly, hitting the earth with bent forearms, and rolling to dissipate the energy of her fall. Luckily, the ground was soft with no unseen hazards. She ended up on her back, staring up toward towering trees, and a patch of dark sky that twinkled with stars.

Against the odds, she had escaped.

Now Patterson must find Scott and take him out if she wanted to free Abigail too.

FIFTY-SEVEN

Patterson got to her feet and looked around. The daylight was almost gone now, but even so, she could tell they were far outside the city. There was nothing but trees in every direction. Except for a clearing that held the block building within which she and Abigail had been kept captive, and a larger log cabin that sat fifty feet distant. Its windows glowed with light from under a porch that ran along the front of the structure.

Between the two buildings was a rough parking area and beyond that a dirt driveway that meandered back through the woods and disappeared into darkness among the trees. Patterson's car stood in the clearing, parked near the cabin. Scott must've used it to transport her here after his aunt administered the drug that knocked her out.

Patterson brushed leaves from her clothes and tiptoed toward the cabin, her senses on high alert in case Scott appeared unexpectedly. On the way, she stopped at her car and tried the driver's and passenger side door handles. If she could open the trunk, there would be a tire iron which would make a great weapon. But the doors were both locked.

She moved beyond the car toward the porch. She mounted the steps, skirting the door, and approached the closest window.

Standing to one side, out of view, she peered cautiously in. The room beyond was a combination of kitchen and dining area. A pine wood table with benches on each side occupied one half of the room. On the other was a small cooking area with rustic cabinets. A partially open doorway beyond the table led deeper into the cabin.

Pictures hung on the walls. An oil painting in an antique gold frame showing a lake with a hump of land that looked very much like Bracken Island. She couldn't tell if it really was Lake Calhoun, or just a generic painting that resembled Scott's favorite dumping ground. On the other wall was another framed picture. This one she recognized. It was a larger version of the family portrait Holly kept on her fireplace mantel. Scott, his mother, and auntie posing innocently for the camera. That happy moment in time, captured forever on film, took on a whole new meaning now that Patterson knew the truth about Holly and her nephew.

Patterson lingered a moment, her gaze roaming the room. There was no sign of Scott. He must be elsewhere in the house.

Patterson continued, moving stealthily back down the steps and around the side of the building. She came to another window. This one looked in upon the living room. A threadbare sofa and two chairs stood in the middle, facing a large stone hearth. A set of stairs flanked one wall, leading up to a second floor nestled within the sloping roof. The unseen room beyond was most likely a bedroom, probably Scott's. Given the cabin's footprint, it was likely there was at least one other bedroom, and maybe two. If Scott was in the living room, she couldn't see him, at least not from this angle. There was another window around the corner to her right. She might get a better view there.

She moved further around the building, heading toward the other window. But then she stopped. There was a shovel leaning against the cabin's back wall. She almost tripped over it in the darkness. If she had, it could have alerted Scott to her presence. Instead, Patterson had found a weapon.

She picked up the shovel. It was nice and heavy with a sturdy handle. Feeling better now that she could defend herself, Patterson moved on toward the window.

Scott was in the living room. He was lying on the sofa, as if asleep. She wouldn't have been able to see him from the previous window because the couch was facing away.

A faint sound of music reached her ears.

She couldn't identify the song, but it sounded like country.

Then she heard another sound. The faint rumble of an engine. She didn't have a view of the driveway from her vantage point, but saw the glow of headlamps reflected on the nearby trees, anyway.

Patterson froze. Someone was driving up to the cabin, and there was only one person she could think of who would do that.

Holly Cartwright.

This complicated things. Now, instead of one foe, she had two. It would be hard to dispatch both of them quickly enough to maintain the element of surprise. She also couldn't risk moving from the back of the cabin until she was sure the coast was clear.

Patterson forced herself to stand still and silent. She watched the glow of the headlights fade as the car moved in front of the cabin, and then go out completely as the vehicle's driver cut the engine.

She didn't dare risk another peek inside the cabin in case Holly had entered already and was facing the window. But she couldn't stay here either. Likewise, she wasn't willing to flee into the woods and abandon Abigail to a grisly fate.

Patterson counted off three minutes, then dared to move. She gripped the shovel with both hands, ready to swing at the slightest provocation, and retraced her steps back around the building. When she reached the front, she saw a second car parked next to hers. She had no idea if it belonged to Holly Cartwright, because she didn't know what the woman drove, but it was a fair assumption.

The question was, what to do next?

She could make a dash for the block building and try to pry the door open with the shovel, releasing Abigail. But that would almost certainly fail, and the noise would bring Scott and his aunt running. Besides, Abigail had already refused to leave with Patterson. She would probably do so again, unless she knew their captor was no longer a threat. Patterson's hastily conceived plan had been to incapacitate Scott, then bring him to the block building and secure him with the same chains he had used to restrain her.

That was no longer an option.

Holly's arrival put her in an impossible situation—unable to rescue Abigail and outnumbered by Scott and his aunt, even if one of them was an old woman. Upon reflection, her only logical choice was to retreat while they were still unaware of her escape. She didn't know the lay of the land, or how far outside Oklahoma City she was, but there must be other houses or a road somewhere nearby. If she could find one and alert the owner, maybe flag down a passing motorist, she could call Mary Quinn and have a SWAT team here in no time.

Making up her mind, Patterson turned toward the dirt driveway intending to fetch help. Instead, she found Holly Cartwright standing several feet distant. In the old woman's hand was her Glock 19M Gen 5 service weapon, the business end pointed squarely at Patterson's head.

FIFTY-EIGHT

Going somewhere?" Holly cooed, her lips curling up into a vicious smile.

Patterson said nothing. She gripped the shovel with both hands, wondering if she could swing it and knock the gun from Holly's grip before she fired.

The old woman was one step ahead. "I think you should drop the shovel before you get any bright ideas." She jerked her head to the left, away from the cars, without ever taking her eyes off Patterson. "In fact, why don't you throw it over there out of reach."

Patterson hesitated, unwilling to dispense with her only weapon, but then realized she had no choice. She pitched the shovel sideways. It landed ten feet away with a thud.

"That's better." Holly's smile had faded now. "Bet you weren't expecting to see me here, huh?"

"I thought you told Scott you were done with him," Patterson said, quickly assessing the situation.

"No. I told him he wasn't to come around to my house anymore. It's too dangerous, thanks to you." Holly's eyes never wavered from Patterson. "But this place is safe. No one knows about it. My husband had a real estate business when he was alive. He taught me a few things. Like how to hide a property's true owner by using a land trust. No one will ever trace the cabin back to Scott or myself."

"So what's the plan now?" Patterson said, staring down the barrel of the gun. "You going to shoot me?"

"Don't be silly. Nothing so messy. Unless you force the issue." Holly's gaze flicked past Patterson toward the cabin. "Scott. Get out here," she shouted.

Patterson stiffened. Any hope of talking her way out of the situation or disarming Holly, no matter how slim, had now evaporated.

"What are you yelling about?" Scott exited the cabin, letting the door slam shut. He stopped in his tracks when he saw Patterson. "How did she get out here?"

"How do you think?" Holly snapped at her nephew. "You screwed up and let her escape. I caught her skulking around outside the cabin with a shovel."

"That's not possible." Scott hurried to join his aunt. He stood looking at Patterson as if he couldn't believe she was there. "I chained her up."

"Yeah, well, not well enough."

"Even if she somehow got out of her collar, there's no way out of the guesthouse."

Patterson couldn't help a wry smile. He called that disgusting, intolerably hot prison cell of a block building a guesthouse. It provided a further window into his twisted mind.

Holly didn't seem to get the joke. "You'd better hope to hell that Abigail is still in there."

"She must be. Door is still locked," Scott said, glancing toward the building. He looked at Patterson with narrowed eyes. "So how did you get out?"

Patterson glared back at him but didn't reply.

His brow furrowed, then enlightenment dawned. "The window."

"I warned you to brick that up." Holly shook her head. "Never listens to me."

"It had bars," Scott protested.

"Which clearly didn't work," Holly shot back. She motioned toward the block building. "We'd better get Little Miss Houdini back inside. I don't have all night."

Scott stepped forward and pushed Patterson. "Move."

"Why?" Patterson knew that if she ended up back in the block building, there would be no further chance for escape. "What are you going to do?"

Holly gave an exasperated sigh. "Just walk or I'll shoot you dead right here with your own gun."

"Okay, okay. I'm going." Patterson realized she had no choice. She let Scott and his insane aunt lead her back to the building from which she'd escaped less than thirty minutes before.

Three large padlocks secured the door. Scott produced a ring of keys and unlocked them one by one, then swung the door open. He gave Patterson a vicious shove, sending her stumbling back inside.

Abigail was still sitting in the same place, with her legs drawn tight to her chest. She didn't look up when the trio entered.

"Kneel over there," Scott said, motioning toward the chain that had held Patterson.

When she complied, he picked it up and placed the metal collar back around her neck, then clicked the padlock closed to secure it. The key Patterson had found was still on the floor where she'd left it. Scott quickly pocketed it, and then turned back to his aunt.

"I'm going to leave you here while I get the drinks from the cabin." He nodded toward Patterson. "Keep the gun on her, and if she tries anything, use it. Don't kill her though. I don't want the bitch to get off that easy. Shoot her in the leg if you have to."

"It would be my pleasure." Holly watched her nephew leave,

then turned her attention back to Patterson and Abigail. "I'll be glad when this is over. It's been incredibly stressful for me."

"When what is over?" Patterson didn't have a lick of sympathy for Holly's stress level.

"You'll find out. To tell the truth, you're showing up at my door might have been the best thing under the circumstances. My poor boy. After they discovered his island, he didn't know what to do. Then you came along and forced us to find a solution. And we did." Holly glanced toward Abigail, then back to Patterson. "Poor Scott. He kept this one longer than usual. Didn't have a choice. But now we'll start another collection in a new place. And your car will be the first one there."

"So pleased I could be of help," Patterson said sarcastically.

"Of course, I've told him to wait a bit before he gets another plaything. He probably won't listen though. He always likes to have one around." Holly's gaze swept the room. "I bet he'll have another guest tucked up here in no time."

"That's enough talking, auntie." Scott had reappeared in the doorway. He carried two glasses of iced tea in his hands.

He moved into the room and crossed to Abigail. As he approached, she stood mechanically and reached for the straps of her shift again.

"No. Not this time," Scott replied. He offered her a glass. "Take this and drink it."

She snatched the glass and drank with fervor.

Scott turned to Patterson. "Your turn."

"I don't think so."

"Drink the iced tea," Scott said forcefully.

"Or what?" Patterson knew exactly what was in the tea, and if she needed any confirmation, Abigail's sudden wooziness and inability to stay on her feet proved it.

Scott's cheeks reddened and Patterson braced herself for another beating, but then he took a deep breath and pushed the glass into her hands. "Drink it."

Holly aimed the gun at Patterson's legs. "Please don't make

me shoot you, my dear. One way or the other you're going to drink that iced tea. You might as well do it while you can still walk."

Patterson realized she was out of options. At least she knew they would not kill her right off. Scott wanted her to die slowly, trapped in her own car. With no other choice, she lifted the glass and drank. Then she waited for the drug laced tea to take effect. It didn't take long.

FIFTY-NINE

When Patterson regained consciousness, she was sitting in the passenger seat of her own car next to Scott, who was driving. The seatbelt was pulled uncomfortably across her chest, and she realized her hands were zip tied behind her back. Her ankles were zip tied, too. He was taking no chances.

Patterson looked around. Abigail was in the back, her head still slumped forward. A chain led from under the seat to her neck, where it was looped tight and padlocked in place. It reminded Patterson of the crime scene photos of Bracken Island. Abigail might be pliant, but Scott was taking no chances.

Her gaze drifted from the captive girl toward the rear window. The night was pitch black, but she could see a second set of headlights behind them. Holly was following along, no doubt to give Scott a ride back after he left Patterson and Abigail to die inside this car.

"Where are we going?" She asked, turning her attention back to Scott, but not really expecting a response.

He surprised her by answering, although his response was chilling. "To a place no one will ever find you. Somewhere I can grow my collection again. I'll need to work harder now, find more girls to replace those I lost on Bracken Island." He sat hunched over the wheel, peering through the windshield and into the darkness beyond. Only the headlights' twin beams proved there was anything beyond the car windows at all except an empty black void. "It's such a shame I'll never get to visit them again, don't you think?"

"I'm sure their families would disagree." Patterson turned away in disgust. After being drugged twice in twenty-four hours, she had a raging headache. But that was the least of her problems. She tugged at the zip ties binding her wrists, hoping there would be some leeway, but they didn't give. "The FBI will catch you, Scott. I want you to know that. You and your aunt. They're closing in. It's only a matter of time."

"Not true." There was a road coming up on their left. Scott slowed and took it. "If they had a clue about me, you wouldn't have come to my aunt's house all on your own. You had no idea, and neither do they."

"It's not too late for me to help you," Patterson said in a last-ditch attempt to reason with him. "When I said I'd make sure your aunt won't go to prison, I meant it."

"You think you're smarter than me, but you're not."

"I never said I was smarter than you, Scott."

"You didn't need to. I can hear it in your voice." Scott was slowing up now as they approached a set of rusting metal gates blocking the road ahead. He came to a stop and turned to Patterson. "I'm getting out for a minute. Don't do anything stupid. Auntie is right behind, and she still has your gun."

"Where do you think I'm going to go?" Patterson asked. "My arms and legs are tied."

"Just warning you." Scott pushed the driver's side door open and got out. He walked past the front of the car and approached the gates. They were held shut with a length of chain attached to a padlock. He undid it and removed the chain, then pushed the gates inward. Satisfied there was enough room for the car to pass through, he returned and climbed back in.

They edged forward, with Holly right behind. As they passed

through the gates, Patterson saw a sign affixed to the one on her side.

No Trespassing. Private Property.

Beneath this was another sign, more ominous than the first.

Danger. Contaminated Area. Do Not Enter.

When both cars were clear, Scott stopped again and repeated the process in reverse, closing the gates.

When he climbed back into the car, Patterson looked at him. "Where have you brought us?"

"It's an abandoned crude oil refining facility. Been closed since the fifties. No one wants to touch it because there are so many chemicals in the soil. Benzene. Xylene. There's even some mercury and arsenic. Of course, it doesn't help that it's so far out of the city. They had accommodation on site for the workers but that was all abandoned too when the complex shut down. Place is perfect for my needs, though. Don't worry. It's been abandoned for decades. No one's going to be coming anytime soon. You'll get to spend a long time here." Scott chuckled. "You won't be alone though."

"How come you have the keys to the place?" Patterson wanted to find out as much information as she could. If she came through this alive, every ounce of data she gathered would help her stop Scott killing anyone else. "I can't imagine you own it."

"I don't need to. It's abandoned. Forgotten. There weren't even any locks on the gate when I came across it. You could just push them open and drive right in. It took me a while to find this place, though. I wasn't expecting Bracken Island to be discovered. Ended up having to keep Abigail longer than I wanted. It's no fun when they stop caring."

"You really are an animal," Patterson said.

"Now, now. Don't flatter me. I already know what I am."

They were approaching the main site now. Patterson could see the shape of buildings looming out of the darkness. There were other structures, too. Chimneys and pipes that ran in all directions. Some led to huge cylindrical drums sitting on concrete footings. Scott couldn't pick a creepier place to use as his new dumping ground.

"Here we are," he said, approaching what must've once been a storage warehouse for oil drums. Large metal barn doors, at least twenty feet tall, stood wide-open, flanking a cavernous interior swathed in blackness. This must be what hell itself is like, thought Patterson, as they passed through the entrance and into the building.

Scott brought the car to a halt.

To their rear, the headlights of Holly's car swept across the space as she followed them inside.

Scott turned the engine off and removed the car keys. He turned to Patterson. "Welcome to your new home."

Patterson said nothing. Scott watched her for a moment, then opened the driver's side door. He came around the car and opened her door, reached down to her legs, and cut the zip ties holding her ankles. Unclipping her seatbelt, he dragged her roughly out of the car, then cut the ties binding her hands too.

Patterson was briefly unsure what was going on until he pushed her forward and walked her to the driver's side.

"Get back in."

Patterson sensed more than heard Holly's approach.

The old woman was still clutching Patterson's gun. "Why is this taking so long?" she asked.

"All right, I'm on it," Scott replied. He turned his attention back to Patterson. "I said, get in."

Patterson glanced toward the gun, then complied, sliding behind the steering wheel. The seat was still warm where Scott had occupied it moments before.

"Put your right hand on the wheel," Scott ordered.

Patterson did she was told.

A set of handcuffs appeared. Scott clicked one bracelet around Patterson's wrist, tight enough that she winced in pain, and clicked the other bracelet around the steering wheel.

"The other hand too." Scott grabbed her left wrist and yanked it up roughly. He pushed her hands together and zip tied her forearms. When he pulled the plastic tie tight, the handcuffs —now trapped between her wrists—dug painfully into her skin. He bent down and zip tied her ankles back together.

"I don't normally take this many precautions," he said. "But since you already escaped once, I can't take the chance. You're stronger than they usually are."

Holly waited for him to finish before speaking. "Did you chain the girl up in the back?"

"I did it before we left the cabin," Scott replied. "She isn't going anywhere."

"Good." Holly was already turning back toward her car. "I hope I never have to come here with you again. Once is enough."

"It was your idea to take the FBI agent," Scott said. "It's not easy dealing with two at once."

"It's done now. Quit griping and let's go."

"One thing, first." Scott reached into his pocket and withdrew two sets of keys. He walked to the front of the car, but instead of putting them on the hood, he tossed them further into the building. They tumbled off into the darkness. Then he turned back to the car and leaned in through the open door. If he was disappointed that Abigail was still out cold, he didn't show it. He moved close to Patterson, his lips brushing her ear, and whispered a parting message. "I'll never stop thinking about you."

Then he slammed the door and walked away.

Patterson heard an engine start. Headlights swept back around the enormous space, and quickly receded. Soon even the red glow of Holly Cartwright's taillights faded into darkness.

Patterson and the unconscious girl in the back seat had been left alone to die.

SIXTY

The decrepit warehouse where Scott had left Patterson and Abigail was so dark that only the vague outlines of skylight windows, high in the roof, were visible. Beyond that, inky blackness surrounded the car. It was quiet too; the silence broken only by crickets chirping somewhere beyond the abandoned refinery's perimeter.

Patterson tugged at her restraints. Between the handcuffs and the zip ties, all she managed to do was scuff the skin around her wrist.

Abigail was coming around now.

Patterson heard her groan and shift in the rear seat. When she moved, the chains securing her clinked.

"Where is this?" Abigail asked at length. Her voice sounded brittle and thin.

"Somewhere Scott found off the beaten track," Patterson replied. "An old refinery site, apparently."

"Is he here?"

"No. He's gone." Patterson pulled her thumb in across her palm and tried to slip her hand through the handcuff's bracelet. The metal dug painfully into her flesh, but she still could not get free. She stopped pulling and let her throbbing wrist have a break.

"Are we going to die here?" Abigail asked, her voice trembling.

"I hope not." Patterson wanted to tell her companion that everything would be okay. The problem was, she didn't believe it herself. As an FBI agent, she'd been in some perilous situations before, but none like this—locked in her own car, far out of the city and in the middle of nowhere, with no means to summon help. The situation appeared hopeless. Scott had picked his new dumping ground carefully. By now he would have closed the gates at the entrance to the property and chained them again. There would be no outward sign they were even here. Assuming anyone was even looking yet. At some point Mary Quinn would notice Patterson missing. She would, no doubt, mount a search. But it would be fruitless. Patterson had not mentioned visiting Holly Cartwright, so they wouldn't even know where to start. In hindsight, this was a bad lapse of judgment. She should have known better.

Patterson felt a rush of remorse. In trying to find out what happened to Julie, all she had done was fracture their family even further. Now her parents would go through life wondering what happened to both their daughters. It would devastate her father. Patterson was all he had left.

Frustrated, she let out an angry scream and pulled at the handcuffs, oblivious to the pain as her wrist chaffed against the sharp metal. Finally, when her fury had turned to exhaustion, Patterson leaned back against the driver's seat headrest, her chest heaving. Blood trickled down her forearm where she'd scraped the skin away in her frantic efforts to free herself.

She stared out into the blackness beyond the windshield. Had Julie endured a similar fate all those years ago? Was this how her sister felt in the last days and hours of her life?

"I'm sorry." A small voice spoke up from the back seat.

"You don't need to be. This isn't your fault," Patterson said, pulling herself together. She resolved to be strong, if only for the terrified girl sitting behind her.

"This is all my fault," Abigail said. "I shouldn't have refused to leave when you got the window open."

"You were scared," Patterson replied. "It's understandable after what you've been through."

"But if I'd climbed out the window like you wanted me to, Scott wouldn't have caught you again. He wouldn't have caught either of us. We could have escaped."

"Maybe," Patterson agreed. "Or maybe not. Either way, it doesn't matter. We can't change the past."

"I'm still sorry."

"I know."

"I wish there was something to drink. I'm so thirsty."

"Me too." Patterson was more than just thirsty. The room in which Scott had kept them was unbearably hot. She had lost a lot of fluids to sweat and could already feel the effects of dehydration. It would only get worse as time wore on. It was night right now and the temperature in the car wasn't too bad, but when the sun came up, it would be another matter. Even though they were parked in a building and under shade, the mercury would quickly rise. A person could go weeks without food, but only three or four days without water, tops. In this environment, trapped in the car, they would be lucky to survive another twenty-four hours.

"I don't like the darkness." Abigail's voice was barely more than a whisper. "I can see things moving. Dark shapes flitting around the car. I'm scared."

"There's nothing there," Patterson replied. "It's an illusion. Your brain is trying to compensate for the lack of visual stimulation. It'll be better after sunrise."

"How long will that be?"

"I don't know." It had been getting dark when Patterson climbed out of the window and escaped the block building. Several more hours must've passed since then, although it was

hard to gauge because Scott had rendered them both unconscious in the meantime. She guessed it was somewhere after
midnight. "We probably have another five or six hours."

"I'm not sure I can wait that long."

"There isn't any choice," Patterson admitted, as much to
herself as to Abigail. "When it gets light, we'll be able to see
exactly where we are. We can reassess the situation."

"It won't do any good. We can't free ourselves."

"That remains to be seen," Patterson replied. Even so, she
didn't hold out much hope that daylight would bring them any
more luck than they currently possessed. "We should stop talking. Preserve our energy. We'll need it."

"Okay." Abigail fell silent for a while, but then she spoke
again. "I told you my name, but you didn't tell me yours."

"What?"

"Back in the guesthouse," Abigail said, using Scott's term for
the block building, "you asked what my name was, and I told
you. You didn't tell me yours."

"It's Patterson."

"What's your first name?"

"That is my first name. My full name is Patterson Lucinda
Blake."

"Oh. That's unusual, especially for a girl."

"I know," Patterson replied. "I guess my parents were feeling
creative when I was born."

"How did they ever even come up with a name like that?"

"My grandmother on my mom's side," Patterson said,
grateful for the distraction. "It was her maiden name. She died
when my mother was little. I guess I was named Patterson to
honor her."

"You got lucky, then," Abigail said.

"How so?"

"Imagine if your grandmother's maiden name was like my
grannie's family name. Higginbottom."

"That would be worse," Patterson admitted.

"Special Agent Higginbottom Blake." Abigail said. "That would be a name."

"I like Patterson better."

"Me too." Abigail's voice was small, faint. "I'll stop talking now."

"Okay. But don't go to sleep. Try to stay awake. If you feel yourself slipping, tell me."

"I'll try."

"Good." Patterson took a deep breath and leaned her head back on the seat. She looked up at the rearview mirror, but Abigail was nothing but a vague, unmoving shape in the back. Her gaze slipped from the mirror toward the windshield and the unyielding dark beyond, and even though she wasn't religious, Patterson mouthed a silent prayer that this wasn't the way her sister had died.

SIXTY-ONE

The hours of darkness ticked by so slowly that Patterson began to think time had stopped moving forward altogether. Behind her, in the backseat, Abigail cried softly for a while, the occasional clink of chains when she shifted position an intermittent counterpoint to her sobs.

Patterson wanted to comfort the distressed young woman, tell her everything would be all right, but knew her words would amount to hollow reassurances neither of them believed.

At some point she must have dozed off into an exhausted half sleep despite her own advice. She was jolted back awake as the first rays of dawn penetrated the warehouse, pushing the blackness back and replacing it with a murky gloom.

Something was moving outside the car.

Patterson stiffened and studied their surroundings, peering through the car's windows, but saw nothing that would account for the strange snuffling and scrabbling sounds coming from somewhere close by.

Abigail had heard it, too. She let out a frightened whimper. "What's making that noise?"

"I don't know," Patterson admitted. "Sounds like an animal. A raccoon, maybe."

"I wish it would stop." Abigail's voice cracked. "What if it's something bigger, like a bobcat or a coyote?"

"It's fine. We're safe inside the car." Patterson shifted position. Her legs were going numb thanks to the zip ties binding her ankles. Her wrists throbbed too, where she'd spent fruitless hours trying to get free of the zip ties and cuffs. The skin was raw and bloody around the bracelet.

She pushed herself up to gain a better vantage point through the windshield to see over the car's hood. Despite the brightening sky beyond the warehouse doors, the interior remained shrouded in long shadows that fell away into a leaden half-light. Strange angular shapes sat silhouetted against the semi darkness. The remains of heavy equipment abandoned when the refinery closed. Birds, roused by the approach of day, flapped in the building's rafters high above. At first, she could see nothing to account for the movement close at hand.

Then she saw it. A rotund shape moving at the periphery of her vision near the front of the car. It had dark, bristly hair and a pointed snout. It shuffled around the vehicle, sniffing and grunting. At one point it looked up and met Patterson's gaze with small beady eyes. This was no coyote. It was a wild hog. A three-hundred-pound battering ram that would turn aggressive in a heartbeat if it felt threatened. This one appeared mostly curious. After giving the car another pass, it turned and sauntered off back toward the warehouse doors where it disappeared out of sight.

"It's gone," Patterson said, trying to allay Abigail's fears. She glanced up at the rearview mirror and saw her companion sitting huddled in the back with the chain wrapped around her neck. She looked small and vulnerable, still wearing the dirty shift. "It was a wild pig. Probably wondered what we were doing here."

"Do you think he'll come back?"

"Who?" Patterson asked. "The pig?"

"No. Scott. Maybe he'll change his mind and take us back to the guesthouse."

"I don't think that's going to happen," Patterson said.

Abigail lapsed back into silence.

Patterson sat staring out of the windshield, trying to ignore the intolerable thirst that left her throat dry, and her lips parched. She felt dizzy, too, and it was hard to keep her eyes open. After less than a day, her dehydration was already bordering on severe. Despite being trapped in the car for only twelve hours, she hadn't felt the need to pee, which was a bad sign. For Abigail, who was malnourished and weak, the situation would be much worse. Later in the day, when the temperature climbed up into the nineties, the car would become an unbearable death-trap. An oven from which neither could escape. They would bake alive.

Patterson swallowed a sob, wincing at the pain in her sand-paper dry throat. She lifted her eyes to the rearview mirror. Abigail was sitting with her head slumped forward again. Her gaze shifted to the back window and beyond, to the open ware-house doors. Soft yellow light was creeping across the ware-house floor, inching further into the building as the sun rose higher. She watched the shadows wither and die under dawn's soft glow and wondered if she was witnessing the last sunrise of her life.

SIXTY-TWO

A bigail, sweetie, are you still with me?" Speaking made Patterson's throat ache, but she knew it would be bad if the girl in the back of the car lost consciousness. No, not just bad. Probably fatal. "Try to stay awake."

Silence was her only answer.

Patterson drew in a long breath, tried to calm the sudden feeling of panic that enveloped her. Was Abigail already dead? Had her unwilling companion slipped quietly away into eternity without so much as a parting whimper?

Patterson tried to twist in the front seat and peer into the back, but the handcuffs prevented her from turning enough to get a good look at the girl.

She looked up at the rearview mirror once more but only saw the girl's head slumped forward, her hair falling in a tangled mess around her downturned face. It was impossible to tell what condition her companion was in.

"Abigail." Patterson mustered all her energy and spoke louder. "Please, say something. I need to know that you're still with me."

Again, there was no response.

A sudden chill ran up Patterson's spine. Her stomach turned

itself in knots. This wasn't the way it was supposed to end. She should have saved the girl, but instead had condemned her to this grisly fate.

Patterson let out a howl of despair and pulled on the handcuffs with all her might. She jerked her arm backwards until the cuffs cut into the flesh of her wrist. Blood flowed down her arm, the steel bracelet digging into the wounds from her previous escape attempt and creating new ones. But Patterson didn't care. She pulled her arm back again and again, ignoring the sharp pain as metal met flesh.

Her movements became frenetic. She slammed her hand against the steering wheel, her knuckles hitting with a jolt, and yanked against the cuffs hard enough to bring tears to her eyes. But freedom remained elusive.

All the while, Abigail didn't move.

Finally, when Patterson had used up the last of her anger, she fell back against the headrest and drew in several long breaths. It was hopeless, she knew. Short of gnawing off her own hand, or breaking every bone in her wrist, there would be no escape. And Patterson didn't think she could do either one of those things. Not because she was afraid, but because she didn't have enough strength left. Patterson was done. There was only one way to leave this car behind and accepting that brought a calmness that wrapped around her like a warm blanket. Patterson closed her eyes, looked inward to the place in her mind where Julie still lived on, and waited for the inevitable as her consciousness slipped easily away.

SIXTY-THREE

P atterson opened her eyes with the realization that time had moved forward. It was no longer dawn.

She felt groggy. Unbalanced.

Shafts of brilliant sunlight streamed down through the skylights, projecting bright oblong patterns upon the warehouse's dusty concrete floor. The gap between the building's doors, reflected in the car's rearview mirror, shone with white brilliance as if she were looking at the gates of heaven itself. And standing there, flanked by those celestial gates, a figure.

Julie.

Patterson must have died at some point during the morning and was now being greeted by her long-lost sister, who would escort her into the afterlife. Except it didn't feel like heaven. It was too hot. Stifling. This felt more like hell. Also, the figure coming to greet her was not alone. Two more unearthly beings followed behind the first, and still more came after that.

Then, as the figure she had thought was Julie moved closer and stepped out of the blinding light, Patterson realized she wasn't dead after all.

She was saved.

It was Mary Quinn, with detectives Ballard and Gimenez

bringing up the rear. They moved quickly toward the car and pulled the door open.

Quinn leaned in, her face a picture of relief. "Thank the Lord. We found you."

"There's a girl in the back seat," Patterson said. She glanced up toward the rearview mirror, praying that Abigail wasn't dead already, suspecting that she was. "She needs urgent medical attention."

"We're on it," Quinn said, motioning to the figures who had trailed herself and the detectives into the warehouse. Not celestial beings, but not far off.

Paramedics.

They opened the back door and began examining the slumped and silent young woman.

"We have a pulse," said one of the paramedics while his partner looked on. "It's faint, but she's alive."

Patterson felt the dread lift, if only a little.

"We need to free her right now," the other paramedic said.

Patterson craned her neck, trying to look in the back. "There are keys to the padlock holding her chains on. The bastard threw them somewhere in front of the car," She tugged her handcuffs. "The key for these is out there too."

"We don't have time to look for them. Her breathing is shallow. She won't survive much longer without medical attention." The first paramedic spoke again, his voice calm despite the dire circumstances. He straightened up and stepped aside to allow a man dressed in a firefighter's uniform to move in with what looked like a pair of oversized bolt cutters. A moment later, the paramedics were lifting Abigail from the backseat, the chain now gone from around her neck. They deposited her carefully onto a stretcher and were soon hurrying back toward the open warehouse doors with their charge.

Quinn looked at Patterson, reading her mind. "She's in good hands. She'll be fine. We're not losing anyone else to the Bracken Island Killer."

"Thank you," Patterson said, smiling weakly.

"Now it's your turn," Quinn said. "Let's get you out of those handcuffs."

Thirty minutes later, Patterson was sitting on a stretcher in the back of an ambulance. There was a saline drip in her arm, pumping fluids back into her body. In the warehouse, a forensics team were examining Patterson's car, going over every inch and collecting evidence. She knew they wouldn't find much. Scott had been careful. He'd worn gloves to drive the car here, just as he had with the stolen truck when he tried to abduct her outside the hotel.

"I can't believe that Holly Cartwright, that sweet old woman who used to monitor whooping cranes for a living, was raising a monster right under her own roof," Quinn said, incredulous.

"Well, she was. Her nephew came to stay with her when he was a young boy to escape his abusive alcoholic mother, and instead of teaching him right from wrong, she leaned into his dark urges." Patterson had spent the last fifteen minutes explaining what had happened. How she received a call from Holly Cartwright, who claimed to have more information. How she'd rushed over there immediately after the confrontation outside police headquarters with Justin Ferrera, but instead of getting a hot lead, ended up drugged and chained to the floor in Scott's remote woodland lair. Now she looked up at Quinn, puzzled. "You've heard my side of it, but I still don't know how you found me."

"If it wasn't for the car your boss arranged for you in Chicago, we wouldn't have. When you didn't make it home last night, I got worried. At first, I thought you might have stayed out blowing off steam. Figured I'd keep out of your way. You were pretty mad at me for stepping between you and Justin Ferrera. But this morning, when I saw your bed hadn't been slept in, I realized something was very wrong. Your phone kept going to voicemail, so I called Jonathan Grant. He contacted the Special Agent in Charge at the Chicago Field Office. They'd used your car in drug operations. It was an undercover vehicle for a while. They had a concealed GPS tracking system installed."

"I had no idea," Patterson said.

"Why would you?" Quinn shrugged. "Luckily, it was still active. We were able to pull the tracking data and it told us exactly where you were."

"Or at least where the car was," Patterson pointed out.

"Right. But given the Bracken Island Killer's MO, and the car's location, we figured there was a good chance we'd find you here."

"And I'm very grateful that you did." Patterson felt moisture welling in her eyes. "I thought I was going to die."

"It also gave us the location of the cabin where Scott took you and kept his victims. It's not registered to either him or Holly Cartwright. On paper it belongs to a retired lawyer who lives locally. The guy's lucky we didn't kick his door in already."

"Holly Cartwright's deceased husband had a real estate business. She used a land trust to hide ownership."

"I've got SWAT teams on standby, ready to go pick Scott up. We're going to simultaneously raid Holly Cartwright's house and the cabin property."

"No." Patterson shook her head. "Don't do that. He's already spooked because I was asking questions. That's what drove him to abduct me. There could be other properties in land trusts registered to other people. Holly Cartwright isn't stupid. If you mount a raid and he gets away, you might not find him before he abducts another young woman. We can't take that chance."

"Then how do you propose we catch him?" Quinn didn't look convinced.

"We use his own urges against him," Patterson said, thinking back to the trap set on Bracken Island by Quinn's FBI colleagues. It hadn't worked there because he knew his dumping ground had been discovered, but this time he was not so well informed. She told Quinn what they must do.

"That might just work," Quinn said once Patterson was finished. "I'll tell the teams to stand down. We'll do it your way."

"Thank you."

"In the meantime, we need to get you to the hospital for a check-up."

"There's no need," Patterson protested. "Once they get these fluids into me, I'll be just fine."

"It's not negotiable. We'll put your plan into action, but first I want to make sure you didn't suffer any ill effects from your ordeal. Take it or leave it."

"Okay. If it means that much to you, I'll go get checked out."

"It does," Quinn replied. She took her cell phone out and dialed a number, then handed the phone to Patterson. "But first there's someone you need to speak with."

Patterson lifted the handset to her ear, afraid that Madeline Kahn, the Special Agent in Charge of her division at the New York Field Office, would be on the other end of the line. But it wasn't the SAC. It was Grant, and he sounded relieved to hear her voice.

SIXTY-FOUR

They had been waiting in the dark warehouse for hours—three teams of agents positioned out of sight around the car. Inside the vehicle sat two store mannequins dressed in the same clothes Patterson and Abigail had been wearing when Scott brought them here. They also sported wigs that matched as close to the previous captives' hairstyles and color as possible. The staged scene was designed for one thing. To convince Scott that his victims were still in the car, at least long enough to allow the waiting agents to move in and arrest him.

"It's been three hours already and there's no sign of him," Quinn whispered to Patterson from their position concealed behind a large and unidentifiable chunk of partly disassembled machinery. "Are you sure he's going to show?"

"He'll be here," Patterson replied. "He likes to check on his victims, see how long they take to die. He won't be able to resist."

"What makes you so sure of that?" Quinn glanced sideways toward Patterson.

"Because he told me as much and he's a creature of habit. By now it will have become a ritual to him."

"I hope you're right," Quinn said. "I stood down two teams

of agents based on your hunch. If he doesn't show up here tonight, we might have lost our opportunity, especially if he thinks we're on to him."

"Your agents will still get their chance. Once we've caught Scott returning to the scene of his crime, they can go pick up the aunt."

"I still can't believe she's involved in all of this." Quinn shook her head. "It just goes to show, you never can tell what a person is really like."

"That's the truth," Patterson admitted. "She fooled me when I spoke to her. I would never have guessed."

"And yet Scott still tried to abduct you outside the hotel. When that failed, he had his aunt lure you to her house."

"I know. Their own paranoia tripped them up."

"Even so, they almost got away with it. If it wasn't for the GPS tracker in that car, we would never have known what happened to you."

"It was a close call, that's for sure." Not for the first time, Patterson's thoughts turned to her father. How close had she came to depriving him of both his daughters? Too close. Operating on her own without the FBI's resources to back her up, she took chances she never would have in an official investigation. Like going alone to visit Holly Cartwright, telling no one of her whereabouts. As one of the few people with official access to the island over the last twenty years, it should have occurred to Patterson that Holly knew more than she was letting on. But like everyone else, the woman's *sweet old lady* act took her in. Patterson had forgotten one of the basic tenets of investigative technique. Assume nothing and suspect everyone. Even when Patterson saw the photo on the mantle, nephew and aunt posing together, she didn't catch on. Blinded by the banality of the old woman's existence, Patterson had assumed Holly was just a potential witness instead of a partner in crime to a sadistic serial killer—a sociopath who might have murdered her sister. Now, more than anything, Patterson wanted to bring Scott's decades long reign of terror to an end. And not just for Julie, but for Abigail and all the other victims who had fallen into his clutches over the years. Not to mention those yet to come if he went free.

"We have movement," Quinn whispered, breaking Patterson's introspection. "There's a vehicle approaching."

Patterson looked toward the open doors of the warehouse and saw headlights approaching through the darkness. The vehicle pulled up close to the building and stopped. With the engine still running and the headlights illuminating the warehouse interior, the driver's side door opened.

A figure stepped out.

Patterson recognized Scott.

He stood for a while, surveying the apparently empty warehouse and Patterson's car.

Patterson held her breath, wondering if he would notice anything amiss. By now a team of agents would have moved to block the abandoned refineries gates, cutting off his retreat. The trap was sprung, and Scott had walked right into it. But Patterson didn't want him to flee. She wanted to be the one who brought him down.

Then, deciding it was safe to proceed, Scott stepped into the warehouse and approached the stationary vehicle that he still believed to contain his latest victims.

Patterson's arm went to her shoulder holster. She quietly withdrew the Glock Jen 5 waiting there. This was not her own service weapon. Holly Cartwright had relieved her of that the previous afternoon. This was a different weapon, provided by the Oklahoma City Field Office.

Beside her, Patterson sensed Quinn drawing her own service weapon.

Scott was crossing the cavernous warehouse floor now. The twin beams of his own car's headlights painted Patterson's vehicle in a bright halo.

Slipping from her hiding place, and still swathed in concealing darkness, Patterson moved into position.

Scott was beside the car now. He bent down and looked through the passenger window, cupping a hand to the glass. For a moment he stayed like that, unmoving, then he jerked away from the window as realization dawned that he was not looking at Patterson and Abigail. He took a couple of faltering steps back from the car, then turned to run.

Patterson was waiting for him.

She stood five feet distant, gun levelled upon him.

He froze, surprised to see her.

Patterson inched forward. Her finger hovered over the Glock's trigger.

Scott's eyes flicked toward the waiting car, engine still idling. His body tensed as he contemplated his chances of reaching the vehicle and escaping.

"Go ahead. Try it," Patterson growled as Quinn, Ballard, Gimenez, and the rest of the joint FBI and Homicide team moved in from all directions, their own guns drawn. "Give me a reason to shoot you."

SIXTY-FIVE

TWO DAYS LATER

Patterson was resting up at Quinn's house. A full checkup at the hospital had revealed no serious damage from the beating she'd taken at Scott's hands while confined in his cabin *guesthouse*. She'd suffered only bruising, which still hurt, but was slowly getting better. Dehydration was the chief concern, and a second course of fluids took care of that. The doctors had wanted to keep her in overnight and administer yet more fluids, but Patterson had insisted on leaving to join the FBI team staking out the killer's new dumping ground. She wanted to be there to arrest Scott. In Oklahoma City, a second team moved in on Holly Cartwright, and she was soon behind bars, too. The pair would stand trial separately. Scott on at least twenty counts of murder, and his aunt on a similar number of accessory charges. Both faced various kidnapping, auto theft, and other associated charges. Given the overwhelming preponderance of evidence against them, neither would ever walk free again.

Abigail was still in the ICU, but would make a full recovery, at least physically. Her parents, who could hardly believe she was still alive after so long, had flown in from Dallas and rushed to be by her side. They found an emotionally broken daughter with a long road ahead but resolved to be with her every step of the way.

But one thing still weighed heavily on Patterson's mind.

Her sister, Julie.

Many of the Bracken Island Killer's victims were still unidentified, and Scott wasn't talking. Despite hours of questioning, he remained stubbornly silent, refusing to tell Ballard and the other investigators the identities of the almost two dozen young women he had abducted, tortured, and killed over the last couple of decades.

But there was one other way to find out if Julie had crossed paths with the Bracken Island Killer. The DNA sample Patterson had provided several days before. She'd been waiting eagerly for the results, even though she was torn regarding what she wanted to hear when they came in.

If Julie was one of Scott's victims, it would mean an end to her quest. She would know what happened to her sister. She could go home. But with that knowledge would come the full realization that Julie had died a miserable death at the hands of a man who kept her locked in the *guesthouse* as his personal toy for upwards of a year or more first.

It was not the answer she wanted.

Patterson was a realist. Not only that, but she worked for a law enforcement organization that dealt with missing persons and abduction cases all the time. She knew the odds of Julie's survival were close to nil. But of all the ways she imagined her sister dying, this was one of the worst.

Which was why, when Quinn arrived home early from work after calling ahead to say she had the results of the analysis, a part of Patterson wanted to hide in the bedroom and pretend it wasn't happening. But that would achieve nothing, so she took a deep breath and went downstairs.

Leah was in the kitchen making coffee. When Patterson entered, she turned with a concerned look on her face. "M will be here any minute. She just texted me. She has the DNA comparison."

"I know," Patterson said. "She called me when it came in but hasn't looked at it yet. She wanted to wait so we can look together."

"You must be beside yourself," Leah said. "Would you like a cup of coffee, or maybe something stronger?"

"I'm not sure I could drink anything at the moment," Patterson said. "But thank you."

"Well, I'm going to have a drink," Leah said, abandoning the coffee. "I'm nervous enough for the both of us." She went to the fridge and took out a half-finished bottle of white wine, then poured herself a glass. "Are you sure you don't want one?"

"Quite sure," Patterson replied.

At that moment, Quinn walked through the door, carrying a manila envelope.

"Are you ready to open it?" Quinn stood at the kitchen island with one hand on the quartz countertop and the other clutching the manila envelope she'd brought from the office.

"I'm so nervous," Patterson admitted. She eyed the envelope with a wary gaze. "I've been going back and forth on what I want the results to be."

"Either way, it's better to know," Leah said. "Whatever the paper inside that envelope says, it's not setting an uncertain past in stone, it's merely reporting a truth that's already occurred."

"I know," Patterson said. She was shaking. All the days and years since her sister disappeared, all the wondering and worrying, might come down to this. A simple sheet of paper that could provide answers no one had been able to give her family in a decade and a half. She looked from the envelope to Leah. "Maybe I will take that wine, after all."

Leah wordlessly took a glass down and poured.

Patterson picked it up, gulped back half the glass, and turned to Quinn. "Do it."

Quinn nodded. She opened the envelope and reached inside, withdrawing two sheets of paper stapled together in the top left corner. The FBI crest and field office address were at the top of the first sheet. Underneath this was the heading Forensic Biology Report. The rest of the page was taken up with a series of strips with black horizontal lines at irregular intervals. The first strip came from the DNA sample provided by Patterson. The rest belonged to the victims. Together they represented the collected DNA fingerprints of herself, and each person found on Bracken Island.

Quinn studied the page for a moment, then flipped to the second sheet containing a summary of the results. She read the page, her lips moving silently. Then she looked up at Patterson. "None of the victim's mitochondrial DNA samples match the one you provided."

Patterson felt suddenly lightheaded. She gripped the counter to steady herself. "So that means—"

Quinn finished the sentence for her. "Your sister was not a victim of the Bracken Island Killer."

SIXTY-SIX

The next morning Mary Quinn drove Patterson across town to The Welcome Inn. There was still one outstanding thread to follow up, and forensics were not finished with Patterson's own car, which had briefly become part of the Bracken Island Killer's new dumping ground.

Patterson made her way into the hotel, with Quinn by her side. When she entered, Hank looked up. If he was surprised to see her, he didn't show it

"Special Agent Blake," he said as she approached the counter. "I hope you've recovered from the ruckus in the parking lot the other day. Nasty business. But the neighborhood isn't what it used to be. Too many unsavory elements hanging around." His eyes shifted toward Quinn. "Police don't have much interest in cleaning it up."

"You really want to go there?" Quinn said, stepping forward. "Some of those unsavory elements you refer to are staying under your own roof."

"Now hold on a minute. No one at this hotel had anything to do with the incident in the parking lot."

"Never said they did," Quinn countered. "But you hired a

criminal with fetishist tendencies who stole from your guests and put their safety in jeopardy."

"We had no way to know Justin Ferrera was going to do that stuff. We ran a full background check, just like we do with all our employees."

"Sure you did," Quinn replied. "Just like you reported him to the police when he was caught sneaking into occupied rooms and watching the inhabitants sleep."

"Look, we fired him. What more do you want?"

"Do I really need to tell you?"

"Okay." Patterson stepped between Quinn and Hank. "The two of you can have this conversation later. All I'm here for is the registration card. Did you find it?"

"Yeah, I found it. Almost didn't bother looking. Figured you wouldn't be back after what happened."

"You wish." Patterson held out her hand. "Give it to me."

Hank eyed her briefly, then sighed and rummaged around on his desk. A moment later he came up with the yellowed index card, which he placed on the counter. "This is it. Not sure what you expect to find. She checked in with her friend, then checked out again six days later."

"So she did check out of the hotel," Patterson said, examining the card. Her throat tightened when she recognized Julie's handwriting and signature. This was another link, no matter how tenuous, to her sister. She looked back toward Hank. "Mind if I keep this?"

"If you don't, it's just going in the trash," Hank replied. "Just like all the other cards in the boxes I had to go through to find it. Figured since I was there anyway, I might as well clean out the storage closet. Been meaning to do it for a couple of years."

"Thank you," Patterson said. She studied the card for a few seconds, then slipped it into her pocket. She looked at Quinn. "This is all I need here. If you don't mind taking me one more place, I'd like to go collect my car if forensics are done with it."

"Sure." Quinn shrugged. "My only assignment today is

making sure you get what you need. The SAC said it was the least we can do after you cracked the case for us and almost got killed."

"What?" Hank raised an eyebrow.

"Don't ask, it's a long story." Patterson turned to leave.

"Wait." Hank stood up. "I found something else when I was looking for the registration card. It was clipped to the back."

Patterson turned back to Hank. "What did you find?"

"This." Hank reached into his desk again and picked up a yellowed, creased envelope. He held it out for her. "Apparently, your sister asked us to mail a letter for her when she was checking out. Looks like something happened, and the address got damaged. We couldn't mail it like that, so we attached it to the registration card in case she ever got in touch again."

Patterson's hands trembled as she reached out and took the envelope. There was a stamp on the top right corner, but the address was unreadable. It looked like someone had spilled coffee on it, which had made the ink run. The only legible part was the recipient's name.

Stacy Trafford.

"You had this all along and didn't tell me," Patterson said, glaring at Hank.

"I didn't know. It was a long time ago," Hank protested. "If I'd remembered, I would've gotten it for you sooner. At least you have it now."

"Maybe the answers you're looking for are in there," Quinn said.

Patterson didn't reply. She just stared at the envelope. Her chest felt tight. Her sister had written a letter to Stacy after they parted ways. A letter that had ended up unread and forgotten in a storage closet for sixteen years.

Now it was in her hands.

"Well, are you going to open it?" Quinn asked.

Patterson snapped out of her fugue. She turned the envelope over, slipped a fingernail under the back flap. The glue was old and brittle. The flap came easily unstuck. Inside was a sheet of folded notepaper. Patterson went to remove it, then hesitated. The last person to touch this paper was Julie. A part of her didn't want to disturb it, as if doing so would break some invisible link with her sister. But she had to know what the letter said. With her heart beating like crazy, Patterson plucked the letter from the envelope and unfolded it. Then she started to read.

SIXTY-SEVEN

The letter was written in blue ink on a single sheet of canary colored notepaper torn from a legal ruled writing pad. Patterson held it in shaking hands while she read, her eyes dancing over Julie's handwriting in a frantic scramble to consume the words.

Hey Stacy,

Hope you're not too mad at me. You're my best friend and it feels strange being here without you. I know you didn't want me to stay, and I understand why, but I really want to complete this trip. It means a lot to me. I hope you understand. You won't believe this, but they found some of our clothes in an alley behind the hotel. It wasn't all of them, but I got my favorite shirt back. Your Levi's were there too. The ones with the rip in the knee that you love so much. I'll bring them back with me, but I can't guarantee I won't wear them. They fit so well. And honestly, I look hot in them.

You don't need to worry about me. I've been doing okay. I met some people a few days after you left. They're really nice and you would like them. They've been looking out for me. And get this, one of them is called Trent, just like the singer in Nine Inch Nails. I know you liked

NIN growing up. Bet you wish you'd stayed now. Doesn't look much like him though, but he's still cute.

They're on the way to Dallas and asked me to go with them. There's plenty of room in their van and it sounds like fun. We leave tomorrow.

Anyway, please don't worry about me. I'm doing fine, and I really am sorry about what happened. I hope you've forgiven me by the time I get back to Chicago.

I'll write again soon, I promise.

Love you lots and miss you loads,

J.

Patterson felt her eyes moisten. She wiped the wetness away with the back of her hand and sniffed. "Julie didn't stay in Oklahoma City. She hooked up with some people and went to Dallas. They all checked out at the same time and rode together."

"That's great," Quinn said. "She was still alive when she left here. You're one step closer to finding her."

"I need to know who she was with after Stacy went home." Patterson turned her attention back to Hank. "Where's the box of registration cards you found my sister's card in?"

"Dumpster in the back alley. Put it there this morning along with all the other boxes."

"You have to get it back," Patterson said. "There are other registration cards I need. Everyone who checked out on the same day as my sister. One of them might go by the first name Trent."

"Come on, lady." Hank shook his head. "Haven't I done enough for you?"

"You really want me to answer that?" Patterson was in no mood to argue with the grouchy hotel manager. If necessary, she would frog march him out to the alley herself, force him into the dumpster, and hold a gun on him until he found what she needed.

"Look, I'm not rummaging through the trash for you. I've said where it is, go find the damned card for yourself."

Quinn stepped forward. "You know, we haven't officially

closed the investigation into the attack on Special Agent Blake in your parking lot. We might need to interview all your guests, maybe even get a warrant to search their rooms."

"What happened in our parking lot was nothing to do with any of the guests here, and you know it."

"All I know is there was a stolen truck parked on your property. A truck put there to enable a kidnapping," Quinn said. "Even if we don't uncover any evidence tying that vehicle to one of your guests, who knows what else we'll find. You don't exactly cater to a high-class clientele."

"You threatening me?" Hank asked.

"What do you think?" Quinn replied.

"All right. Fine." Hank shook his head and stood up with a scowl on his face. "I'll go find the dang box and bring it back in here. That make you happy?"

Quinn looked at Patterson and then back to the hotel manager. "That depends how successful you are finding those registration cards."

"If they're in there, I'll find them." Hank was already making his way through the office to the rear door. "And then I never want to see the pair of you ever again. Deal?"

"Sounds fair to me," Quinn replied. "Now hurry up. I'd rather not spend any more time in this disgusting hovel than I need to."

Hank ignored the comment. He tromped through the door and slammed it behind him. Ten minutes later he was back with a cardboard storage box. Twenty minutes after that, the two FBI agents were walking away with all the registration cards from the day Julie Blake checked out of the Welcome Inn. One or more of them, Patterson hoped, might contain a clue regarding what happened to her sister next.

SIXTY-EIGHT

Patterson sat on the bed in Mary Quinn's spare bedroom. After leaving the hotel, they went and picked up Patterson's car, which was now parked on the road outside the house. They also recovered her service weapon, which had been found at Holly Cartwright's house. She was relieved to have the gun back and felt foolish for having lost it in the first place.

It was now early evening. The registration cards and the unsent letter Julie had written to Stacy were sitting on the comforter in front of her. There were four cards. The first had one name. Simon Bailey. The next card contained her sister's details, along with those of Stacy. On the third were a pair of names. Trent Steiger and Mark Davis. The final card also had two names on it. Martin Wright and Karissa Harper. Under the names on that card, someone had scrawled a message accompanied by a smiley face.

Sunrise at TexFest.

Patterson had no clue what the message meant, or which cards related to the people her sister had traveled with. But it was a place to start.

Her gaze shifted to the letter for the hundredth time. She reached out and touched it as if doing so would provide some magical glimpse into her sister's last days. She withdrew her hand and picked up one of the registration cards. Could she track any of these people down? It would be difficult without the Bureau's resources, especially given how much time had passed and with nothing but their names to go on. She didn't even know which of them were traveling together, how old they were, or if she was looking at three separate groups with no relationship to each other. All she knew for sure, was that her sister had left town with one or more of the people on these cards.

She placed the card back on the bed and reached for her laptop.

At that moment, her phone rang.

It was Grant.

She scooped it up and answered. "Hey. I was going to call you later."

"Now you don't need to," Grant said. "How are you doing?"

"Pretty good, considering." She told him about her visit to the hotel, and discovery of the letter detailing her sister's decision to head south.

Grant listened without interrupting and only spoke when she was finished. "At least you have a direction to continue your search now."

"It would be a lot easier if I wasn't out here on my own without FBI support."

"That's why I called." Grant's tone turned serious. "I've just gotten out of a meeting with Madeline Kahn. She was less than pleased."

"Shit. I was hoping she wouldn't find out about what happened here."

"Are you serious? An FBI agent under her supervision gets kidnapped and almost murdered after meddling in a case against the express instructions of her superior, and you think she wouldn't hear about it?"

"I wasn't meddling. You told me not to investigate the Bracken Island Killer, and I didn't. It's not my fault the search for my sister overlapped with that case."

"Semantics. You stepped over the line, and you know it."

"Even if I did, there's nothing I can do about it now." Patterson paused, a horrible thought occurring to her. "Did I get fired?"

"No. If Madeline Kahn wanted you gone, you'd be hearing about it from her, not me," Grant said. "Mainly because I'd probably get fired right alongside you."

"Sorry. Did you get in a lot of trouble?"

"Let me put it this way," Grant replied. "I'll need to keep my head down from here on out if I don't want to end up transferred to an RA on a glacier in Alaska."

"Hell. That bad?" RA stood for Resident Agency, an outpost in an area too small to have a field office. "But look on the bright side. I'll probably get transferred there right alongside you. At least we'll be together."

"This isn't funny, Patterson."

"I know." Patterson steeled herself for what was about to come. "What's my new punishment?"

"Surprisingly, nothing. Actually, just the opposite."

"What?" Patterson was confused. "Why?"

"Because your meddling ended up catching a serial killer who's been operating unchecked for more than two decades. Something no one else could do. Not only that, but you've now saved victims of two different serial killers in the last month. They already have a new nickname for you around the office."

"What's that?"

"The Alchemist."

"Huh? I don't get it."

"Because you appear to have a knack for screwing up big time and somehow turning your faux pas into pure gold." Grant chuckled. "You also put Madeline Kahn in an impossible situation. If she pushes you out of the FBI, she looks petty and vindictive. She also wouldn't be able to take credit for your unintentional accomplishment. And if there's one thing we know about the SAC, it's that she loves to score points that might move her further up the chain."

"She wants some of the credit for catching the Bracken Island Killer."

"She wants all the credit she can reel in. Which is why the narrative has now changed. As far as anyone outside the three of us is concerned, your off-the-books investigation into Julie's disappearance was actually a meticulously planned deep cover operation that happened to catch a prolific serial killer."

"What?" Patterson's head was spinning. "Are you serious?"

"There's more," Grant said. "Since you haven't yet resolved the puzzle of what happened to your sister, she had no choice but to make Julie's case an official investigation. It was the only way for the deep cover operation story to hold water. As of right now, you're officially reinstated for fieldwork, and will receive the full backup of the FBI in your search for Julie."

"I can't believe this," Patterson said.

"Believe it," Grant replied. "Congratulations. You're back on the team."

———

Forty minutes later, Patterson told Grant that she loved him and hung up. She leaned back on the bed and allowed herself a rare feel-good moment. Her reinstatement made the search for Julie so much easier. With the information she'd learned from Julie's letter, Patterson's next stop would be Dallas. The city had a large and well-staffed field office, and she could now use those resources to her benefit. Relieved that she wasn't in trouble, and optimistic she would find her sister now she had the FBI's might behind her, Patterson jumped up off the bed and went downstairs to tell Quinn and Leah the good news. Tomorrow she would leave on the next leg of her search for Julie, but tonight she wanted to celebrate with new friends.

ABOUT THE AUTHORS

A. M. Strong is the pen name of supernatural action and adventure fiction author Anthony M. Strong. Sonya Sargent grew up in Vermont and is an avid reader when she isn't working on books of her own. They divide their time between Florida's sunny Space Coast and a tranquil island in Maine.

Find out more about the authors at
AMStrongAuthor.com

Made in United States
Troutdale, OR
06/26/2023

10807461R00202